Book of Secrets

Book One of the Vital Secrets Series

D.F. Hart

2 Of Harts Publishing

The Vital Secrets Series

Visit 2ofharts.com to sign up for my newsletter and get a special bonus supplement to the series!

Follow me on:
BookBub
Facebook
Goodreads

Copyright © 2019 by D.F. Hart
Library of Congress Control Number: 2019905525
ISBN: Softcover 978-1-7330454-2-1
eBook 978-1-7330454-3-8

All rights reserved. No part of this book may be reproduced or transmitted in any form or by any means, electronic or mechanical, including photocopying, recording, or by any information storage and retrieval system, without permission in writing from the copyright owner.

This is a work of fiction. Names, characters, places and incidents either are the product of the author's imagination or are used fictitiously, and any resemblance to any actual persons, living or dead, events, or locales is entirely coincidental.

Custom Cover Design and Artwork commissioned for
D.F. Hart by:
Rocking Book Covers

Published 2019 by 2 Of Harts Publishing
Arlington, Texas

Acknowledgments

To my husband, who supplies flowers, chocolate, and lemon bars at just the right times and celebrates every step forward right along with me.

To fellow DHS alum Michael C. Miller, who with patience and good humor endured several FBI-related questions.

Last but certainly not least, to all those who encourage me to keep writing, mostly by saying, "Oh my God, what happens after that?"

I thank you all.
Let's go find out, shall we?

D.F. Hart

Book of Secrets

D.F. Hart

Prologue

"Morning. Hey, there was a package that came for you. It's on your desk."

"Thanks." FBI Agent Nathan Thomas continued down the hall to his office in the BAU division. He hung his jacket on the back of his chair, then stared thoughtfully at the plain, brown box in the middle of his blotter.

Hmmm. No return address, no distinguishing marks on the package.

The label was made out to him.

Problem is, I haven't purchased or ordered anything lately, and if I had, it would have been shipped to the house, not to work.

He wasn't expecting any case-related packages, either.

He thought for a moment before ringing the lobby.

"Does anyone know if this thing went through the scanner?" he asked.

"Of course it did. Everything does. Standard safety protocols."

"Just checking."

He hung up the phone and frowned for a moment, then pulled on latex gloves, got out his pocketknife, and began to carefully open the package. He waded through layers of packing peanuts until he came to a six-by-nine-inch manila envelope.

Nathan's pulse quickened.

I have a bad feeling about this, he thought as he pulled the envelope out of the box. He turned it over carefully and used his knife to cut along the bottom seam to preserve any DNA evidence on the gummed flap. Tilting the envelope slightly to one side, he shook it a little. Some Polaroid pictures and a folded paper fell out.

Nathan's heart fell as he glanced at the photos – pictures of fifteen different young, obviously deceased women, with long, dark hair and staring eyes that were once a pretty blue. He unfolded the paper and read it.

Give her back, Nathan, and it will stop.

Chapter One

"BEL!"

Loud humming.

"Hey, Bel!"

Loud humming.

"BELLA AMSEL!"

Bella Amsel turned off the hair dryer. "*What?*"

"Bel, have you seen my calculator?" Stacy called out as she rummaged through the computer desk drawers.

"It was on top of the TV two days ago," Bella answered, and flipped her hair dryer back on - then sighed and turned it off again as Stacy appeared in the bathroom doorway looking panicked.

"Oh, Bel, help me find it. I gotta be across campus for my Trig final in half an hour," Stacy pleaded.

"I thought you were a human calculator," Bella said dryly as she moved to the living room and lifted couch cushions.

"I love you too, smartass," Stacy snapped as she stomped down the hall to her room to check it again.

Meanwhile, Bella wandered into the kitchen, spotted the

wayward calculator on top of the microwave, retrieved it, and headed back into the living room to wait patiently.

Stacy came barreling down the hallway and stopped in her tracks when she spied the prize in Bella's hand.

"You found it. I really DO love you!" Stacy flung herself at Bella and hugged her before grabbing the calculator. She turned her loose and began hastily shoving things into her backpack.

"Don't you want to know where I found it?"

"No time," Stacy trilled as she headed out the door. "Gotta go. Professor B will throttle me if I walk in late again."

Shaking her head, Bella retreated to the bathroom to finish getting ready herself. Today was an important day. She had been selected to interview with the Metzger Youth Institute for a tutoring position in the fall.

The first cool thing about it was she would be getting electives credit for it. The second cool thing was she was only a sophomore; most of these positions were filled by seniors or graduates. But her four-point GPA and her ability to speak French, German, and Russian fluently had landed her on Student Services radar.

The third, and perhaps the coolest thing about it, was that she would be getting paid. *Paid.* To speak in languages that she loved with all her heart, and to teach others to speak them, too. This would be a dream come true if it happened. She'd be able to hang up the apron she wore while working the coffee bar in the student union building once the fall term started.

"Not that slinging double half-caf foamy latte is a bad thing. But it would be nice to earn more than minimum wage," she remarked to her reflection.

Not to mention having the Metzger Youth Institute at the beginning of one's resume couldn't do any harm either. Bella smiled as she checked herself one last time in the mirror.

Here's to the future, she thought as she knocked back the rest of her orange juice before brushing her teeth.

Mikel stopped on the landing and stared at the stunning creature walking toward him.

Well, not actually toward *him*. Toward the headmaster's office just to the left at the base of the stairs. He could not stop himself from watching her; slender but curvy, with glossy, jet-black hair down to her waist that swayed as she walked. She looked straight ahead and didn't notice him.

She's perfect, like a china doll.

Which was a weird thought, even for him. He viewed most everyone and everything around him as inanimate, set there purely as tools for his entertainment and use. The only person he'd ever had any sort of positive feelings for was his father. But the girl he'd just seen struck his senses in a wholly different and completely new way.

Had Mikel Metzger been wired like other twenty-eight-year-olds, he might have recognized the feeling for what it was – love at first sight. But for him, anything other than contempt for those around him was foreign, so he didn't know how to process what was welling up inside him. He found himself wanting to follow her, touch her, hold her, possess her. It unnerved him.

He crept down the stairs, close enough to the open doorway to hear her say, "Hello, I'm Bella, nice to meet you, Mr. Wallace," before the headmaster closed the door for their meeting.

Bella. My angel's name is Bella, Mikel's mind repeated dreamily as he made his way to the elevator. *She must be here for one of the tutoring positions.*

Mikel decided he would do whatever it took to make sure she got one.

The ringing buzzer signaled the arrival of a visitor.

"Yes?" Stacy said into the intercom.

"It's Brad."

Stacy pressed the button. "C'mon up."

Then, knocking on Bella's bedroom door, she called out, "Hey."

"I'll be out in a sec. The money is on the coffee table."

Stacy scooped up the cash and met Brad, their pizza deliveryman and her boyfriend, at the door with a kiss.

"Man," he said, walking into the kitchen, "a tip, *and* a kiss? How many other sustenance-procurement technicians do you treat like this?"

"Sustenance-procurement technicians?" Bella said, laughing as she strolled in. "Seriously?"

Stacy mock pouted in the kitchen doorway.

"So, are we really your last stop this time, or is your boss going to be a jerk again?"

"Yes, you are," Brad said, putting his arms around her. "I made sure that this was my last one for the night."

"How've you been, Brad?" Bella asked as she got out three plates and some sodas.

"Fantastic. As a matter of fact, I have awesome news." Reaching for a slice, he continued, "When I graduate next month, I have a job lined up already. I've accepted an offer from the biggest accounting firm in Los Angeles."

Stacy squealed and hugged him.

"That's wonderful," she exclaimed. "And it fits perfectly into our plans."

"So, you two are moving to California?" Bella said. "I thought all that was up in the air."

"Well, we had pretty much decided to leave here already," Stacy answered. "The pivot point was who was going to offer Brad the best deal, Boston or Los Angeles."

She took his hand and continued, "But we really wanted it to be L.A. so I could go to Cal Tech."

"When are you going?" Bella asked.

"I'll be leaving to find a place out there in the next week or so," Brad said. "They want me to start August first."

"And I'll finish out the fall here, then move out there over the holiday break. With any luck, I'll be taking classes at Cal Tech come spring. I've already sent my application, so it should all work out," Stacy finished.

"Well, I have some pretty cool news myself," Bella said with a twinkle. "I had my interview out at the Metzger Youth Institute today. I think it's down to me and one other person. Hopefully, I'll hear something within the next week."

Stacy squealed again, and hugged Bella tightly.

"That is just so awesome. When would you start?"

"September," Bella said. "Unless I can rearrange my summer schedule to start sooner."

Mikel paused with his knuckles on the door.

God, it's tiresome having to pretend to care what people say, he groaned inwardly.

But it was the only way to obtain the information he wanted.

He rapped on the door and entered.

"So, I was just wondering how the tutor search was going," he said as casually as he could manage.

Wallace looked up from his screen.

"Very well. As a matter of fact, we've hired all but one. I'm particularly impressed with the languages tutor candidates. They're both fluent in French, German, and Russian, and each would give our kids some much-needed support in their studies."

Subtlety was not Mikel's strong suit. Trying his best to sound nonchalant, he asked, "Is one of them the dark-haired girl that came in today?"

"Why, yes, as a matter of fact she is," replied the oblivious headmaster. "The single thing that works against her is she's only a sopho-more. Brendan, however, graduates next month, which means we could have him full-time without having to work around his school schedule."

"I see," Mikel said, his mind racing. "Glad I don't have to make the choice."

He made more inane small talk and worked his way out of the headmaster's office. Free at last, he surreptitiously glanced at the visitor sign-in log. *Brendan C. Jones* was written in a strong hand, along with his address.

"Well, Mr. Jones," Mikel murmured to himself as he walked out to his car, "I'm sorry, but you're not *my* first choice."

Bella hung up the phone and came dancing into the kitchen.

"You got it, didn't you?" Stacy asked, holding her breath.

"Yes, yes, yes!" Bella exclaimed and was immediately knocked short of breath by Stacy hugging her tightly.

The phone interrupted their celebration.

"I'll get it," Bella offered.

"Hello?" she said cheerily. Then, "Oh, hi Granpa, I was going to call you later, I have the most amazing news..."

Her voice faltered and she grew silent.

"*What?*" she said, alarmed.

Hearing the change in Bella's tone, Stacy came out to the living room to see Bella still on the phone with tears in her eyes.

"Okay," Bella managed. "I'll be there in the next couple of days. Love you, too."

She hung up the phone, looked at Stacy, and sobbed, "Granma's cancer came back."

"I thought you were going with the young man," Adolf frowned as he looked at the list.

"I was going to," Wallace replied, "but he hasn't returned my calls in three days, so I guess he found a better offer. I'd wager the young lady's more proficient than he is in Russian anyway."

Just then his desk phone rang. He answered, listened, offered sympathy, and finished his conversation with, "Of course my dear. We'll make do until you can get here. Take the time you need with your family."

Hanging up the receiver, he looked at Adolf and said, "Speak of the devil. That was her. I'm afraid her start date with us may be postponed. Poor thing, she has a family emergency back East."

The following evening, on the outskirts of town, a property owner called authorities to report an abandoned car in the open fields behind his place. The policeman responding to the call found the body of a young man in the trunk. The victim still had his wallet and credit cards, and the car was registered to him. There were no obvious injuries, no suspects, no trace evidence, and no witnesses. The murder of Brendan C Jones would become a cold case by the New Year.

"Happy New Year, Granma," Bella said, trying to cheer up the hospital room.

No response.

Bella moved closer to the bed. Rose was sleeping deeply, no doubt from all the medications they were giving her. In June, Dr. Gable had opted to try surgery again to solve the problem. But on the operating table, they found that Rose's ovarian cancer had already spread to her entire abdomen. There was nothing to be done surgically.

Now, after six months of aggressive chemotherapy treatments, Rose was just about out of strength. Her beautiful dark hair had long since disappeared. Bella's had barely grown back out to shoulder length – she'd had much of her waist-length tresses cut off to fashion a wig for Rose.

Bella sighed and stepped out of the room to talk to Melanie, Rose's nurse for the night. Melanie was a robust, black woman with a Southern drawl who had been a nurse for twenty years. She was one of Bella's favorites.

"How'd she do last night, Mel? And be honest," Bella said.

"Not good, baby girl," Melanie answered. "We've had to increase her pain meds. Doc Gable will be around in a few minutes. He's going to want to talk to you and your grandfather."

Laying a motherly hand on Bella's shoulder, she continued, "I've been prayin for her, and for you two, since I met ya'll. But baby girl, what she's going through right now, it ain't livin. You know that."

"I know," Bella said, a single tear escaping down her cheek. Sniffling, she said, "Granpa went down for a cup of coffee. I guess I should go get him."

She found him leaving the cafeteria, two cups in hand.

He saw her, smiled wanly, and said, "Figured you could use some hot chocolate." He handed her a cup.

"Mel says Doc Gable wants to talk to us. He's making rounds now," Bella told him. "So, we should probably get back up there."

Manfred nodded silently. As they stood waiting for the elevator, she looked at him.

God, he looks tired – and old, she thought. *He's aged a hundred years since June.*

They took the elevator up without speaking. Doc Gable was coming out of Rose's room when the doors opened. He motioned them to the family waiting room down the hall.

"I think it's time to make service arrangements, if you haven't already," he said as gently as he could. "There's nothing else I can do for her except keep her as pain-free as possible until she passes."

Tears in his eyes, he continued, "I've been racking my brain trying to think of something. But I'm out of ideas. The latest tests indicate the cancer has metastasized into her bones..."

His voice broke.

"Doc Gable, you've been brilliant, and you've been there for us," Manfred replied, his voice thick with emotion. "But sometimes there just isn't anything else that can be done. You've done your best; it's just my angel's time to go."

He put an arm around the young doctor's shoulders.

They made their way back down the hall and went in to sit with Rose. Around sunrise on January second, she sighed deeply once, and was gone.

"Go back to school, honey," Manfred said, gazing out of the living room window at a snowy January eleventh. "You already took off early when she got worse. If you don't start the spring semester, you could be dropped from the University. Not to mention your internship you were telling me about."

"Are you sure, Granpa?" Bella asked again. "I don't want to leave you alone."

"I know, Bellissima, and I appreciate that," Manfred answered, sitting down next to her and taking her hand. "And I know how hard this is, believe me. But your Granma would want us both to have a good cry and then get on with living."

"Well, we've been here before, and certainly done the first part of that," Bella said, laying her head on Manfred's shoulder.

"Yes, we have," Manfred said, hugging his granddaughter. "Now, once again, we have to move to the second part. I'm going back to teaching when my university reopens next week. You should go back to yours, too."

The apartment seemed cavernous without Stacy's cheerful clutter spread everywhere. Bella shut the door and leaned against it, exhaling slowly. She walked into her room and put her suitcase down, then turned and headed down the hall into the bathroom. She filled the tub, then undressed and sank into the warm water, trying her best to let her mind go blank.

She hadn't realized until now how exhausting it had all been. She'd traveled back and forth from Phoenix to Virginia a handful of times since that fateful call in June. Then, in early December, when Rose took a turn for the worst, she'd powered through her finals early – *thank God for understanding professors* – and hopped on a plane.

The last month had pretty much been a blur; every waking moment spent at the hospital, then the funeral service, and lastly, the plane ride back to Phoenix.

She thought back to when she was eight and her parents had died. It was a sudden and horrifying hock, and it completely sucked. This time, it was announced, so to speak. Instead of quick and unexpected, Granma's decline had been slow and brutal to watch. And it, too, completely sucked. Even if someone had had the stupidity or nerve to ask which was easier to deal with, Bella wouldn't have been able to answer.

Her stomach growled to get her attention. *Food.*

Now there was a thought. Bella realized she hadn't eaten all day. She pulled the plug on the tub and stepped out, reaching for a towel. Wrapping it around herself, she tucked the corner in at the top and turned to the mirror absentmindedly.

Wow. I really do look different with this shorter hair, she thought. *But I kinda like it. Easier to manage, anyway.*

She put on her 'comfort clothes' – yoga pants and an oversized sweatshirt -and went to the living room. Reaching for the phone, she dialed Ping's Palace and ordered her usual chicken fried rice with mushrooms and bean sprouts, and an extra eggroll. She fixed a cup of hot tea and settled in on the sofa to watch TV while she waited for dinner to arrive.

Then it occurred to Bella – this was the getting on with living that she and Granpa had talked about. She was managing it. It might not be easy, but she was doing it.

Mikel came awake with a start.

Where am I? his mind raced.

I'm in my room, of course Where the hell else would I be?

But he knew why he was disoriented. The face he'd been picturing in his dreams almost every night for six months was more vivid than usual. His angel.

Bella.

"I must see her again," he said aloud in the darkness. "I must make her mine."

He felt the familiar strain of penis against pajama bottom and fought to clear his mind. He knew he could have anyone he wanted. There were several women right here in the complex he could bed if he wanted to.

But he didn't want them. He wanted Bella.

Sighing, he rolled out of bed and pulled on his clothes. There was only one other way he knew to soothe the heat that surged through him.

Striding out into the hall, he approached what looked to be a broom closet door. He opened it, placed his palm on the scanner, and was rewarded with a red elevator door opening. He punched in his keycode, then pressed the button for Sub-Level Three. Once the door opened at his destination, he repeated the security protocols and then a retinal scan to access the tunnel entrance.

Mikel traveled through to the decontamination chamber and suited up. He pressed the keypad at the far end, walked through the negatively pressured antechamber, and entered his workrooms.

Stopping at the first station, he picked up the clipboard and murmured, "Good evening."

Bella's smile grew as Tommy, an introverted eleven-year-old, recited the alphabet in near-flawless French. By the time he reached the end, she was beaming.

"Excellent. You're doing brilliantly, Tommy," she said.

He blushed and said, "Thanks to you, Miss Bella."

She looked at her watch and said, "Oops. You have a history class to get to, I believe. And I have a major test this afternoon. See you after Thanksgiving?"

"Yes, ma'am."

He gathered up his books and headed toward the door. He turned, his hand on the doorknob, and said carefully, "Je pense que vous êtes jolie, Mademoiselle Bella!" before scurrying out.

The sentiment made Bella misty.

Two months ago, he was so shy he would barely speak to me at all, she mused. *Now he tells me he thinks I'm pretty!*

For a kid with so many walls built up, it was a huge stride forward.

She placed her books and notepad in her backpack and slung it over one shoulder almost on autopilot, her mind already churning about the Economics test she would endure this afternoon.

Bella walked into the foyer toward the front entrance, and immediately had the sensation of being watched again. She glanced around but only saw a small group of students heading into the library. None of them were paying her any mind.

Weird, she thought. *I swear to God it feels like someone's watching me.*

Trying her best to quell the goosebumps on her arms, she continued out into the sunlight.

From his vantage point at the monitor, Mikel watched her go.

I've really missed you, angel, he thought.

His dreams of her had continued while he'd been gone. Father had interrupted the vital progress in his workroom to send him back to Macapa to deal with some personnel issues that had come up at the mines. What was supposed to be a one-week trip had stretched on forever.

Fortunately, he'd been able to cover his tracks well. The labor foreman that had become such a pain in the ass would never be found – Mikel had made sure of that - and his disappearance quelled the uprising. Smoothly doctored maintenance records took care of the rest.

When he returned in February, he'd been ecstatic to see that Bella had indeed started as the languages tutor. Without Father's knowledge, he'd expanded the security feed to send images to his workroom computer, then set up his terminal for auto-recording. He routinely waded through the security tapes to isolate videos of her. Now he could watch his angel all he wanted, in real time or in play-back, even when he had to work.

He *was* spending more and more time in the workroom these days. The new test subjects he'd been working with had developed serious complications; he would have to start completely over with new ones. The frustration at being set back was immeasurable.

Once I find the right mix, we can proceed, my love, he thought as he caressed the close-up still shot of Bella's face lovingly.

Adolf leaned back in his chair in quiet contemplation. He'd spent this beautiful November afternoon reviewing student files and had found several promising candidates in this newest batch of kids. Each of them had perfect or near-perfect grades in their studies; each of them was tall and blond; and each of them showed interesting scoring results on the psychological testing. Even the ones that stood out as major disciplinary problems would be manageable once Mikel perfected the serum.

He reached for his desk phone and punched in a four-digit number. He waited patiently until his protégé answered.

"Mikel, what's the status?" he inquired smoothly.

"We're almost there," Mikel replied. "There's one small permutation left to overcome, but I've just about got it, Father. I want to try one last round of test subjects just to make sure."

"Of course, Mikel, whatever it takes," Adolf answered soothingly. "Just get it done."

Mikel pressed the disconnect button and leaned back, smiling wolfishly. He'd already chosen the perfect candidate.

But first he needed to tidy up his workroom.

Chapter Two

"Oh Bel, you're gonna come, right?" Stacy pleaded over the phone. "I know it's short notice, but it would mean the world to us if you were here."

"Wouldn't miss it, Stacy," Bella answered. "As a matter of fact, I'm putting a bag together now. Where are you staying?"

"Planet Hollywood. We already booked you a room. Are you flying or driving?"

"I was thinking I'd drive it, but I found a deal on a round-trip. Southwest flight 627 landing there around nine. Pick me up at the airport?"

"You know it. See you in a while, Bel!"

Bella hung up the phone and smiled to herself as she threw a couple more things into her suitcase.

Thanksgiving break as a bridesmaid in Vegas...

Not quite what she'd planned, but she was genuinely pleased for Stacy and Brad. And it beat spending the short holiday break all alone in the new one-bedroom apartment she'd just moved into.

Granpa had called a couple of weeks ago and sheepishly asked if she would be okay on her own for the holiday. Great Uncle Max had finally convinced Manfred to take a vacation; the two widowers were on a single seniors' cruise in the Bahamas.

She quickly reviewed the contents of her suitcase, then added her hairbrush and other toiletries into the mix. Snapping her suitcase shut, Bella moved it into the living room by the front door.

She made sure her answering machine was turned on, grabbed her purse and keys, then headed out the door. Locking it securely behind her, she made her way to the elevator, then down to the truck.

Traffic and the trip through security were both lighter than she'd expected. She made it to her gate with twenty minutes to kill. Bella plugged her earbuds into her iPod and opened the paperback she'd brought.

———

Mikel needed a break. The coolness of a desert night was providing little comfort for his aching muscles. He was disposing of his test subjects.

The serum was a complex mix and was designed to insert itself into the subject's brain tissue and nerve fibers, remaining dormant until activated. He'd tried several delivery methods but only found two that worked the best – injection as a direct approach and suspended in liquid as a subtle one. Activating the serum was childishly simple – a press of a button. Once activated, the serum would essentially function as a mind-control agent that could be operated via electronic signal. Nanotechnology was a wonderful thing.

And it had worked like it was supposed to, in the rats and the monkeys he'd begun the trials with.

In late September, he'd decided to make the move to human subjects. He'd taken the first of four trips across the border into Nevada. Each time he found, befriended, drugged, and brought back a transient nobody would miss. Three men, ranging in age from forty-five to seventy, and one old prostitute in her mid-fifties.

But this first batch of human specimens had been a complete

disaster. Instead of allowing for remote control of the individual's brain activity, the serum had attacked the host when activated, causing seizures, psychotic rages, and massive aneurysms.

He'd buried three of them already and was digging the hole for the fourth.

Should've started with the big one first, he grumbled to himself. *That one will take twice as big a hole to cover him properly.*

Finally, the hole was finished. He grabbed the last body by the legs and strained to pull the man out of the truck's bed.

You'd think a homeless degenerate would be skinnier, he thought disgustedly.

Dragging the stocky man by the feet like a sack of garbage, he stepped around the edge of the hole. Gravity assisted him in placing the body.

He rested for a moment, then picked up the shovel and filled in the last hole. Grabbing the small, leafy branch he'd pruned from a tree at the Institute, he swept it back and forth over the graves to minimize obvious signs of digging. Then, he carefully walked backward toward his truck, erasing his tracks as he went. He drove slowly back to the main road, then turned right for the twenty-mile drive back to Phoenix.

Mikel had taken great care to strip his subjects of any personal possessions. These items had been locked in the workroom safe. Now he might have to burn them. He saw no reason why the bodies would ever be discovered, and even if they were, no one would be able to link them to him. Still, it might be better to get rid of it all.

Bella stood on her balcony, watching the lights twinkle up and down the Strip. The wedding had, quite frankly, been classier than she thought. For some reason, she had envisioned Brad and Stacy exchanging vows in front of an Elvis impersonator and surrounded by the musical cacophony of slot machines.

She sighed and went back into her room to remove the sky-blue, floor-length dress Stacy had rented for her. Hanging it up carefully, she made her way into the bathroom and turned the water on for a nice hot shower. Attending a wedding in Vegas just made her realize how alone she felt.

Well, maybe I can cheer myself up in the casino later, she thought wryly as she washed her hair. *Maybe I'll meet a tall, dark stranger who happens to love literature and languages as much as I do.*

"Yeah right," she said aloud. "With my luck, he'd either be married, gay, or a criminal."

Laughing to herself, she stepped out of the shower and toweled off. Seriously – Who was she fooling? She'd only had one serious relationship in her whole life. Bella and Anthony had dated through high school. At least until the senior prom, when she caught him making out with the homecoming queen. He'd had the nerve to blame it all on Bella because she wouldn't, as he put it, 'prove her love for him.'

Jackass.

After that, she'd written off boys for the foreseeable future. But seeing Stacy and Brad beaming with happiness as they exchanged vows and rings had awakened a longing in her, a desire to not be isolated anymore.

She sighed again, pulling on jeans, a sweater, and tennis shoes.

"What the hell," she said aloud to no one. "Let's hit the slots and see what happens."

She tucked her money and her room key into her pocket, hooked her cell phone to her belt, and set off. She stopped in the gift shop and bought a pack of smokes and a lighter before making her way to a bank of penny slots. It was a bad habit she had picked up, and she really needed to quit, but she was in no mood for self-recrimination or analysis.

Putting a twenty into the machine at the end of the row, she lit a cigarette, selected her bet amount, and pressed 'spin' half-heartedly. Bella looked around the casino and people-watched a bit, only barely paying attention to her machine. It seemed that everywhere she looked she saw nothing but happy couples.

God, this would be so much more fun if I had someone to talk to, she thought wistfully.

Her machine beeping and blinking caught her full attention. A fifty-dollar win on a fifty-cent bet.

Not bad.

She smiled to herself as the credits added to her total.

"Nice spin," came a voice from the seat to her right.

She turned and looked into the most amazing hazel eyes. Her field of vision widened to take in a chiseled face, attached to a muscular body. He was the most handsome man she'd ever seen. She felt herself smiling back at him.

"Um, thanks," she said, slightly flustered. "It's the luck of the draw, I guess."

"Pretty darn good luck, I'd say," the vision before her responded. He held out a hand.

"My name's Nathan Thomas."

She hesitated, then shrugged her shoulders and shook his hand.

"Bella Amsel."

"What brings you to Vegas, Bella?" Nathan asked. "Besides good luck on the machine."

"Marriage," she replied as she pressed the spin button again. "My best friend got married today."

"Oh, good. At first, I thought you meant your own," Nathan replied. "That would have been awkward."

They both laughed.

"What about you? What brings you here?" Bella asked him.

"Fun," he said. "I start my new job next week, so I thought I would blow off some steam before I hit the ground running."

"What type of job?" she asked. "If you don't mind my asking."

"Law enforcement," Nathan replied. "I got a Bachelor's in Criminal Justice and spent two years with the Virginia State Troopers. But," he said leaning a little closer to her and dropping his voice, "I recently graduated from the FBI academy, and I go into the field next week. So, I'm taking a little vacation first; sort of a 'happy graduation to me'."

"Congratulations," Bella said sincerely. "Quantico is beautiful."

"You've been there?"

"Virginia's my home state. I grew up in Manassas," Bella explained. "And my grandfather teaches languages and literature at the University of Virginia. But he's done some guest lecturing at Quantico, and I got to go with him once. When I was about twelve."

There was a comfortable silence.

"And," she continued, leaning closer to him and looking him straight in the eyes, "I was taught to not talk to strangers, and to always ask policemen for ID."

Laughing, Nathan drew out his wallet and showed her both his identification and his badge. "Satisfied?"

"Very, thank you," Bella said. "Now I can keep talking to you."

"That's wonderful," Nathan said. "But only if you let me buy you dinner."

"That would be nice," Bella said, trying to be nonchalant as she scouted for a wedding ring.

He caught her surreptitious gaze, and said solemnly, "I'm not married, Bella. Not even dating anyone, not for a long time."

She flushed crimson and managed, "It never hurts to check."

Nathan stood.

"Come on," he said, extending his hand. "Grab your bounty of winnings and tell me about yourself over some nice Italian food."

"Sixty-five dollars isn't exactly a bounty. But Italian food happens to be my favorite," Bella said with a smile. "So now I couldn't tell you no even if I wanted to."

She took his hand.

Bella cashed in her ticket, and they strolled leisurely down the Strip to the MGM.

"The place is called Fiamma, and it's excellent," Nathan told her.

"I tried it about a year ago when I was here for *my* best friend's wedding."

They were graciously ushered to a cozy table in the corner. For the next three hours, they ate and talked and laughed. Nathan talked about his family and upbringing; he was the youngest of four and the only boy. Then he listened as she shared her journey with him, and held her hand when she talked about her parents' and her grandmother's deaths.

Over tiramisu he asked her, "So, a degree in literature to go with all those languages. What are your plans?"

"Well," she said, "I've had an opportunity to work with troubled kids as a languages tutor for the last several months. And I've found I truly enjoy it. I foresee working with children in some form. I'm not sure what age bracket yet, though."

She took a sip of her hot tea before she asked, "And what about you? What led you to law enforcement?"

"Two generations of my family were D.C. cops," he said. "I guess it's in my blood. And working as a trooper got me some valuable experience on the ground. But I decided I wanted to be a criminal profiler. I want to be more proactive in identifying and catching the bad guys *before* they can do damage, rather than just chase them once they do. So, I applied to the FBI."

Dessert was cleared and beverages refilled. Then Nathan took her hand again, and asked, "So, when do you leave for Arizona?'

"My flight is at four tomorrow," she replied softly, savoring the touch of his hand on hers. "What about you?"

"Mine leaves at six," he said.

They were both quiet for a long moment.

"Bella," he said gently, reaching over to touch her cheek, "I know we just met, and forgive me if this sounds stupid, but... oh hell," he muttered. "Never mind."

"What?" she asked, a little breathless.

"May I kiss you?"

She flushed again, but her eyes did not leave his as she whispered, "Yes."

He smiled, leaned in, and gently traced her lips with his. A thunderbolt shot through her, all the way down to her toes. She shuddered involuntarily from the sudden heat that burned in her.

"Are you all right? Did I upset you?" Nathan asked, his eyes filled with longing and concern.

"No," she said. "I just haven't been kissed in a really, really long time."

"That surprises me, quite frankly," Nathan replied. "You're stunning, and you're one of the most intelligent people I've ever met. I'm amazed you're even single."

"Well, I don't know about the rest of that, but I'm most definitely single," Bella said. "In fact, this is the first date I've been on since high school."

The waiter appeared with the bill.

"Let me settle this, and then let's get out of here," Nathan said quietly.

When he wouldn't hear of at least letting her pay her portion, she nodded silently. In her head, she was thinking all sorts of things, none of which were proper, especially with someone she'd just met. But the images in her brain refused to go away. She wanted to spend the night with this man. She wanted to feel his mouth, his skin, his body on hers.

Isabella Rose, get hold of yourself, her inner matron intoned. *What the hell are you doing? You've only known this guy for about three hours.*

But she realized she really didn't care. She wanted to be with him tonight and the future could be sorted out later.

"Bella?"

She pulled out of her inner conflict and smiled at him. "Are you ready to go?'

"Yes," he said, returning the smile.

They left the restaurant arm in arm, heading back toward Planet Hollywood.

"Nathan?"

"Yes?"

"It's my turn to ask something awkward."

He laughed. "Okay, shoot."

She stopped and turned to face him. Taking hold of both his hands, she took a deep breath. "Like you said, we just met. But it feels like we've known each other for a long time."

She blushed a deep, deep red and took the plunge.

"I cannot believe I'm about to say this to you, but... what I mean is, this is not like me, but... *dammit*... I want to know if you want to... um... come to my room with me," she finished in a whisper and looking at the ground.

She felt him let go of her hands. She closed her eyes and cursed inwardly.

Christ, I finally meet a great man and I scared him off, she thought. *I am such an idiot.*

Then she felt two strong arms wrap protectively around her and his breath on her hair. He was shaking, she could feel it.

"Bella," he murmured throatily. "I know how you feel; I know where you're coming from."

He tipped her chin upward until she opened her eyes and looked at him

"I will come with you, to talk. Nothing else will happen unless and until you are absolutely ready for it. Okay?"

"Okay," she said simply.

They reluctantly broke the embrace and continued their walk back to the hotel.

They rode the elevator hand in hand and in silence. Her heart was racing so hard she had trouble swiping the key card to her room.

"Here, let me," Nathan said gently.

He opened the door and held it for her. She made her way past him over to the little fridge and pulled out two sodas to occupy her shaking hands.

Suddenly, her words came out in a tumble.

"I'm so sorry. You must think I'm a slut or something. I swear to God this isn't normal behavior for me, at all, ever. I've never even..." Bella's voice trailed off in complete embarrassment.

"Why would I think that?" Nathan prodded as he filled two glasses with ice. "And what makes you think I've ever done it, either?"

Bella was flabbergasted. "Seriously?"

"Completely," he admitted as he opened the sodas and poured. "I know it's not hip or cool or the norm, but yes, I am a twenty-six-year-old virgin. I had opportunities to change that, of course, but I wanted to wait for the right woman. For someone special."

"I know what you mean," Bella said. "After Anthony cheated on me because I wouldn't put out, I decided not to bother with dating anymore. I figured that if a boy I had known for years could turn out to be that shallow, all the rest must be, too."

He walked over to her and handed her a glass.

"We're not all like that, Bella, not by a long shot," he said. "And I'm sorry you had to go through that."

He took her hand and led her out onto the balcony.

"You know, this is so ironic," Bella said, almost in disbelief. "About five hours ago, I was standing in this very spot, feeling very isolated and sad because I realized I'm tired of being alone. I even daydreamed about meeting some tall, dark stranger," she added, poking his side as she noticed Nathan grinning at this bit of news.

"And wonder of wonders, here you are. So, where do we go from here?" she asked as they looked at the traffic and lights up and down the Strip.

"Well, I definitely want to see you again, as much as possible, regardless of where tonight leads," Nathan said. "We met for a reason, and I'll be damned if I'm going to let distance or anything else get in the way of getting to know you."

Setting his glass down, he turned and wrapped his arms around her.

"I want to spend the night with you, Bella, even if we just talk all night."

She sighed and laid her head on his shoulder.

"Nathan?" she said in a small voice.

"Yes, Bella?"

"I'm so glad I met you."

They went back inside and talked until somewhere around three a.m. before drifting off in each other's arms.

Just before nine a.m. Bella stirred. Slowly she became aware of Nathan's arm draped protectively over her and his deep and even breathing lightly fanning the side of her neck. She slowly turned her head and gazed in wonder at this gorgeous man snuggled beside her.

Wow was all she could think. *So, this is what a "we" feels like.*

It was the most comfortable feeling in the world to see him beside her. She studied his face, so peaceful in sleep. Long, dark lashes, high cheekbones, chocolate-brown hair, just a hint of a cleft in his chin and a touch of five-o'clock shadow. And now those amazing hazel eyes were open and looking back at her.

"Morning," he murmured, tightening his arm around her waist. "Sleep well?"

"Very well," she replied. "I've never woken up with anybody before."

"Me neither, but I like it. I like it a lot," he said sleepily, softly stroking her cheek.

At some point during the night, he had removed his shoes and shirt. Before she could stop herself, she ran the palm of her hand across the muscular landscape of his bare chest and watched his eyes awaken and take on a sparkle.

Christ, he's built, she thought.

Lost in the feel of him, her hand began to slide downward toward the six pack of his abdomen. The sparkle became a fire of longing in his eyes.

Nathan put his hand over hers.

"Bella? You might want to be careful. I've got willpower, but I'm not invincible."

Bella leaned forward and kissed him, long and hard. Against his mouth she whispered, "I'm ready if you are."

He moved his head back slightly so he could see her eyes. "Are you absolutely sure about this?"

"I'm more sure about this, about you, than I have been about anything, ever," she stated. "I want to be with you. Make love with me, Nathan."

Now it was Nathan's turn to blush.

"Bella," he said gently, softly. "You have no idea how tempting you are. But I don't have any..." he faltered a bit, then continued, "I don't have any protection with me. Are you on the pill?"

She smiled, a little frustrated. "No. And you're right, we shouldn't do this without being prepared." Bella sighed. "I know it's the right choice, but I sure don't have to like it."

At this, he bellowed with laughter and hugged her tightly.

"I know," Nathan said. "But if we're willing to wait until we *are* prepared, I have a feeling it will be spectacular."

He kissed her gently, then continued, "Let me buy you breakfast at least. And I want to make plans to see you when you're home for Christmas."

They were interrupted by Stacy calling to arrange to meet for brunch at eleven. Bella hung up, turned to Nathan, and said, "Do you mind running the gauntlet? I want you to meet Stacy and Brad. They're the whole reason I'm even in Vegas."

"I would love to," Nathan answered. "Tell you what. I'm going back to my room to get cleaned up. I'd stay here and do it but seeing you in any state of undress at all would completely wreck what little self-control I have right now. I'll be back in half an hour."

She smiled at him.

"Did I mention I'm glad I met you, Nathan?"

"You did," he said. "And I feel the same way. See you in a bit."

She kissed him again at the door and watched him all the way to the elevator. Then, Bella closed her door and couldn't stop herself from doing a little dance across the room.

He is so amazing, she thought, unable to stop smiling as she headed for a shower.

Two floors up, Nathan also couldn't shake the stupid grin as he shaved.

She is so beautiful, he mused as he relived their meeting. Waking up with her had been phenomenal.

He dressed, packed up his things, and headed out to the elevator to return to Bella.

Chapter Three

THEY CHECKED out of their rooms, left their bags with the concierge, and headed to the restaurant.

"Bel!" Stacy squealed as they approached.

"Good morning, you old married people you," Bella said, giving her best friend a hug and Brad a peck on the cheek.

"Who's your friend, Bel?" Stacy asked, eyes gleaming with curiosity.

"Stacy, Brad, I'd like you to meet Nathan," Bella answered. "We met last night at the slots."

She could tell Stacy was brimming with questions, but to Stacy's credit, she reined herself in and said sincerely, "It's a pleasure to meet you, Nathan."

Small talk was made, and the meal ordered. Then Stacy excused herself to the ladies' room. The look she shot Bella meant it needed to be a group trip.

The bathroom door had barely closed before Stacy started in.

"Bel, he's gorgeous, and obviously quite taken with you, I might add," she said. "Tell me all about it."

Bella recounted the whole story.

"So, you guys spent all night together, and you didn't have sex?" Stacy asked.

"No, we didn't," Bella answered. "Not that the chemistry isn't there. But we decided to wait a while."

She looked over to see Stacy teary eyed and smiling. "Bel, that is so beautiful," Stacy said, sniffling a little. "So romantic. Old-fashioned but so sweet."

Bella sighed contentedly, and said, "It is, isn't it? I never thought I'd find someone with the same values as me, but here he is."

"He's easy on the eyes, too," Stacy chimed, poking Bella in the ribs. "Now, let me fix my makeup right quick and we'll get back to our Prince Charmings. And," she added, glancing at Bella in the mirror, "when the time comes, I already know the perfect bridesmaid dress to wear at your wedding."

At the table, meanwhile, Brad had been peppering Nathan with questions.

"I'm sorry if I seem a little pushy. It's just Bel's like family, that's all. Just watching out for her," Brad said.

"I would expect nothing less from her friends," Nathan replied. "I get where you're coming from. She's special, one of a kind. That's why how fast or slow this goes is up to her. I just want to be around her."

Wow, Brad thought as he listened to Nathan speaking. *He really means it.*

Brad looked at Nathan and quietly said, "You're all right in my book, man."

"Thanks, Brad," Nathan answered. "It may be old-fashioned, but it matters to me what the people closest to her think, too. Speaking of which, maybe you and Stacy could get me in contact with her grandfather. I'd like to meet with him when I get back to Virginia."

"Be glad to," Brad said.

The conversation returned to general topics when they saw the ladies returning. An hour later, they were saying their goodbyes.

Brad extended his hand to Nathan and said, "It was great meeting you. We'll see you again?"

To which Bella replied, "Most definitely."

Nathan smiled at her.

"Your friends are amazing," he told her as they made their way to the casino floor to kill time before the trip to the airport. "And protective."

Bella laughed. "Sorry if Brad was a little, well, pushy."

"Funny, that's exactly the word he used," Nathan replied. "But it doesn't bother me. In fact, I appreciate how loyal your friends are. It just reinforces my opinion that you're very special."

And he lightly touched his lips to hers as she blushed and smiled.

She wrapped her arm around his waist and said, "And so are you. Now, let's see if my machine is lucky again today, shall we?"

Mikel sat in his car, surveying the street. Although he had one test subject already in his workroom, he'd decided to bring one more and had made the drive yet again to Vegas. Now he was parked just down from Planet Hollywood, scouting for a good candidate.

Ah, yes, over there. A woman, maybe thirty at the most, obviously a prostitute, with long, brown hair and curves. She will do nicely.

He started to get out of his car and froze in complete shock. *Bella.* His angel was coming out of the hotel. He blinked rapidly to make sure his eyes were actually seeing her.

Then the shock turned to mind-numbing rage as he noticed the man with her. They were obviously acquainted; Bella had one arm laced through his. He watched in disbelief as they placed bags in the open trunk and then got into the cab together. When the cab pulled away from the curb, it took with it his intention to secure another test subject. He immediately swung out and began to follow Bella's cab.

Who is that bastard? Bella is MINE! his mind screamed.

Bella and Nathan sat snuggled in the cab, talking and laughing, lost in their little world.

Mikel could see how close their silhouettes were, and it turned his stomach. When the cab reached the airport, Nathan helped her out of the car and grabbed both their bags from the trunk while she paid the driver. Neither of them noticed the man with white-blond hair four cars back.

As he watched them go into the terminal, Mikel flung his car into park with a curse, got out, and slammed the door. He had taken three steps toward the entrance when he was stopped by a security officer.

"You can't park there. It's for taxis and hotel shuttles only," the officer announced sternly, pointing at the posted signs.

Mikel glowered silently at the man and returned to his vehicle. Cursing again in frustration, he jerked the transmission into drive and pulled out from the curb without looking, narrowly avoiding a passing minivan.

That cheating bitch. She'll pay for this, he seethed. He turned sharply and headed back to the Strip.

Cindy had been, well, bored. Clients had been few today. So it was a pleasant surprise when the handsome, muscular blond approached her.

I hope he's hung like a bull to match the rest of that body, she had thought wickedly. *Might as well have some pleasure with business.*

A bit of suggestive talk back and forth, and now she was sitting in the front passenger seat, popping her gum and making small talk as he drove.

"Hey," she said. "We're heading out of town?"

"Yes," he replied, staring straight ahead. "My place is just outside the city limits. You'll like it; it's beautiful."

"Cool, baby," she said, and gave her attention to the passenger-side window. She people watched until there were no more in view.

As he turned off onto a side road, she finally decided to ask more questions about where they were going. Turning to speak to him, Cindy was met by a fist to her mouth, followed by a rag of chloroform.

"Coming."

Bella opened her door to face two dozen long-stemmed red roses in a huge vase. She signed for them, took them, and thanked the deliveryman before shutting and locking the door. She made her way to the kitchen on autopilot, her nose stuffed close to the bouquet. Bella set them on the counter and sighed with pleasure as she read the card.

I miss you already, Bella – Nathan.

Her head had been filled with thoughts of him since they'd parted ways yesterday afternoon at the airport. She was obviously on his mind, too.

A groan as she came back to consciousness.

"Please." Her tongue hurt from where she had bitten it.

No response. She tried again.

"Please don't hurt me anymore. I'll do whatever you want," Cindy managed through bruised lips and broken teeth. She knew he was there – she could hear him breathing, but she could not see him. She was blindfolded. Not that it mattered. Both eyes were swollen shut anyway from his repeated blows to her face, her dark-brown hair matted with sweat, tears, and blood.

Her body tensed. She began to panic as she heard him coming closer. She struggled to no avail; he had adjusted her position and now had her lying face down, hands bound over her head and her legs strapped down spread-eagle, with a pillow under her pelvis.

It was forty hours in and counting, and the smell of sex and the battered woman's terror permeating the air made Mikel grin from ear to ear.

What had started out as another test subject had quickly become something else. He had noticed when he chloroformed her that her eyes were the same color as Bella's. As a matter of fact, she resembled his angel quite a bit. His obsession took over. Mikel had thoroughly used Cindy, repeatedly, painfully. The act itself to him was not fascinating in the least. What was fascinating, though, was that at the point of climax he always saw his angel's face, called his angel's name. Whether this tramp noticed or not he neither knew nor cared. These visions of Bella were overpowering and addictive.

Now he edged closer, wanting another fix, becoming more aroused as Cindy continued to beg. "Oh, I know you will - because you don't have any choice. You can scream if you want to, you know," he finally answered. "Knock yourself out. This place is soundproofed."

"Mr. Amsel," Nathan said, striding into Manfred's office at the University. "Thanks for meeting me."

"Well, I admit my curiosity's up about you, ever since Stacy and Brad called to tell me about Bella's new man," Manfred responded with a grin. "Have a seat."

Manfred already knew quite a bit about Nathan, having done a full background check in addition to asking around about him at Quantico. But he chose to remain silent for a bit and see firsthand what this young man was made of.

Accepting the chair offered to him, Nathan leaned forward and said, "Mr. Amsel, I'll get right to the point. I met Bella last week in

Vegas, and I'm completely captivated by her. I'm here to ask your permission to date her, sir."

Noticing Manfred's raised eyebrows, he added, "I have very strong feelings for her, more than any woman I have ever met. And I know it's the twenty-first century and she and I are both adults. But I just didn't feel right about not asking you first."

"Well, son, Bella's got to make her own choices. She's certainly old enough, and modern enough," Manfred replied. "The fact you've come to me and introduced yourself and asked my opinion means a great deal to me personally. That was the standard back in my day. It speaks volumes for you and the way you were raised that you keep that tradition."

"So," Manfred continued, "my answer to you is yes, if Bella chooses to see you, that's fine with me."

He leaned back and favored Nathan with a smile.

"Now that's out of the way, tell me more about yourself."

"Hello?"

"Bella. It's Nathan."

God, he sounds sexy on the phone.

She pulled it together and said, "Nathan, the roses you sent are absolutely gorgeous. Thank you."

"I'm glad you like them. Listen, I'm flying out to Flagstaff on business tonight. If you're available, I can drive from there to Phoenix on Friday afternoon when I'm done. I'd like to see you."

"I would really like that, Nathan." Bella beamed as she twisted the phone cord around her finger.

"Great. It's a date. I'll call you when I leave Flagstaff?"

"Sounds good. I can't wait to see you."

"Me either. See you Friday, Bella."

"Bye."

Neither of them knew it, but they both did the same silly little happy dance when they got off the phone.

"Mr. Wallace? Do you have a moment?" Bella asked after knocking on the doorjamb.

"Certainly, Bella. Come right in. How was your Thanksgiving?" the headmaster asked as he motioned her to a chair.

"It was really nice," she answered. "Sir, I know you're busy, but I need to know if you've seen Tommy lately?"

"Not that I recall, not in the last couple of days anyway," Wallace responded, frowning. "But then again, we have over four-hundred kids here right now."

"Well, he missed our tutorial session yesterday and again today," she explained. "He's been doing so well, and he's been so excited about them, that it surprises me he's missed them."

The headmaster got up and moved over to a filing cabinet. "Tommy Bennett, right?"

"Yes."

He thumbed through, then extracted the boy's file.

Returning to the desk, he murmured, "Ah, here we are. It seems he was signed out of school the day before Thanksgiving by his uncle. I wasn't in that day, but the paperwork's in order, and Shelly filed it for me."

"Wow," Bella said. "I'm a little surprised he didn't tell me he was going home for the holiday."

"He may not have known," Wallace said gently. "Many of these troubled kids are troubled because their families are, well, loony. It may have been a last-minute thing. Still," he continued, still frowning, "he should have been brought back already, unless they signed him out permanently."

He flipped through the documents again.

"Yes, see, right here," he said, showing the pages to Bella. "For whatever reason, his family has opted to completely withdraw him from the Metzger Institute."

"I hope he's all right. He's such a sweet kid, and he has such promise," Bella said woefully.

Wallace patted her shoulder awkwardly.

"There, there, my dear," he said. "All we can do is hope for the best."

"I appreciate your time, Mr. Wallace," she said, rising to shake his hand. "I'll let you get back to your work."

"Anytime, dear."

He replaced the file in the drawer and returned to his desk as she left his office.

Mikel's ears perked up when he heard her voice. The bug he'd installed in the headmaster's office was of the finest quality; he heard their entire conversation as clearly as if he had been physically in the room. Mikel watched the monitor as Bella made her way out the front door.

Then, he walked softly down the hall to check on workroom two, where the subject of their conversation remained in a drug-induced sleep, before moving to workroom three to pay Cindy another visit.

Hearing his angel's voice had reignited his need for a fix.

"Bella? It's Nathan. I'm headed to Phoenix."

"Wonderful. Do you want to have dinner here, or go out?"

"How about there. Order in, or cook?"

She laughed.

"I'm equally good with either. I'm more interested in getting to spend time with you. Food's a bonus."

"Hmm," he said. "Chinese?"

"I know a great place, and they're quick, too. How do you feel about mushrooms and bean sprouts?"

"I like them both."

"Good, then I will order my usual and we can share; their portion sizes are huge."

"Sounds good to me. Just get a couple of extra egg rolls?"

"Of course."

"I should be there in about two and a half-hours, give or take," he said.

"And I will have food ready when you arrive," she responded.

She hung up reluctantly and busied herself with tidying up the apartment a bit. Then she brewed some iced tea, grabbed a shower, and ordered the food from Ping's. Her timing was perfect; he arrived just after the food did. She was setting plates when the intercom buzzer rang again, and she pressed the buzzer to let Nathan up.

She walked over to the door with a fork in each hand, looked out the peephole, grinned, and opened the door.

"Well, hello," was all she got out before he swept her up in a kiss. They moved backward into the apartment as one, Nathan pausing just long enough to close the door with his foot, while Bella took one arm from around him long enough to throw the deadbolt and drop the forks to the floor. Their pulses raced in time as their mouths and tongues intertwined.

With an effort, he lifted his mouth from hers, and his voice was hoarse with desire as he murmured, "God I missed you. In case you didn't notice."

She snuggled her face into his neck and breathed in his scent.

"I missed you, too. In case you didn't notice."

They stayed there for a time, arms around each other, reveling in the moment.

Then, she lifted her head and said teasingly, "You know I love this, but fried rice is better hot."

"No argument here. I'm starving," he answered as he watched her retrieve the hastily discarded silverware from the floor.

Following her to the table, he began scooping rice and placing egg rolls onto the plates while she got out more forks.

As they ate, Nathan said casually, "How's your week been?"

"Not too bad," she said. "One of my favorites at the school got withdrawn by his family over the break, though. Good kid, really bright. I just wish I'd had a chance to say goodbye."

She shrugged her shoulders. "It is what it is, I guess. Maybe they'll realize how happy Tommy was at school and let him return at some point."

"I'm sorry, Bella," he said. "But I'm sure he's fine."

He took another bite of fried rice and sounded nonchalant as he said, "Oh, by the way, I met your grandfather the other day."

"Really?" Bella asked. "Cool. Was he lecturing at Quantico or something?"

"Nope," Nathan replied. "To be honest, I went to see him at the University."

Bella put her fork down and rested her chin on her hand, intrigued.

"Why?"

"Honestly?"

"Of course."

"Well," Nathan said, dabbing his mouth with a napkin, "I'm a little old fashioned. I met you, I've fallen for you, so I went to ask your father – or in this case, your grandfather – for permission to date you."

She smiled. "And what did he say?"

"He said Bella's old enough and modern enough to make her own choices. He also said it impressed him that I would – how did he put it – 'keep the tradition' and ask. Then," he continued, gesturing with his fork, "he said if you chose to see me, that would be fine by him."

"Nathan Thomas," she responded, "I absolutely choose to see you. And I think it's sweet you kept the tradition."

Later, as they stood in the kitchen rinsing plates, she asked, "So, when do you have to be back in Virginia?"

"Not until Monday," he said, putting the leftovers away. "I built in some time to spend with you."

"In that case, let me show you something."

She took his hand and led him down the hall.

His breath caught as she opened her bedroom door. LED candles and rose petals graced the room.

He turned to her and said, "Are you sure?"

"Yes," she said, looking into his eyes. "And this time, we're prepared."

He swept her up into his arms and carried her to the bed.

"Have you lost your *mind?*" Adolf screamed as he smashed his glass against the wall.

Mikel remained silent. He had never seen his father like this before. Beet-red face, cords standing out on his neck, a vein pulsing ominously at the left temple.

"Your little side project could ruin us, you ungrateful bastard!"

"Dad, I'll take care of it."

"Damn right you will. *Tonight*, Mikel. And if you ever pull another stunt like this again, so help me God, I will take you out myself. Are we clear?"

"Clear, Dad."

Adolf stormed out of the room.

I deserved that, Mikel said to himself.

He had become so addicted to seeing the Bella visions that he'd been neglecting everything else. Adolf couldn't reach him by intercom, so his father had come down to check progress on the serum and found him with Cindy.

Well, what was left of Cindy, Mikel amended with a sadistic smile.

The spark that had defined Cindy had short-circuited after

almost one-hundred hours of misuse. Now, she was just... there. He was impressed she had remained connected as long as she did.

He'd hoped to be able to assuage his father's rage by using her as a demonstration of all his research and testing. Unfortunately, her broken mind rendered her completely unresponsive to the serum. He had tried several times to activate it; the only measurable responses were slight convulsions before the brain waves returned to minimalistic readings.

Now, she had to go. She wasn't even able to help him see the visions anymore. Without her cries, her screaming, her begging, the level of arousal needed just wouldn't come. He had tried.

Sighing, he filled the syringe and injected her at the base of the skull. He had found that for lethal doses, this tended to be a place often overlooked during a routine autopsy; good old Mr. Jones had been dispatched the same way, and that case was cold.

Where to put her? He thought for a moment. The place outside Phoenix where he'd buried the others was the perfect spot for this sort of thing. Would it be pushing his luck to take her there, too?

Mikel mulled it over as he watched the brain waves go flat. He checked for a pulse in her carotid and found none. Satisfied, he detached the monitoring wires, removed the rings and earrings she wore, and hummed as he wrapped the body in plastic bags for transport.

Tommy, my boy, it's all you I guess, Mikel reflected as he rechecked Cindy's room one more time to ensure no trace of her remained. *You get to be the star of the show after all.*

And the show would start as soon as he got back from the desert.

Adolf stood at his office window and watched Mikel's truck pull out of the main gate. He took another sip of his favorite brandy and again willed himself to calm down.

Reckless. Unfocused. Damn that kid.

Hopefully, he had gotten Mikel's attention. Adolf had been very careful over the years to rein in his temper. The last time it got the better of him he was almost caught with the manifesto and a sworn enemy went unpunished. That was a lifetime ago. Since then, he'd prided himself on remaining cool and calm despite the circumstances. Until tonight, he'd kept the beast under control rather well.

But seeing Mikel with that woman had set him off. There was no time, no room, for anything other than complete loyalty and dedication to the Reich and its resurrection. Animalistic urges had no place whatsoever at this table.

Adolf turned and went to sit in his armchair. He swirled his brandy and contemplated the fire; it relaxed him and helped him think. He would have to be more vigilant about his son, make sure Mikel stayed focused. That much was certain.

Of course, he didn't know about Mikel's obsession and the increasing power it had over him. He did not know that because of it, Mikel's loyalty to him might well be tested in the future.

If he had, he would have been much more worried than angry.

Chapter Four

"You've got to be kidding me," Mikel muttered, looking through his night vision binoculars.

He was lying on his stomach on a rise overlooking the burial site. On his approach, he'd noticed lights up ahead where there should have been darkness. He'd pulled over, killed his truck's engine, and walked the remaining quarter mile to scope it out.

What he saw had him on edge.

A party? Here? With all the open spaces around, these dumbass teenagers had to pick this one spot?

Above the rock music, someone screamed.

He followed the noise and trained his focus over to the right. He saw a rather drunk and extremely frightened girl pointing at something foreign poking up from the earth. One of the boys in the group walked over and bent down, making sweeping motions with his hands. Suddenly, he stood up and backed away quickly, gagging, reaching for his cell phone.

It was a shoe, with the owner's foot still inside.

Mikel put the binoculars down and dropped his head to the ground in disgust.

Fuck.

Trying to be as silent as possible, he maneuvered back down the slope and hustled back to his truck. He started it, turned around, and drove several hundred yards by moonlight before he dared to turn on the headlights.

He got back to the main road and was on it just long enough for the dust he'd kicked up to settle again, when he saw the two police vehicles hauling ass toward him. He slowed and pulled to the shoulder, then watched his rearview to confirm they were heading toward the underage drinking party.

Dammit. Think, Mikel, think. Are you sure you didn't miss something? he asked himself.

Yes, he was. He specifically recalled gathering up any jewelry or wallets they'd had. He'd specifically chosen the ones he did because they were anonymous and disposable. No one would miss them. No one would care. Even if they could be identified, there was absolutely nothing tying them to him. He'd even taken care to wipe his footprints that night.

Mikel exhaled slowly and pulled back onto the road. Stashing what used to be Cindy would have to wait until he could find another place.

On the outskirts of town, it came to him.

Smiling wolfishly, he veered left and headed for the construction site he knew to be nearby. A new bridge was being built. He had noticed workers assembling the column molds a couple of days ago. Whistling softly to himself, he maneuvered his truck into position and killed the lights. He sat for several minutes, watching, listening to make sure he hadn't been seen.

Just off to the left, he spotted what he was looking for – the huge hole in the earth for the first piece of the column mold to be placed into. He risked shining the flashlight on his keychain down the hole. It was perfect. No telling how deep that damn thing was.

He waited another few minutes to be safe. No one had seen him.

Mikel quickly moved to his tailgate and lowered it silently. He scooped up his broken rag doll, walked the twenty feet to the edge of the hole, and dropped her like a sack of garbage. He stood still in the darkness for a minute or two. No one had heard him.

He resisted the impulse to laugh out loud as he let his truck slowly coast backward to the street. If anyone saw him now, they would assume he had car trouble. Another few minutes spent with the hood up, pretending to fix it, and he was ready to return to the Institute.

The following morning Mikel watched with interest as the pretty redhead on the news relayed the breaking news of five bodies discovered; four in the desert, and a badly beaten woman discovered at a local construction site. Information was sketchy and the news anchor promised to keep him updated.

You do that, he thought. *Keep dreaming. There's nothing to tell.*

Bella and Nathan were unwittingly discussing Mikel's handiwork as they walked into the grocery store.

"I'm telling you, Bella, you should learn to shoot," he stressed as he opened the door for her. "That woman they were talking about yesterday on the news? Her body was found not far from here. You need to be able to protect yourself."

"I know," she sighed. "I've thought about it off and on since Stacy moved out. The apartments are quiet, and I've never had any trouble at all. But being alone makes you rethink your safety."

They grabbed a cart and started down the produce aisle.

"Fresh mushrooms?"

"Absolutely," she said. "I'll sauté them. They'll go great with the steaks."

Nathan placed the mushrooms in the cart and said, "I gotta tell you, food shopping with someone is a hell of a lot more fun than doing it all by yourself."

He leaned down to kiss her but was interrupted by his cell phone.

"Thomas," he announced, winking at her.

Then his face hardened, and a glint came into his eye as he signaled that he needed a minute. He was frowning in concentration as he listened.

A-hah, Bella thought. *So that's his "work face".*

"Yes, sir. Well, I am actually in Phoenix already, sir. I can be there in half an hour. Who's the POC? Harrington? Right. Will do."

Nathan hung up his phone and looked at Bella.

"Duty calls. I need to get to the ME's office as soon as possible. Can you hold dinner for me?"

"Absolutely," she said. "Let's hit the checkout lane. It sounds like you don't need to be late."

"Dr. Harrington? Nathan Thomas, FBI. Nice to meet you, sir."

"Nice to meet you, Agent Thomas. Let me show you what we've got so far."

The medical examiner strode over to the row of images he had on display. He pointed at the first and said, "Do you see that?"

Nathan moved closer.

"It looks like some sort of wound."

"It is," Harrington said. "And I've seen it before, on an unsolved case from back last summer. Brendan Jones. A young man found stuffed in the trunk of his car. Still had all his personal belongings on him. He had the same puncture wound at the base of the skull. This one," the doctor pointed to a second picture, "is his. The rest of these are from the five bodies recently discovered, none of whom had ID on them."

Nathan looked up and down the row. "Doctor, we have a serious problem here."

"I agree completely, which is why I called the FBI," Harrington said solemnly. "It would seem we have a serial killer operating in the Phoenix area. Six victims that we know of. I've already had copies made for you of all my autopsy reports, notes, pictures, everything."

He pointed to a box by the door. "It's all yours, Agent Thomas."

Nathan shook hands with Harrington and hefted the box.

"Let me get started on reviewing all this," he said. "With any luck we'll be able to build a pretty good profile."

"I hope you can catch him quickly," Harrington said. "We've managed to identify three of the bodies so far. The two women's fingerprints were in the system for previous prostitution arrests. We've not released this next bit of information yet, but it turns out he's also a cop killer. The third victim was a Vegas detective."

"Hold that announcement for a couple of days, if you can," Nathan replied solemnly, the glint back in his eye. "I'll be in touch."

Bella's living room had become a makeshift office. Nathan sat, surrounded by photos and frowning as he read the case report on Brendan C Jones.

Bella called him from the kitchen.

"Dinner's ready."

He looked up and smiled.

"I'm so sorry, Bella," he said in frustration. "When I said I'd spend some time with you, I really did mean it. But this," he gestured to all the papers, "this is just... wow. I've got to try and get ahead of this guy."

Bella walked over to him and turned white. With a trembling hand, she picked up a photo of Brendan.

"I knew him," she said flatly. "He was my competition for the internship at Metzger. We were all shocked when his body was found. I just thought it was a mugging gone bad or something. Is he connected to these others?"

"It's a strong possibility," Nathan conceded. "All six of these people had the same strange wound on the back of their necks."

She set the photo back down and took Nathan's hand.

"Let's eat while dinner is still warm," she said. "And maybe we can talk about what type of gun I should learn to shoot."

Later, as Bella slept, Nathan eased open the case file of victim number two, a prostitute named Cindy. His hands started to shake, and his pulse quickened as he looked at her most recent mug shot. The resemblance was eerie — he had to do a double take to make sure it wasn't Bella.

He closed the file and stared into space, his mind working what he knew so far like puzzle pieces.

The next morning over breakfast, Nathan blurted out, "Bella, please come back to Virginia with me. Today."

She rolled her eyes.

"Look, I know this case has got you rattled, but I can't leave yet. I've got finals the next three days. I've got this week at Metzger to get through. *Then* I can go," she retorted. "I'll be fine, really. I talked to Granpa this morning and he's flying out to drive back with me."

"I don't want to leave you here by yourself. It's not safe. But I have got to go back to my office. I need to wash all this through the computer models and get a handle on it so we can catch this guy."

Nathan ran his hands through his hair, and she noticed the worry on his face.

"What are you not telling me?" she demanded.

"Nothing," he lied with a straight face.

He wasn't about to let her know that one of the victims, the one beaten and brutalized, could have been her twin. He wasn't about to let her know that that, combined with the first victim being her competition for a job, had him spooked.

Bella was a part of this somehow. She was on this whack job's radar. He *knew* it. He knew it down to his toes. But there was no hard evidence, nothing he could show her or tell her, just a big, really bad gut feeling.

And so, he lied.

"Nothing," he said again, looking into her eyes.

Two days later, Mikel almost choked on his coffee as he watched the same redheaded news anchor reveal that one of the bodies found had been identified as that of a Las Vegas detective, who went missing while working undercover on the Strip.

Well, that explains a well-fed transient, he thought bitterly.

They had already identified Cindy and that other bitch, too. He felt claustrophobic. Getting up, he paced his main workroom, running his hands across his face.

The only bit of good news lately was that the serum was finally right. Tommy had been inoculated with no side effects whatsoever. He even maintained his appetite.

Mikel returned to his notebook and re-read his last entry, then dialed his father's office.

"You need to come down," he said. "I want you to see this."

At his office in Virginia, Nathan was also pacing.

"No pattern. No discernable pattern at all," he said again. "There's no commonality in the victims. Different ages, races, backgrounds. No known connection between any of them, except the fact that they were all killed by the same lunatic. And the only thing that shows that," he clarified, pointing to the pictures, "is this damn wound at the base of the skull."

"Agreed," said Steve Brown, Nathan's boss. "I also think a detective being killed doesn't signify anything either. I think our perp was snatching what he thought were degenerates, people no one would miss. Detective Allen just happened to be working undercover in the wrong place at the wrong time."

"I do think the killer is male," Nathan continued. "And he must have used some sort of drug to incapacitate or subdue his victims. Allen wasn't a little guy, and he had combat training. He would have put up a fight if he sensed trouble."

Silence followed.

"I want to go to Vegas," he said. "I want to canvass the areas where our three identified victims were last seen, show their pictures, ask around. Maybe somebody saw this guy and just doesn't realize it."

"We'll get you out there by nightfall," Steve said.

Nathan strode to the door.

"And Nathan?"

"Yes, sir?"

"Carry your sidearm."

"Impressive, Mikel. Very impressive." Adolf nodded approvingly as he watched the demonstration.

His son was talented, no question. With a few keystrokes, Mikel transformed Tommy from a thoughtful and well-behaved child to an aggressive, violent warrior who responded only to Mikel and Adolf's voices and who was completely malleable. Another couple of keystrokes and Tommy was normal again, apparently with no recollection of anything.

"Get as much ready as you can, as quickly as you can," Adolf said to Mikel. "I want to begin inoculating the rest of the students and staff in the next day or two. And arrange for a dose to travel with me. I have a pain-in-the-ass senator I have to meet on Friday on the Hill. It's time I poured him some very special wine."

"I'm worried about her, sir," Nathan said.

"Call me Manfred, please," came the reply. "And I can see why you'd be worried, given what you just told me."

"You're flying out to drive back with her, right?"

"My flight is already booked. I head out late Friday afternoon. You just concentrate on finding this guy, Nathan. I'll watch over Bella. We'll see you in a couple of days."

Mikel frowned as he watched the on-screen exchange.

"Tommy?" Bella said, approaching the subject.

"Oh, hello Miss Bella."

"I'm so glad to see you. I heard your family had taken you out of school. I'm guessing they changed their minds?"

Unsatisfied, Mikel punched in a sequence of keys and hit enter. He smiled as he watched Tommy's vacant face curve into a snarl.

"I don't care what you heard. Stay away from me, you stupid bitch!"

As Tommy stormed off, Mikel chuckled and zoomed in on Bella to see her reaction. He felt like shit when he saw the devastated look on her face.

She stood there, mouth agape and tears coming to her eyes, then shook her head slowly, wiping a tear from her cheek as she walked away.

Mikel hung his head. Feeling guilty was new to him, but it melted what little heart he had to see her with tears on her face.

I'm so sorry I made you cry, angel. I won't do it again. I promise, my love.

Nathan caught a break in Vegas. An old, black hooker who went by the name Sweetness had seen Cindy get into a car with a blond man.

"And Lord have mercy, that man was stacked, let me tell you," Sweetness exclaimed over the coffee Nathan had bought her. "Muscled, fine body, with a pretty face to match. At least from what I could tell. I was, you know, catty-corner from them so I didn't get the full-on look. I didn't think nothin' of it at the time, except maybe a little jealous of Cindy. When I heard ya'll had found her body, I asked the other girls 'round here. Nobody seen her since she left with that man. I know he involved, baby. I feel it."

"What about the car?" Nathan pressed.

"Nothin' big there. Old, beat-up, gray four-door. You know, the kind looks like they been too long as a rental. They get beat to hell used, then just sold outright."

"Yeah, Sweetness, I know the kind," Nathan said.

He slid a card across the table.

"Listen, you think of anything else, hear anything else, you call me, okay? And watch yourself."

"They is one other thing," she said. "There was a dude 'round here, Crazy Joe, they called him. Loony but harmless, sweet, you know? Anyway, he was down here every day, like clockwork. Ain't nobody seen him in a couple months now. He may be one of them other ones ya'll got."

She gave him a description of Crazy Joe, and she was right. He was one of the two John Does in cold storage in Phoenix.

Next, Nathan hit a few used car lots in the area. He finally found one man about a mile and a half from the Strip that remembered a strange encounter.

"Guy had a wad of cash, wouldn't sign anything," the lot manager said. "I told him I wouldn't do the deal without a signature, and he walked away."

"How long ago was this?"

"Couple months, maybe three. He was agitated, you could tell. But he was trying to stay mellow about it, ya know? Like he didn't wanna attract attention. Then, about a week later, I come in one morning and notice I'm short one on the lot. I ask my guys if anyone moved it without filing the papers. They say no. I double check the inventory, and yeah, one's missing. A crappy little gray four-door, the most worthless one I got, go figure that."

"Did this guy happen to be blond?"

"Yeah. Didn't get a real good look at his face though; he had a ball cap on and mirrored shades. 'Bout six-four, I'd say, and muscled. And way blond hair, I mean, almost white."

"Anything else you can tell me?"

"Yeah, he had a really small tat on the side of his neck, kinda behind his ear. It was wicked looking. That Nazi symbol thingy, with blood dripping off it. I really think it pissed him off that I noticed it. He wouldn't tell me when I asked where he got it. Wasn't too long after that he left."

"Man, you've been really helpful," Nathan said sincerely, passing him a card. "You happen to see him again, give me a shout, all right?"

"Absolutely."

Bella sat for a moment to cool off. Although the apartment had come furnished so she didn't have to deal with moving furniture, she still had several more boxes' worth of clothes and books and things to pack up. She was beginning to wonder if it would all fit in the truck bed.

She grabbed the next box and headed down the hall. As her hands busied themselves, her mind wandered back to Tommy's outburst yesterday afternoon. It had broken her heart. Whatever had happened to him over the break, it had changed him. The sweet youngster with so much promise that had become her favorite student was now cold and distant.

Her ringing phone pulled her back.

"Hello?"

"Hey Bella, it's Nathan."

"Hi! How's the case going?"

"I'm in Vegas for a day or two digging around. I should be flying back sometime tomorrow evening at this rate. And so far, I've gotten some good leads. Are you doing all right?"

"I'm good," she said.

He heard the tone.

"Bella, what's wrong?"

She burst into tears and told him about Tommy.

"It'll be all right, Bella. Sounds like maybe that kid has got a lot going on at home that he's having trouble processing. He's – what – ten, you said?"

"Uh-huh," she answered, sniffling.

"Well, speaking from experience, boys that age have a lot of trouble expressing themselves. You know, we pull a girl's hair when we like her, things like that. Whatever's going on with him, I'm sure it will pass, Bella. Just be there for him if he comes to you. That's all you can do. Okay?"

"Okay."

"I'll see you in a couple of days, all right?"

"See you Sunday. And hey," she told him in mock seriousness, "no picking up any chicks in Vegas."

"No worries. I already picked up the one I want to spend time with," he replied earnestly.

It was magic. All she had to do was hear his voice, and she felt better. She returned to packing with a little spring in her step.

He's right, she reflected. *Ten-year-old boys are all over the map. Whatever's going on with Tommy, I'm sure it will work itself out.*

She sighed as she counted the boxes again, then headed to the phone book. Flipping through, she found the number she needed and dialed.

"Hello," she said. "I need to rent a really small pull-behind trailer."

Chapter Five

AH. *The privileges of wealth. One's own plane meant no annoying baggage searches,* Adolf thought and smiled. The special canister Mikel had rigged for him didn't have to pass through security.

His limo pulled up to his hotel. Adolf casually retrieved his attaché case with the canister in it and nodded to the driver who held open his door.

Making his way across the lobby, he favored the desk clerk with a smile.

"Hello again, Mr. Metzger, wonderful to see you," the striking blonde said. "Your usual accommodations are ready."

"A pleasure as always, Marjorie."

He strolled leisurely to the elevator.

He settled into the spacious penthouse, then dialed the senator to invite him over for lunch the following day. That accomplished, he hung up, then dialed the Institute.

"Mikel, how are things there?"

He and his son chatted for a bit before Adolf ended with, "I will be back sometime tomorrow. Keep working on what we talked about."

"Yes, sir."

He made two more calls, the last one to room service. He decided on the lobster.

As he feared it might be, Manfred's flight on Friday had been postponed an hour. Old Man Winter had been making life difficult for travel plans today. Hopefully, he would be able to get out during the break in the weather they were mentioning on the radio. If he didn't leave tonight, he might not be able to at all until sometime early next week. He settled into the little bistro nearest his terminal gate to wait it out with a cup of coffee.

Adolf smiled silkily at the young woman behind the counter.

"I need a flight to Phoenix," he said.

His private plane had developed some sort of trouble so he would have to fly commercially. Not that it mattered. His luggage could now safely pass through any security device.

She consulted her monitor, then smiled.

"We have flight 856 direct to Phoenix. It's scheduled to leave at six p.m."

"Any first-class seats available?"

"Yes, sir, you have your choice of rows four, five, and seven, as well as aisle or window."

"Row four, window, please."

He casually strolled through security and took a seat just beside the gate counter, glancing at his watch. About a thirty-minute wait. While he waited, he relived his earlier victory.

The senator had arrived precisely at twelve-thirty, punctual as always. Lunch had been right on time as well. Adolf had plied the man with small talk, exquisite food, and a vintage chardonnay.

What the senator didn't know was that both his wineglass and his water also contained a fast-acting sedative. Once he was out, Adolf had injected him with the serum.

Two hours later, the man woke, groggy and disoriented.

"Where am I?" he had slurred.

"In my hotel room, remember? We met for lunch to discuss the plant," Adolf had said reproachfully from across the room. "But you seem to have overdone the wine."

He gestured to the two empty bottles he had arranged at the Senator's place setting.

The Senator winced.

"Wow. That would explain the headache," he had managed. "I never had a problem with the hard stuff. But wine screws with me, every time."

He attempted to stand, then sank wearily back into his chair.

"Honestly, I cannot continue to maintain a business relationship with you if you can't stay sober long enough to discuss the details," Adolf had announced, playing it to the hilt. "Stay here and sleep it off. When you're ready to be serious, come see me at the Institute."

He glanced at his watch, then continued, "If you'll excuse me, I have another meeting, and then I must head to the airport."

He'd had great difficulty containing a smile as he pretended to storm his way out of the room, leaving a confused and chastened senator in his wake.

"Attention all passengers for flight 856 non-stop to Phoenix. We will begin boarding shortly," came the brisk announcement over the intercom and pulled a smiling Adolf back to the present.

Within ten minutes, first class passengers had been seated. Now the business class and coach passengers began to file down the narrow aisle. Adolf looked up idly at the people shuffling past him and was stunned.

The professor? After all these years? On the same damn plane? Surely not.

He got up and moved out to the aisle, with the pretense of

retrieving something from his bag in the overhead storage compartment. As he did so, he glanced down the cabin toward the back of the plane. It was him, all right, he was sure of it.

Adolf sat down again, trying to hide his smile as he turned his attention to the window.

I can't risk killing him on the plane, he thought, *but I can damn sure handle him once we land.*

The revenge he'd waited so long for was just hours away, and the thought made him giddy. He pulled out his cell phone and sent a quick text to Mikel.

Meet me at the airport yourself. There's been a change of plans. Flight 856. Come armed.

He hit 'send', then turned off his cell phone per the flight attendant's pre-takeoff instructions.

"What are we doing?' Mikel asked as Adolf climbed into the car.

"We are following those two right there," Adolf responded tersely. "Just do what I tell you."

They circled the parking lot slowly until they saw the truck heading toward the exit.

"Don't lose them, Mikel, but don't get us seen. I mean it," Adolf snarled.

They followed, hanging back about fifty yards. When the truck pulled over and stopped, Mikel coasted to a stop on the opposite side of the street and doused the headlights. From this angle, he could tell it was a man and a woman but not much else. The woman had some sort of ball cap on, throwing a shadow across her face. They walked into an apartment building that Mikel recognized, though he would never dare admit it to his father. To do so would reveal his obsession with a certain Institute employee – an obsession best kept secret.

Mikel turned and looked at his father with a raised eyebrow.

"This is about settling a long overdue score," Adolf said. "It must look random, accidental."

And he explained what he wanted done.

Adolf finished with, "Do what you want with the woman if she comes back out. But he dies. Understand?"

Mikel nodded his understanding and stepped out of the car. Silently, he crossed the street and settled into the deep shadows by the front entrance, waiting for his prey to appear, the blade tucked out of sight in his sleeve.

"So, did you get everything packed up?" Manfred asked, strolling around the apartment.

"Finally," Bella said. "I did a few boxes each day this week, so it actually wasn't bad. But I discovered I have accumulated more stuff than I thought. So, I called and planned for one of the little bitty U-Haul trailers to pull behind the truck. I thought we'd pick it up first thing in the morning."

"How's your young man, Bellissima?"

"Great. Except for catching this wicked case, that is. It's pretty big, Granpa. If he can figure this creep out and stop him, well, it would be impressive for his first case out of the academy. Although if you were to ask Nathan, he's not even thinking about that part."

"I know for a fact he's not even considered that part. His focus is on stopping this lunatic, which is where it should be."

Manfred paused and then changed topics.

"So, am I right in assuming wedding bells at some point?"

Bella laughed.

"Granpa, we *just* started seeing each other."

"Just saying. I was young once, too, you know." He smiled, putting an arm around her shoulders. "And it was love at first sight with your grandmother. I managed to wait six whole dates before popping the question, when I really wanted to ask her after the first five minutes."

Bella got misty.

"So, you're all right with my dating him?"

"I'm more than all right with this. I hope you get to experience the same kind of magic Rose and I had. A deep and abiding love, Bella. That's what I wish for you, child."

His eyes took on a wistful glaze.

"I miss her, Bella. I really miss her."

"I know, Granpa. Me too."

Manfred sighed and smiled.

"How about we go get that Italian food now?"

"Sure thing."

They locked the door and headed down the stairs. Halfway down, her cell phone rang.

"Hi Nathan, hang on just a sec," she said, beaming at her grandfather.

He smiled at her and held his hands out for the keys.

"I'll give you some privacy. Meet you at the truck," Manfred said, and kissed her cheek.

He continued down the stairs, smiling to himself as he heard her talking in that awestruck tone.

True love.

He was so happy Bella seemed to have found it.

Manfred walked out the front door of the building and paused, staring up at the sky.

Rose, I miss you, and I wish you were here, he thought.

"Manfred?"

A man's voice saying his name snapped him back to reality.

"Yes?" Manfred said, looking around.

"I have a gift for you, from Adolf Werner," said the voice behind him.

Manfred turned.

Nathan's conversation with Bella was interrupted by her screaming, "No! Granpa! Oh my God..."

"Bella, what's going on? Bella? *Bella?*"

The only response was distant screaming and what sounded like a struggle. She had dropped the phone, then the call dropped completely.

Nathan spun a hard U-turn in the middle of the intersection, then began to haul ass toward Phoenix, wishing like hell rental cars had lights and sirens.

He dialed nine-one-one, gave his name and title and said, "There's something going on at two-forty-two Pine Road in Phoenix. Send an ambulance, then put me through to the police chief, please."

A few anxious moments passed before the man came on the line.

Nathan explained the situation and said, "I need someone to call me back and tell me what the hell's going on there. I'll be there as fast as I can."

Next, he called his boss and filled him in.

Then he hung up the phone and floored it.

Bella was in the fight of her life.

She'd been walking out the door, talking to Nathan, when she saw the man come into view from the left. She heard the man say something about a gift from someone. She saw her grandfather turn toward him. In slow motion it seemed, she saw the stranger's right arm raise up, and the glint from the overhead light reflecting off the knife in his hand.

Without any thought for her own safety. she ran forward, screaming. It only took a few seconds, but in that time the man had stabbed Manfred repeatedly. Her grandfather lay crumpled on the pavement.

She howled like a wounded animal and charged, jumping on the man's back, dropping the phone as she did so. She screamed and kicked, scratched and clawed. He shrugged her off like a mosquito. She charged him again. A vicious backhand struck her face and took her breath away. She felt the sting of the blade as it sliced her arm.

Determined not to give up, Bella yelled a warrior's yell, and ran at their attacker again. Then, time seemed to stop. She felt a pain in her chest like she had never known. She looked down at her sweatshirt, quickly saturating with her blood.

A massive left hook to the face knocked her ball cap off completely. She fell backward to the ground, slamming her head against the pavement.

As she started to lose consciousness, the last thing she saw was the man who had stabbed her leaning closely over her. She could see his lips moving, see his ghostly gray eyes, and then she slid into blissful darkness.

Mikel was absolutely crushed.

Manfred had gone down easily. Then all hell had broken loose behind him. The woman was fighting with all she had. He fought on autopilot, managing to land knife thrusts once to her arm, and once in the chest.

He didn't know it was his angel until he struck her the second time, and her baseball cap flew off. Seeing her lying there, bleeding by his hand, burned him to the core.

He knelt over her.

"Bella, angel, are you all right? Angel, please speak to me. Forgive me."

Then he felt rough hands on his shoulders, pulling him to his feet.

It was Adolf.

"Mikel, we must go. The police are coming. Move, Mikel. Now, goddammit!"

Mikel let himself be manhandled to the passenger seat and sat there blankly as Adolf sped off into the night.

"Stay with us."

IV drip started.

"Pulse thready, BP ninety over sixty, pulse ox eighty-five. Sounds like a punctured lung. Lost a lot of blood. Starting plasma."

A faint rhythm, now stronger. A gasp for air.

"Call ahead and tell them to prep a surgical suite, stat."

"Already did."

"How's the other one?"

"Dead at scene."

"Stay with us. Stay with us. You're gonna be all right. You're a fighter. Stay with us."

Darkness again.

Lights flickering. Hallway? White walls. The sensation of being lifted, then lowered again. More lights.

A woman, leaning close.

"Just relax, we've got you."

Darkness.

Nathan made it to the hospital a full half-hour before the surgeon came out to relay any news. He switched back and forth between sitting with his head in his hands, and pacing. He jumped to his feet when the door to the waiting room opened. Then, his shoulders sagged.

"You must be Nathan," said a booming but kind voice. "I'm Max Jones. I work with Manfred. I came as quickly as I could."

Nathan half-heartedly extended a hand.

"Any word?"

"No." And he held his head in his hands again. "No one will tell me anything. Not a thing."

He lifted his head and looked at Max, his eyes filled with tears.

"I can't lose her, I just can't."

"I was there the day Bella was born," Max said gently. "Manfred and I have been friends since 1945. They're tough people, Nathan."

And he rested his hand on Nathan's shoulder to comfort him.

The door opened again. It was the head surgeon.

"Amsel?"

Max and Nathan nodded.

The surgeon sat down across from them.

"Bella is serious but stable. She lost a lot of blood. We gave her a unit of plasma at the scene, and three units of blood once she got here. She has two hairline fractures, one at the back of her skull and the other on her right cheekbone. She also sustained a severe concussion, a stab wound to the chest that collapsed her right lung, and a slice on her arm that needed fifty stitches, in addition to cuts and contusions on her face where her assailant hit her."

Nathan's fists doubled up at this news; Max patted his shoulder.

The surgeon continued, "We took her into surgery to repair some damage and successfully re-inflate the lung. She'll be staying here the next several days, but I see no reason why she won't make a full recovery."

Nathan's relief was palpable.

"And Manfred?" Max asked solemnly.

"We tried to resuscitate him, both on scene and once he arrived here. I'm sorry, but the damage was just too great."

Max lowered his head and was silent for a moment. When he cleared his throat and spoke, it was raw with emotion.

"What's the next step?"

"The hospital chaplain will be by shortly. Please let us know if there's anything else at all we can do."

"Keep taking care of her," Nathan said earnestly. "When can I see her?"

"She's still in recovery. We'll be moving her to ICU tonight because of the blows she took to the head. When they are severe enough to cause hairline fractures, we want to keep a close eye on things. So, she'll be in ICU for observation for probably thirty-six to forty-eight hours, then to a regular room for a couple of days after that. My OR nurse, Alicia, will come let you know when we move her to ICU. It shouldn't be much longer."

"Thanks, doc."

They watched the surgeon step out to talk to a uniformed officer and what looked to be a detective.

Max exhaled.

"I just lost my best friend. Because of a mugging."

Nathan looked at him and saw the grief.

"I am so sorry, Mr. Jones. I only met him once, talked with him a couple of times. But I could tell he was a good guy."

"You don't know the half of it, son," Max said, with a mournful smile. "We were friends for over sixty years. Hell, he was like a brother. He was one of the most decent men I have ever known."

"You stay with Bella," he said, rising. "I'll be back to see her later. I have calls to make and services to arrange. Do me one favor, Nathan. Don't tell her about Manfred, and don't let anyone else either. Not until I get back. Okay? She'll be devastated. I want to be there for her when she hears. She is the granddaughter I never had."

"I promise, sir."

"Mikel."

No answer.

Adolf tended to the deep claw marks on his neck. His patient sat catatonic.

"Mikel, drink this."

Adolf worked the glass of brandy into his hand and waited.

No movement.

Sighing, he sat beside his son and maneuvered the glass up to Mikel's lips.

Mikel drank, swallowed, shuddered. He blinked several times, then slowly turned his head to look at his father.

Adolf was amazed to see he was crying.

"I killed her," Mikel sobbed like a little kid. "I killed my angel."

Adolf pressed him for more information, but Mikel was unresponsive. Finally, Adolf decided sleep would be best.

He guided Mikel to his room, took off his shoes, and tucked him in. He stayed until Mikel fell asleep.

Then he headed for Sub-Level Three.

Nathan and Max went into the hallway and approached the men that had been talking to the surgeon.

The one in the suit said, "I'm Detective White, and this is Officer Maguire. He was first on scene."

Handshakes were made.

"Your lady friend's one hell of a fighter," White said. "The ER team told me they recovered a lot of the perp's skin from under her nails. If the bastard's DNA is anywhere on file, we should be able to get a match."

"Something tells me we'll have a prior sample to match it to," Nathan said grimly, then brought up the multiple homicide case he was involved in.

"Cindy, the victim that was raped repeatedly. Bastard didn't bother to wrap it, so we have a DNA sample. My gut tells me it will match the skin Bella got."

Then he shared his belief that at least part of it tied to Bella somehow.

"Cindy looked so much like Bella that they could have been twins. Brendan Jones was Bella's competition for the internship. I don't believe these are coincidences. I have no hard evidence to back this yet, just a strong gut feeling. So, I'm asking that we at least consider instructing the hospital to screen anyone that calls in asking a bunch of questions about Bella. If they're not on a list that Max and I make, they get told that she's dead. Please. If he knows she survived, he may try it again."

White nodded.

"I'll ask up the chain, but yes, I agree it's the safe thing to do. Let me call the chief." And he stepped away.

A woman in scrubs stepped forward.

"Mr. Thomas?"

Nathan whirled around.

"I'm Alicia. We've got her settled in ICU. Please follow me."

He turned back to the trio.

"Talk later?"

"Absolutely," Max said, with White and Maguire nodding in agreement.

He bolted down the corridor.

<hr>

She looked so frail, so tiny.

The entire right side of Bella's face was bruised, with an ugly black bruise centered on that beautiful cheek. That and the ebony of her hair seemed to make her skin snow white, almost transparent. Her knuckles were banged up from pummeling her attacker with all her might. Her right forearm was swathed in bandages.

Nathan pulled a chair up as close as he could, and gingerly took her right hand in his. She was still out from the anesthesia and the pain medications. He leaned forward, touching his forehead to her bed. All the worry and fear wrung out of him in silent tears.

Then he felt a delicate hand, feather-soft against his hair. He lifted his head and saw those blue eyes gazing at him drowsily.

"Hi baby," she whispered before drifting back into sleep.

She danced between dream and lucidity for a time, and it was a strange dance. Her eyes darted back and forth behind closed lids. She shuddered several times. Every muscle in her body seemed to tense, and just when Nathan thought he ought to get the nurse, she relaxed again.

He had been sitting at her bedside for two hours when she began to moan. It was the sound of a wild animal, cornered, fighting to survive, and it broke his heart.

Bella's eyes popped open wide, huge, and now she was trying to scream, trying to sit up, fighting off the attacker from her dream.

"Bella, it's me. It's me. You're safe now, baby. It's Nathan," he repeated over and over.

But it seemed she couldn't hear him, still struggling blindly against an apparition.

He pressed the call button frantically.

"Yes?" said a voice through the speaker.

"Help her," he pleaded.

Moments later, the nurse came through the door with an IV sedative. She injected it into the mainline and in another few moments Bella calmed and returned to sleep.

"What's happening?" a frightened Nathan asked.

"She's sustained a trauma to her head," the doctor who had just entered the room explained. "So, it may take longer for the cobwebs to clear, so to speak. Concussive injuries like hers can be tricky. She's also survived a horrific attack. What you just saw may be her mind replaying it."

"Do you think she'll remember it once she comes to?"

"Hard to say. It really depends. Some people never regain the memory of the incident. Others remember every detail. Some only have little pockets of memory. They may recall seeing the other car run the light, for example, and then it fast-forwards to remembering the airbag deflating, with just a blank space in between."

She put a reassuring hand on his shoulder.

"The best thing for her right now is sleep. The body can do amazing things to heal itself. Of course, with a concussion we'll follow standard protocols. We'll be waking her every hour or so to check progress. And we'll run at least one more CAT scan while she's in ICU."

Another nurse poked her head in.

"Mr. Thomas? You've got friends in the waiting room."

He looked at Bella.

"Go take a little break," the doctor said gently. "She's in good hands. If she wakes before you get back, we'll come get you, I promise."

Nathan walked down the corridor to see Max, Stacy and Brad all standing there. His eyes filled with tears as Stacy held out her arms.

"God, Stacy, we almost lost her," he managed.

"But we didn't,' she said, patting his back. "She's tough as hell. That's one of the things we love about her."

They walked over and sat down, and Nathan brought Stacy and Brad up to speed on everything that had happened.

"Full recovery? Oh, thank God," Stacy said.

Chapter Six

*H*IS *ANGEL? What the hell did that mean?*

Adolf was determined to find out. As soon as he was sure Mikel was asleep, he went to the one place where an answer might be – Mikel's workrooms. The kid spent almost all his time down there. Flipping on the light, he went to the computer and entered the login password.

INVALID LOGIN flashed in ugly red letters.

What the hell?

Adolf re-entered the password and got the same error message.

Mikel had changed the login for this terminal. Why? Only he and Adolf even knew about this level, much less had access to it.

He thought for a moment, then typed *"Angel"*.

WELCOME, MIKEL displayed on the screen.

Adolf didn't like this one bit, and he had a feeling it was about to get worse. He pulled up file after file that had nothing whatsoever to do with the Reich, or with the research, or with anything that was supposed to be most important. Every single one of them was about Bella.

Monitoring her movements around the campus, video, audio,

pictures, journal entries about her. He opened one picture and gazed at it for a long time.

That explains the woman he had down here, Adolf reflected. *They could have been sisters.*

His son was quite obviously obsessed with the granddaughter of his worst enemy.

And the sad part is, you read her last name when Wallace showed you the new tutor list, and you didn't connect the dots, his mind chanted.

Well, she was dead now, along with that blaspheming bastard. And he was about to help his son get over her and get back on track.

One by one, all the pictures, videos, pages and pages of lovesick ranting got dragged and dropped into the recycle bin. Then the press of a button. Done. Bella was history, and now Mikel could move on.

"What did you just do?" Mikel said from the doorway, a little too calmly.

"Protecting you," Adolf responded, caught off guard. "Protecting *us*. She's dead. If anyone had ever seen what you had on this computer, it would have been used against you. You stalked her, Mikel. For months, from what I could tell. How do you think all that," he gestured to the computer, "would have looked, especially now that she's dead?"

"She's dead because of *you*!" Mikel raged at the top of his lungs. "You had me do your dirty work, and now my angel is *dead*! And you think you can sneak down here and take her from me again, take all my memories?"

Fists clenched, he walked slowly toward his father. "What, you think you can reset me like some fucking *machine*? That I won't love her anymore because her pictures are gone? Is that what you think? *Is that what you think?*"

Adolf began to back away slowly. Something was very, very wrong here. Mikel had gone somewhere Adolf couldn't reach him.

Mikel continued his slow approach, deliberately keeping himself between his father and the door. The look on his face was feral.

"Mikel, get hold of yourself." Adolf's tone turned dangerous. "Don't let some tramp cloud your judgment. You need to focus. Don't blow everything we've worked for all these years."

"Some *tramp*? Fuck you, old man. We both know I can take you. I'm the perfect example of Hitler's 'master race', remember? You said so yourself," Mikel taunted, edging closer.

Adolf searched his peripheral for something – anything – he could use as a weapon. He noticed a pair of scissors on top of a small cabinet.

"Go for it. Please. I want you to," said the man he'd raised.

Adolf faked right then lunged left. His left hand clasped around the scissors as Mikel closed the distance between them to two feet.

Then Adolf stepped back, disbelieving, looking down at the red flower blossoming in his chest. The smell of gunpowder filled the small room as he stumbled back into the wall and slid down.

Mikel leaned down over him.

Adolf remained alive just long enough to see those gray eyes filled with hate a few inches away from him and hear his son say, "Your Reich was a pipe dream. Welcome to reality, Adolf."

"Bella, angel, are you all right? Angel, please speak to me. Forgive me."

Bella's eyes opened, frightened, darting around the room. Then she frowned.

Where the hell am I?

"Hey, baby. You're awake."

She turned her head and looked into those hazel eyes she loved so much.

"Hi," she said weakly. "Where am I?"

Nathan sighed.

"You're in the intensive care unit at Phoenix Memorial," he said, gently squeezing her hand.

"And we're very glad to see you awake," came a voice from the doorway.

She looked and saw Stacy, Brad, and Max standing there.

She closed her eyes.

"We were attacked."

"We know, baby," Nathan said softly.

"I was on the phone with you," she said. "And then I saw this guy come up to Granpa, and I heard him say something about a gift from someone named Werner? And the guy had a knife."

She frowned as she remembered more.

"He stabbed my Granpa, Nathan," Bella revealed. "So, I went to stop him, and we fought, and I hit my head, I think. But I remember him leaning over me, speaking to me, and then... nothing."

"Did you say Werner?" Max asked, with a strange look on his face.

"Yes, Werner. And I remember exactly what the guy looked like. Even his tattoo."

Now Nathan had a strange look.

"Tattoo?"

"Yes. On his neck. A swastika with blood on it. Nathan, he knew my name," she continued. "He called me by name and asked me to forgive him."

Max and Nathan exchanged 'we'll need to talk outside in a bit' looks.

Bella tried to sit up and winced.

"Ouch. Man, I hurt *everywhere*. I thought I just hit my head?"

"Baby, you took a knife to the chest. They had to re-inflate your lung. You also have a severe concussion, a couple of hairline fractures, and fifty stitches under that arm bandage," Nathan told her.

"How's Granpa doing? Is he in ICU too? When can I see him?"

They all were silent for a moment before moving closer to her, dreading the answer to the question, knowing it would break her heart.

Max came and sat. He took her other hand.

"Bella." He paused. "I don't know how to tell you, but, he's gone, honey. I'm so sorry."

"Oh, no, no, no," Bella began to sob. She pulled her hands free and covered her face.

Nathan rubbed her arm gently and Stacy patted her leg, trying to comfort her.

After a time, she dropped her hands from her face and looked into Nathan's eyes. She was still crying, but now he could see she was also pissed.

"Get someone in here who can draw," she said evenly, wiping away tears. "I remember his face. Let's catch this guy."

"That's the Bel I know and love," Stacy announced, wiping away tears of her own. "I told you guys she was tough as hell."

Mikel sat and stared at Adolf for some time. His father's words still burned in his ears.

Don't let some tramp cloud your judgment.

But she wasn't some tramp. She was his whole world.

Self-serving bastard. It was his insistence on settling some ancient wrong that had caused Bella's death.

Well, the king of hypocrisy was dead now. And everything Adolf had was now Mikel's to use as he liked.

"But it won't bring back my angel," he muttered bitterly.

I wish it could. Oh, how I wish it could.

Sighing, he got to his feet. Time to clear the trash out of his workroom again.

"His eyes were just a little further apart. And gray, like a winter storm," Bella urged.

The tech pressed a few keys, then said, "Like this?"

Bella began to shake.

"Exactly like that," she managed. "That's the man that killed my grandfather and attacked me."

The tech turned to Nathan.

"She's got one heck of a memory. I've never worked with anyone who remembered so many details, and I've been doing this for ten years."

"Nathan," Bella said suddenly. "Someone else was there."

"What?"

"Someone else was there. This man was leaning over me, calling my name and asking me to forgive him. Right before I blacked out, someone put their hands on his shoulders and pulled him up. And they said something."

She closed her eyes, frowning with the effort of recollection.

"Dammit. I can't remember. I know it's important, and I just can't remember."

She opened her eyes, frustrated. Nathan could see her becoming increasingly agitated.

"That's enough for now, Bella," he soothed. "You're doing great. Take a little break, okay? I'm sure it will come back."

He saw the tech out, then closed the door and returned to her bedside. Bella looked exhausted.

Stroking her hair, he said gently, "Bella, maybe you should try to get some more sleep. You look worn out."

"Anyone else who patronized me like that would get it with both barrels," she replied with a wan smile.

"But you're right. I'm tired. So, I'll sleep, and when I wake up, let's try again. I just know I'm missing something really important," she added, tears coming to her eyes. "Okay?"

He touched his lips to hers.

"Okay," he whispered.

Mikel stuffed Adolf's body in the trunk of the Jag, smiling at the irony.

There you go, father, one last ride in your favorite car. No one said it necessarily had to be up front.

Smiling ghoulishly, he climbed behind the wheel and fired it up.

Now he was in the desert, coming up on the burial site. The plan was simple. It needed to look like Adolf had been overcome with guilt and killed himself in the same place where the victims had been dumped.

Mikel had even gathered up the belongings he had hung on to so he could plant them in Adolf's car, along with a suicide note confessing to it all. He signed Adolf's name very convincingly.

As he'd hoped, the site had been processed then forgotten. He pulled up to within ten feet of the now open graves. Mikel placed Adolf's body behind the wheel and the gun in his lap, having previously wiped his own prints off of it. He scattered the victims' possessions on the passenger seat and floorboard after pressing them into Adolf's hands. Lastly, he put Cindy's torn bikini briefs in Adolf's left hand.

Then he walked back to the main road. A spring came to his step as he began the twenty-mile hike back into town. Twenty miles was a small price to pay.

"Mikel."

"What?" Nathan said.

"I remember now. The person who walked up and pulled the man leaning over me away. What he said was, 'Mikel, we have to go.'"

Bella swiveled her head to look at him.

"The creep who killed Granpa is named Mikel," she repeated, with a steel edge to her voice.

Five days later, Bella and Nathan were watching television in her hospital room, waiting for the nurse to come back with discharge papers.

"I'm ready to get the heck out of here," Bella muttered, walking over to the window to gaze outside wistfully. "I've been in here a week. Enough already."

Then something coming from the television sparked her interest.

"Turn that up," Bella said, turning from the window.

Nathan increased the volume. The local station was reporting a breaking story – Adolf W. Metzger, philanthropist and international businessman, had been found dead in the same location where four bodies had been discovered not long ago. Police had confirmed the presence of several suspicious items at the scene and were investigating the death as a possible suicide.

"Is that Metzger, as in Metzger Youth Institute?" he asked.

"Yes," she said simply. "Wonder what's up with that."

The screen flashed to the ribbon-cutting ceremony. As the old video rolled of Adolf's welcome speech, Nathan turned to ask Bella something and was instantly concerned. She had gone white and was leaning heavily against the bed.

He crossed the room in a split second.

"Bella, are you all right?"

"That's the voice," she stammered, clinging to him to try and steady herself. "That's the voice I heard say 'Mikel'."

Nathan's phone rang.

"Thomas," he said sharply, then listened.

He asked a few questions, listened again, then ended with, "I'll be there as soon as I get her settled."

He called Max.

"You on your way? Good. There's been a development. We'll see you at the apartment. Stacy and Brad are already there."

"What's going on?" she asked as he hung up.

"That was Detective White. The items found with Metzger's

body tie back to my case. I need to get out there. Max is about ten minutes out. We'll meet him at your place."

He turned and smiled at the nurse who had finally appeared with the paperwork.

Mikel could not believe his eyes.

He just had left the apartment complex after leaving flowers on the sidewalk where Bella died. His face had been on the news the past few days, so he'd dyed his hair brown and was wearing tinted contact lenses and mirrored shades.

As he made the right turn to get back out to the highway, a vehicle passed him. The man behind the wheel looked vaguely familiar, but Mikel couldn't place him.

The woman in the passenger seat, however, Mikel would have known anywhere.

Mikel u-turned at the first opportunity and drove slowly back toward Bella's place, trying to remain calm and unnoticed.

It can't be her. I called. I called the hospital, they said she was dead. Even the news said two were killed, not one.

He pulled slowly into the campus parking lot across the street and watched. Her companion got out, then went around and helped her out. Mikel could see the sling on her right arm. He could see that she moved gingerly toward the building, pausing and leaning on the man for support when she saw the flowers lying on the sidewalk. He could also see the man kiss her and stroke her hair.

It is! Bella. She's alive! My angel is alive!

He thought he would weep with joy.

Then he remembered where he had seen the man before. On the Strip outside Planet Hollywood, getting into a cab with his angel.

His belly burned hot with anger.

Those bastards. Tricking him. Letting him believe his angel was gone.

They'll pay for that, every single one of them. Starting with that pretty boy who is trying to steal my woman.

His smile was a vengeful one as he sped away.

"Wow, Stace, you've never hugged me this softly before," Bella said as she returned her friend's embrace.

"Well, I figure you're still banged up, so I'll wait for a real hug 'til you're all better," Stacy replied with a mischievous grin. "Then watch it, sister."

"Stacy, I need to leave," Nathan said. "Max should be here any minute. I'll fill you all in right quick, then I'll have to take off for a while."

"Go right ahead," Max announced as he walked in. "The gang's all here."

He told them about the phone call from Detective White.

"I need to get over there," he said. "White says there was personal stuff belonging to each victim inside Adolf's car. He's working on obtaining a warrant for the Metzger Institute."

Bella shook her head.

"I met him, talked with him, several times. He just didn't figure as the serial killer type. He always seemed very, I don't know, elegant, I guess."

"Well, a DNA profile will tell us a lot," Nathan said. "We know it won't match the skin samples the hospital collected from you, because you know it wasn't Adolf that attacked you. But," he continued, "if his DNA comes back as a match in—" he stopped himself from mentioning Cindy's rape, "other areas of this case, then we have real reason to believe it was actually Adolf and this Mikel character working together somehow."

To Bella, he said, "Please do me a favor and stay inside, okay? We don't know if Mikel may be watching this place or not. I really don't want him knowing you're still alive. If he believes you to be dead, you're safe. Okay?"

"Okay," she mock pouted. "But can we at least order Ping's? I've been on hospital food all week."

He laughed and held her close.

"Absolutely. Order the usual for me, too."

Over her shoulder he mouthed to the others, *Don't let her out of your sight,* and got three thumbs-up in reply.

"Good," she said. "I'm off to the shower, Nathan. See you when you get back."

She and Stacy went down the hall.

"Did you see the flowers someone left outside?" Nathan asked Max quietly.

"Yes," Max said solemnly. "Fair sized bouquet, too."

"What flowers?" Brad said. "There weren't any when Stacy and I got here."

"When was that?"

"I don't know. A half-hour, forty minutes ago, maybe."

Nathan raised an eyebrow.

"Follow me," he said.

The three men walked outside and tried to look casual as they bent to examine the fresh flowers. Mixed in with the fragrant arrangement was a wide swath of ribbon that said *Rest in Peace, Angel.*

"Holy shit. He's been here. Today," Nathan breathed, then stood upright.

"Brad, see what you can do about arranging to ship her stuff home. Max, call the airlines. See if you can book us a flight out of here first thing in the morning. I'll be back as quick as I can."

"I'm coming with you," Max chimed in. "If this Adolf character is in any way responsible for my best friend's death, I want to know about it. And something tells me he's not who he seemed to be."

Nathan hesitated.

"You both go," Brad offered. "Stacy and I will stay with her. Besides," he continued, indicating the weapon strapped to his right calf, "I'm packing, just in case."

Nathan grinned.

"Look at that, a bean counter that's armed."

"No sense taking chances," Brad grinned back. "Call and let us know what's going on."

He headed back inside.

"Let's go, Max," Nathan pointed to his rental car. "And you can tell me why you think Metzger's not what he seems to be on the way."

As they drove the twenty miles out to the scene where Adolf's body had been found, Max filled Nathan in on the history that he and Manfred had shared regarding one Adolf Werner. Nathan almost hit the curb at one point.

"Werner? As in, the name Bella heard the man say to Manfred before he stabbed him?"

"Yep," Max answered bitterly. "After the night we barely missed him in the graveyard, he went off the grid. No clue where he was. His name was on our lists, but he never pinged on the radar anywhere. Now I know why."

He pulled out his cell phone and continued, "So now I'm gonna call in some favors and have Adolf Metzger's background looked into. Maybe we'll find the transition point where he went from one identity to the other."

"I agree," Nathan said. "And maybe it will also lead to how this guy knew this Mikel creep."

He turned down the dirt road toward the scene as Max dialed. He waved to Detective White as he put the car into park.

"Hello again, Detective. Thanks for calling me," Nathan began as he stepped out of the vehicle. "What do we have?"

"Take a look," White replied, motioning to the Jaguar, now roped off with yellow tape. "We've not moved anything yet, just roping off the car and taking pictures. Coroner should be rolling up at any moment. Check out what the DB's holding in his left hand; something tells me we've already met who they belong to."

His phone rang just as the coroner's van pulled in behind Nathan's car.

"Be right back," he said to Nathan, then flipped open his cell and walked over to greet the ME.

Nathan glanced at Max, who had just hung up his phone.

"Okay, I've made arrangements for this guy's prints to be run through all available databases," Max informed him. "If my hunch is right, that man is actually Adolf Werner, not Adolf Metzger."

White and Dr. Harrington came back over to join Nathan and Max by the tape barricade.

Nathan introduced Max and the doctor, then said, "Are we ready, gentlemen?"

They nodded their assent. A uniformed officer raised the tape and they ducked underneath and approached the car.

As they walked, White mentioned, "The chief called me just now. Our warrant for the Metzger Institute should be ready within the next hour or so."

Now it was Nathan's turn to make a call. He reached the Flagstaff office and arranged for four agents to join him in Phoenix when the search warrant was served.

Putting away his cell phone, he looked at the group and announced, "We've got FBI backup en route. With any luck, they'll get here right about the time we get that warrant in our hands."

Harrington immediately went around to the driver's side to confirm death and take a liver temperature; the others concentrated their initial efforts on the contents of the vehicle to give the coroner room to work. But Nathan did notice the torn bikini briefs in Adolf's lifeless hand.

Cindy's, gotta be, he thought bitterly.

The next thing that caught his attention was something shiny on the passenger floorboard.

Pulling on gloves, he asked White and Harrington, "Are we clear to move things?"

White replied, "As far as I know, yes. My guys have taken all the pictures we need, along with written notes detailing item location. Doc?"

"My part is done here as well, except for loading the body for transport. Help yourself."

Nathan gently opened the passenger door, reached in carefully, and pulled the shiny object from its resting place. He recognized the number on it from the case files. It was Detective Allen's badge. He motioned to one of the crime scene techs, who brought over an evidence bag. Then, he and Max walked around to the driver's side where they could see the face better.

"Is it him?" Nathan asked Max.

"I believe so," Max said. "Keep in mind the last time anyone saw him – at least that I am aware of – is when an asset identified him as being in Berlin in November 1989. Snowbird would be able to tell us right away if this was him or not; she was a sharp old bird. But she's gone now, died years ago. And Manfred," Max continued solemnly with a little hoarseness to his voice, "Manfred would have recognized him immediately."

He coughed.

"Anyway, prints should tell the tale. Now that Germany's one big happy family again, we'll be able to access any prints that East Germany built on their people. The way things were back then, trust me, they kept tabs on everyone. So, we should get a hit."

One of the techs pointed out, "Hey, got what looks to be a suicide note here."

It had fallen to the driver's side floorboard. Picking it up gingerly with tweezers, she bagged it and sealed it before handing it to Nathan. He in turn showed it to Max.

"Is it usual to type the whole thing but actually sign your name?"

"Interesting point," Max conceded. "I'm not sure. Maybe Harrington or White would know."

And then the light bulb went on in Max's head.

"I'm glad he did, though. We have a sample of Adolf Werner's handwriting on the back of an old picture. Maybe there's enough of a sample here in his signature to compare. Just to make sure he actually signed it."

"What are you driving at?"

"Nathan, look at this purely as a profiler for a minute. This guy was sharp. I mean *sharp*. He disappears underground for almost thirty years without leaving a trace, surfaces again just long enough to pull whatever it was out of that damn wall, then disappears again until now. Only now he's got a new name, with no obvious or readily traceable link to his past. Does that strike you as the kind of person that would be sloppy enough to keep souvenirs from victims, or commit suicide out in the open like this?"

"No, it honestly doesn't," Nathan answered. "It doesn't mesh together at all. I guess I have been leading with my heart on this one, especially lately."

Max put his arm around the young man's shoulders.

"As have I," he said. "No shame in it. Feeling deeply about a case can inspire you to new heights to solve it. You must learn when you need to put that part aside and be impartial and logical about it. And that, my boy, takes some agents years to master."

Chapter Seven

"God, I feel almost human again," Bella announced as she and Stacy walked into the living room. "I can't wait to get these stupid bandages off for good, though. Thanks, Stace, for helping me with my hair. I don't think I could've managed it by myself with this arm."

"No problem," Stacy responded. "And I learned just now that if I ever get bored with chemistry and math, I'd make one heck of a nurse. We got you cleaned up without flinging too much water everywhere and look at how pretty those new bandages are. I do pretty good work."

The doorbell sounding caught them by surprise at first.

"Ping's!" Bella squealed like a little kid.

"I'll get it," Brad called out and strode toward the door.

He paid the man and brought the food to the table. Bella stood for a moment, eyes closed, breathing in the fragrant aroma.

"I will never take the smell of good Chinese food for granted again," she sighed contentedly.

She went to grab plates and was immediately shooed away by Stacy.

"We've got this," Stacy admonished. "You go sit down. I'll bring you a plate."

Then, "Oh, honey," as she noticed Bella beginning to cry.

Stacy went and put her arms around her.

"You... you sounded like Granma Rose just then," Bella stammered into Stacy's shoulder. "Now I've lost them both, Stace..."

There wasn't much Stacy could do besides hug her best friend while she wept.

Mikel paced like a trapped leopard in his main workroom, back and forth, back and forth, lost in thought.

The initial shock at seeing Bella alive had been replaced with both a need to punish those who tried to keep them apart, and a huge longing to take her into his arms and profess his love. But she had at least one person with her, presumably all the time. She still had a sling on her right arm, and she didn't look that stable walking into the building; no one in their right mind would leave her alone right now.

Be rational for a moment, his mind counseled. *If you use the proper enticement, it doesn't matter if she's alone or not. Find something she holds dear and use it as bait. She will come to you.*

Yeah, right. Like what?

Mikel didn't have access to her outside the Institute. He had wanted to go to her house and plant some bugs, so he could see and hear her all the time, but the opportunity had never presented itself, and then after he thought she was...

Don't go there! His mind warned. *Do not go there. That part's over now.*

As he paced and debated with himself, he happened to glance absentmindedly at his computer console and stopped pacing. There, on his screen, walking from one class to the next, was the answer to the problem.

Mikel picked up his phone and dialed an extension.

"Mr. Wallace? Could you please locate one Tommy Bennett, and could you and he please meet me in my father's office in, say, twenty minutes?'

He could hear the headmaster starting to make some excuse not to, so he leaned over and tapped a few keys on his computer, then pressed send.

A second later, he heard Wallace respectfully say, "Yes, sir."

"Come to think of it, Wallace – round up all the chosen. And let's meet in the war room instead."

"At once, sir."

Mikel smiled as he hung up the receiver.

Nanotechnology rocks.

A squad car pulled up on scene and the chief himself got out.

"Here you go," he said, handing the warrant to White. "Freshly approved by Judge Walker."

Nathan finished the phone call he was on.

"That was my agents," he said. "They're about forty minutes away; they'll meet us out there."

He turned to Max and said, "Let's head to the ME's office. We can get those fingerprints scanned in and sent to Langley, then go out to the Institute."

To the chief and White he asked, "You guys en route?"

"In a few," White replied. "My guys here need to wait for the tow truck so we can get this hot rod back to the evidence garage. I'll give you a call when we gear up to head to the Institute. Any guesses on needing SWAT, Chief?"

"I wouldn't think so, it's a school full of kids," Nathan pointed out.

"I agree. But we'll have them on scene and on standby, just in case," the chief answered. "If anything happens, they can breach within three minutes. Besides, it's the Christmas break, so there should be fewer people around."

"See you there," Nathan called as he and Max climbed back into his car for the trip to Dr. Harrington's.

As they drove, Nathan called to check on Bella.

Brad answered and said, "Hang on a second," then walked down the hall to Stacy's old room.

"We're doing as well as can be expected here," Brad said in response to his inquiry. "Chinese food and tears. She's really starting to deal with her loss now. Stace is doing her best to keep her spirits up, but it's hard."

"Put her on, please," Nathan answered.

A long pause, then a sniffly, "Hello?"

"Hi baby," Nathan said. "How are you feeling?"

"I miss him, Nathan, I just... miss him." Bella sobbed.

"I know, Bella, and I'm so sorry." He switched topics to try to focus her attention on something else. "You're saving me some fried rice, right?"

"Yes, I am, and nice try. I really think I just need to cry for a while, and then sleep."

"Try to get some sleep, baby. I'll be back as quick as I can. Okay?"

"Okay."

"See you in a while."

Hanging up the phone, he sighed deeply.

"It tears me up that she's hurting like that, and there's not a lot I can do to make it better," he confided to Max.

"I think I'll go lie down," Bella said to Brad and Stacy as she replaced the phone in its cradle. "I'm exhausted."

"Well, you've been through a lot," Stacy agreed. "Physically, psychologically, and emotionally, and it all takes its toll. We'll hang out here with you until Nathan gets back, okay?"

"Thanks, guys." Bella smiled. "I love you both, I hope you know that."

"We do," Brad replied, hugging her gently. "We love you, too. And we'll be out here in the living room if you need anything."

Bella turned and made her way to her room.

"Are we clear?"

"Yes, sir!" the three young voices answered in unison.

"You know your assignments. Dismissed."

"Yes, sir!"

Nate and Chris filed out, but Tommy and Mr. Wallace remained.

"Tommy, Mr. Wallace," Mikel said. "Listen very carefully. This is what I want you to do."

When he finished, he made each of them repeat it back to him. Then he smiled.

"Excellent, Tommy," he told the boy. "Now, go with Mr. Wallace to his office, and get it done."

"Yes, sir."

About ten minutes after Bella had retreated to her room, the phone rang again. Stacy answered.

"Hello?"

A child's voice, crying.

"Miss Bella? Oh, Miss Bella, you need to come. I need you."

"Wait, wait, calm down," Stacy soothed. "This is Stacy, Bella's friend. Who is this?"

"Tommy," responded the small voice, crying harder now. "She's my tutor, and I'm in trouble, and I don't know who else to turn to. She must come. Please. Please, can I talk to her?"

"Hold on just a second, sweetheart," Stacy said gently.

She went to Bella's room and knocked on the door. "Bel?"

"Yeah?" Bella said sleepily.

"A kid named Tommy's on the phone for you. He's crying, Bel. Says he needs you."

Bella came fully awake, fumbling for the phone at her bedside.

"Thanks, Stace, I got it," she spoke into the receiver, then heard the click as Stacy hung up the living room phone.

"Tommy?"

"Oh, Miss Bella, I'm in serious trouble. You must help me. You must come. I know I can trust you."

"What's going on, Tommy?"

"I don't want to tell you over the phone. I don't feel safe. Please, Miss Bella, please come and get me."

"Of course. Where are you?"

"At the school. Oh, Miss Bella, please hurry. I don't know how much longer..."

And then he screamed.

The line went dead.

"Tommy? Tommy!"

Bella bolted out of bed, fumbling for her shoes.

"Stacy," she yelled.

Stacy and Brad came quickly down the hall.

"We've got to get out to the Institute. Now. Tommy's in trouble. I don't know what's going on, but it's big. He was talking to me and then he screamed and then the line went dead."

Brad frowned. "Nathan told us to stay here, Bella."

"He's *ten*, Brad. He's just a kid. And he was obviously scared to death about something," Bella snapped. "I have to help him. He's counting on me. You can stay if you want, but I'm going."

"You won't be able to drive very well with that bad arm," Stacy said. "So we're driving you. But we're gonna go and find the kid, then bring him back here. Got it?"

"You're the best, Stace." Bella smiled. "Let's go."

Brad shrugged his shoulders.

"Fine," he muttered. "I know better than to argue with you two. But I'm gonna call Nathan and tell him what's going on."

Tommy put down the phone and asked, "How was that?"

"Absolutely perfect," Mikel replied. "Great job."

To Mr. Wallace, he said, "Remember, I want her alone. If she brings anybody with her, we will incapacitate and subdue them only. No killing—yet. And be ready to raise the barricades when it's time."

"As you wish, sir."

Nathan left Max at the ME's office. Somewhere at the FBI's main lab a supercomputer was comparing prints from a dead man in Arizona to fingerprints on file around the globe.

They had talked to Detective White, who had mustered personnel at the station.

"Let's head out there as a unit," he suggested. "Your agents just pulled up here anyway, and the chief wants to run through the game plan before we get out to the Institute."

"Sure," Nathan said. "Be there in a bit."

"I'm staying here," Max told him. "I want to be able to track our progress with the fingerprint match."

"Sure," Nathan replied. "I'll keep you updated on what we find at the Institute."

He headed to police headquarters about ten minutes away.

Nathan joined the others in a conference room at the station and ran through a quick briefing about the roles each person would play onsite at the Institute.

"Logan. Your men ready?" The chief asked the SWAT team leader.

"Armed and ready, sir."

"Everyone clear on their assignments?"

They all nodded their assent.

"Dismissed. Let's head out. It's a half-hour drive."

"Great, just great," Brad said, as they neared the turnoff to the gates at the Metzger Institute. "Nathan's phone is going straight to voicemail."

"I'm sure he's busy, and we won't be here that long," Stacy pointed out. "Why don't you just send him a text? He'll be able to retrieve that even when he's on a phone call."

"Sorry, baby. I'm so tired that I didn't think of that," Brad said with a sheepish grin, and shot off a quick message to Nathan's phone.

"Okay, here we are," Stacy announced. "Now, Bella, let's go find Tommy and get the hell out of here."

They walked into the main hall and were immediately met by the headmaster.

"Bella? Thank God you've come. I found Tommy Bennett a short time ago. He's very distraught. I have him in my office. He managed to tell me that he called you and you were coming, but nothing else. He was sobbing when I found him, and he hasn't stopped."

Bella's face filled with concern. "Take me to him, please, Mr. Wallace."

"Right this way."

They all went into Wallace's office.

Mikel witnessed the exchange and smiled to himself.

All according to plan so far. Now for the next step.

About twenty minutes away, in the police convoy, Nathan reached for his phone to call and check in on Bella again and was dismayed to see his battery was depleted.

"Seriously?" he said, plugging it into the charger. He'd have to try again in a little bit.

"Miss Bella!" Tommy exclaimed, running to her.

She hugged him as best she could with one good arm.

"Oh, sweetie. Are you all right?"

"He's just fine," came a silky voice from the doorway.

Bella, Stacy, and Brad turned to see a tall man with white-blond hair and eerie, gray eyes strolling languidly toward them, weapon drawn. On either side and just behind him were two students, each about five-ten to six feet and muscled, and each with a wicked-looking knife in his hand.

They spun back to appeal to Mr. Wallace for help—and noticed he also now held a gun.

"What the hell?" Brad exclaimed, reaching toward his own weapon.

"Not a good idea," the man intoned reproachfully, and shot him in the left knee.

As Brad screamed and collapsed, clutching his leg, the newcomer smoothly instructed Wallace, "Please relieve our guest of his sidearm."

"Yes, sir." Wallace roughly pulled up Brad's pant leg and wrested the weapon out of reach.

"You *bastard!*" Stacy started toward the man who'd shot her husband with menacing intent.

Bella grabbed her by the arm.

"Stace, no," she pleaded. "He'll shoot you."

"My angel is most definitely right about that," the gray-eyed man admitted. "Male or female really makes no difference to me. Unless it's Bella, that is. My angel," he finished almost dreamily.

Bella was shocked to realize he was blushing a little. He was nervous talking to her. He was trying to hide it, but there was a slight tremor in his hands.

This man is mentally unstable, Bella realized. *He will go off at the slightest provocation. I can't let him hurt Tommy or Stacy.*

Pushing Stacy and Tommy behind her, Bella took a deep breath and stepped slowly forward.

"Why do you call me that?" she asked very gently.

"Because you are," the assailant said, his color deepening, a little shocked by the question. "I have loved you since the first time I saw you, almost a year ago now."

"Sir, my friend is bleeding. Can Stacy please go to him and put pressure on the wound?"

He shrugged. "Why not. I don't care about them one way or the other. What matters is you. My angel. And please, call me Mikel."

Bella turned her head slightly, without taking her eyes off Mikel, and said carefully, "Stacy, take my bandage off my arm and use it like a tourniquet to bind Brad's leg. That should lessen the blood flow. Then look around and see what's in here that you can use to put pressure on it."

Suddenly Mikel moved to within touching distance of her and Bella willed herself not to shrink back.

"Does it hurt?" he asked, pointing to her as Stacy unwound the bandage.

Although she certainly didn't want to, Bella kept her voice soft and non-threatening when she answered.

"What exactly are you referring to, Mikel?" she asked, gazing at him solemnly. "My face where you hit me? My arm where you sliced me? My chest where you stabbed me? Or my heart you broke when you killed my grandfather, the only blood relative I had left in this world?"

His face drained of color, and she was amazed to see tears in his eyes.

"So now you're an orphan, too. Bella, I didn't know it was you, I swear to God," he began. "It wasn't until your hat came off that I knew it was you. It crushed me to think I killed you. My angel. My love."

Stacy interrupted.

"Mr. Mikel?" she said timidly.

He looked at her, his face filled with irritation.

"Yes?" he snapped.

"Can one of your people help me find some towels or something for Brad's leg? You see, he's the love of *my* life, and I would be heartbroken to lose him."

Mikel's face softened just a bit.

"I certainly understand that. Nate," he said to the young man to his right, "run to the second-floor bathrooms, and bring back several towels please."

"Yes, sir." Nate clicked his heels, saluted, and left.

Five minutes from the Institute, Nathan checked his phone again. Almost three quarters of a battery again. Good. He unplugged it from the charger. Immediately, it signaled that he had a new message.

He flipped open the phone, read it, cursed, and pulled over sharply to re-read it again. It was from Brad.

One of Bel's students called. In trouble. We're going to the school to get him.

"That is not good at all," Nathan muttered. No way in hell that was coincidental; his heart and head agreed on that one.

He tried calling Brad. It rang four times and went to voicemail, so Nathan sent a text back. Then he called Detective White.

"White? My phone's been dead, no battery. I charged it and just saw a text I missed from Brad. He, Bella, and Stacy went out to the Institute. Something about one of her kids in trouble. That was," he glanced at his watch, "fifteen minutes ago. Now I can't get them at all. I think Mikel's behind it somehow."

"Hang on."

White filled in the chief, who was riding shotgun.

"I'm back. We're now going in hot. Chief is on the radio passing the message on to Logan about friendlies inside as possible hostages. SWAT's not on standby anymore, Nathan."

"Roger that," Nathan said. "Kick this convoy in the ass and let's get there."

Back in Wallace's office, all conversation had stopped when Brad's cell phone began to ring. He didn't dare reach for it, not with three armed men present and a fourth coming back any minute. After four rings, it stopped. Then it started to beep incessantly.

Mikel raised an eyebrow.

"Means I have a new text message," Brad explained.

"Well, well, let's see it then," Mikel responded, motioning to Tommy to retrieve the cell phone as Nate returned with a stack of towels and took them over to Stacy.

Bella tried to hold Tommy to her, but he wrestled free.

"Let go, you stupid bitch. I don't take orders from you. Mr. Metzger's the boss."

He strode triumphantly over and snatched up Brad's phone, marching it straight over to Mikel's outstretched hand.

"Good job, Tommy. How about we power you down for a while?" Mikel said casually.

He leaned forward and typed a command into the open laptop on the desk. Tommy immediately went to the loveseat in the corner of the room and fell fast asleep.

"What... what was *that*?" Bella asked, eyes wide with fear.

"Sorry, my love, I forgot to mention – when I haven't been obsessing over you and I being together, I've been perfecting a mind-control serum that my father insisted on. As you can see," he indicated those in the room, "it works quite well. Took a while to perfect and the first few human test subjects were hit and miss, but I got the kinks worked out. And the brilliant part is, that nanotechnology, my angel, can be controlled, activated, and deactivated with a few computer keystrokes."

"Where is your father, Mikel?"

"Oh, I killed him," he responded nonchalantly. "When we thought you were dead, he went into my workroom and deleted everything about you off my computer. Said you were just a phase, a distraction, a tramp. That's not true, so he had to go. Now, let's see who's so anxious to get a hold of our friend here."

He read the text and turned crimson with barely repressed rage.

"Nathan?" he demanded. "Is this the same Nathan you cheated on me with? That pretty boy who *stole* you from me, Bella?"

The convoy pulled over about three-hundred yards from the gate. Nathan got out of his car and hustled to the front to talk to the chief, White, and Logan.

"We have a blueprint of this place?" he asked.

"Yeah," Logan said. "You missed that part in the briefing. This ain't no regular school. According to what we found it's also got sub-levels. Anybody puts those in a place like this, I would guess has enhanced security on those levels."

"Great," Nathan muttered, running his hands through his hair.

"Relax, sir," Logan said kindly. "My guys are well trained. Instead of bringing up the rear, we'll go in first, that's all. We've got accessible points on the side of the building here and here," he indicated on the blueprints. "This gives us an advantage. No reason to give them a heads-up by going through the front door."

"Okay," Nathan exhaled heavily. "Someone give me a radio. The second I hear 'all clear' I'm going in after Bella."

He went back to his car to strap on the bulletproof vest the Flagstaff agents had brought for him.

Wow. I have got to get him calmed down or we're all dead, Bella thought. *Nathan, hurry the hell up and get here already.*

"Mikel," she purred, walking forward slowly to place a hand delicately on his arm. "Forgive me. Please forgive me. I didn't realize you loved me. I've never met you before today, Mikel, so how could I know? Why have you waited so long to come to me?"

He gulped. She could feel him trembling from her touch.

She moved closer, gently stroking his cheek.

"Can we be alone? I really want to spend some time alone with you, Mikel. And I think it's brilliant what you've done with the serum. I'd love to know more. Can we go somewhere, just the two of us?" Bella said sweetly, gazing up at him with what she hoped to God looked like love and adoration.

He let his breath out slowly, heavily, and lowered his weapon.

Yes, she thought. *Now if I can just keep him calm and preoccupied, help should be here soon.*

"Bel," Stacy hissed.

Bella put her hand up to quiet her.

"It's all right, Stacy," she said, gazing into Mikel's eyes. "It's okay. My new love and I are going somewhere more... private."

Then she turned and looked at Stacy and Brad. It was a look that only a close friend could have deciphered.

Roll with me here, it said. *Or he'll kill us all.*

"Sure," Brad managed to say convincingly. "Lovers need to be alone." He squeezed Stacy's hand.

Bella threw a smile that said *here goes nothing* at them before turning her attention back to Mikel.

"Please, my love," she said imploringly.

Mikel straightened his shoulders.

"Let's go to my father's office and have a drink, shall we?"

He gestured toward the door.

To Wallace, he said, "Keep an eye on these two," then, "Follow me," to the two muscled teens behind him.

"Nate, Chris, take up positions in the hallway. I don't want us to be disturbed. Understood?"

"Yes, sir." Both boys snapped to attention.

Mikel held the door to Adolf's office open for Bella, and said, "Please, come in. There's so much I want to talk to you about."

Softly, he closed the door.

Chapter Eight

NATHAN'S PHONE RANG.

"Thomas," he snapped.

"Max here. Got a match on the prints – I was right. Metzger is Werner. And there's something else. ME says no way it was suicide. He estimates Adolf was shot from about two feet. He was murdered somewhere else then staged out in the desert."

"Good info, Max. Hey, we have stuff happening here. Let me let you go. I'll call you back." He hung up the phone just as his radio crackled to life.

"Tango to Delta."

"Go Tango."

"At entry point window. Have observed four, that's zero-four, individuals, crossing the main hall. Three are hostile, one is a friendly, over."

"Do you have a position, Tango?"

"Two hostiles remaining in hallway. I don't see any weapons. Third hostile matching suspect's description went with the friendly into some sort of room, north side, center of main hall."

Christ, that's got to be Bella, Nathan thought despondently as he listened.

"Any sign of the other two friendlies, Tango?"

"That's a negative, Delta."

"Roger that, Tango. Wait one."

Logan consulted his map. "The room they went into looks to be a big office, probably Adolf's."

"Any way to see inside from out here?" Nathan asked.

"Not without being seen. See that big set of windows to the left of the front door?" Logan said, pointing at the building. "That's the room they're in. No way to get eyes on that without being spotted; there's no cover we can use to get there."

He keyed his radio.

"Delta to Tango."

"Go Delta."

"Can you neutralize the hostiles in the hallway?"

"Request permission to use tranquilizer darts, Delta. They're just kids."

Nathan and Logan exchanged looks.

Then Logan told his team, "Tango you are clear for non-lethal, over."

"Roger that, Delta. Stand by."

The three-person assault team switched from their handguns to their tranquilizer guns.

The entry point they had found on the blueprint was a service entrance coming out to the main hall about thirty feet from their targets. The door was locked from the inside, so the team went to work on the hinges with a blowtorch to minimize noise. This accomplished, the team lead called Logan again.

"Tango to Delta."

"Go Tango."

"Door breached, team in position. Ready for diversion, over."

"Roger that, Tango, wait one."

A fourth team member, dressed as a deliveryman, drove a flower van into the parking lot. He got out and went to retrieve a ridiculously large bouquet from the back of the van, as well as his tranquilizer gun, which he tucked into his shoulder holster under his jacket.

He murmured, '*nonlethal ready, flowers being delivered*' into the mike hidden between his uniform and bulletproof vest.

Hearing '*you're a go, Alpha*' from Logan in his comms device that looked like regular headphones, he cranked up the iPod in his front pocket a little, grabbed the flowers, shut the van doors, then headed toward the front door of the building.

"Package on the way, Tango. Stand by."

"Roger, Delta. Standing by."

In Adolf's office, Bella was trying her best to remain calm and play her part, but she was having more and more trouble. As soon as the door was closed behind them, Mikel had thrown his gun onto the loveseat, pulled her into his arms, and kissed her.

It repulsed her to the very core. Her grandfather's murderer stuck his tongue down her throat and his hands roamed up and down her body. But she saw no other way to keep him from becoming lethal other than to play along. So, she kissed him back, although she would sooner have shot him.

And if I can just get to that gun, I'll be happy to, she told herself.

She pulled herself free from his octopus-like hands and said breathlessly, "Wow, you sure can sweep a girl off her feet. But we have the rest of our lives, my love. How about that drink?"

"I apologize, my angel," Mikel said sincerely. "I've wanted to hold you for so long that it got the better of me. What's your poison?"

"Scotch on the rocks, please."

She wandered to the window and gazed toward the front gate, thinking wistfully of Nathan. She turned back toward Mikel, her mind racing with how to get out of this situation.

Mikel was grinning at her.

"Not what I expected from a petite flower such as you. I think I'm going to enjoy discovering all your little secrets, Bella," he said with a sickening leer as he poured out a very healthy serving and handed it to her.

Inside, she was cringing. His touch alone was enough to make her vomit. And the idea of having sex with this man?

Over my dead body, my 'love', she thought disgustedly.

But outwardly, she giggled and flirted and kept up the charade.

"Hey, sweetie, tell me more about the serum," she said. "That really does sound fascinating. It must have been challenging."

While he was pouring his drink, she moved surreptitiously to the loveseat, rearranging the throw pillow so that it covered the gun. Then she wandered back in front of the window.

Swirling her drink, she said, "So was it difficult? How long did it take?"

Good choice of topic, she told herself. *Look at him strut over here toward me to share his genius with me. At least he'll keep his hands to himself for a while.*

He leaned against the desk, enjoying her attention.

"Well," he said, "I actually had the idea for it when I was twelve..."

As Nathan watched the fake deliveryman prepare to make his approach, a glint of something reflecting in those big windows caught his attention.

"Hand me the binoculars," he said tersely.

He trained them on the windows, and there Bella was, holding a glass. The sunlight was bouncing back against the liquid she was swirling with a trembling hand, and her eyes were rounded with terror.

Nathan watched as she closed her eyes and swallowed hard, then forced a pleasant expression onto her face before she turned away from the window.

Hang in there, baby, he willed her silently. *It's almost over.*

He looked at Logan.

"Can your sharpshooter take out someone in that room with the big windows?"

Logan looked offended by the question before saying, "Martinez. Come here a minute."

The deliveryman went up the steps and entered the front hall.

"Delivery," he announced.

He walked toward the receptionist's desk to set the flowers down. Chris, the one closest to the front door, immediately tucked his knife into its scabbard and went to intercept the intruder. Nate, further down the hall, also came forward, stopping with his back to the service entrance.

Outside the service door, the team heard the code phrase 'rush delivery' from their counterpart talking to Chris. They silently worked the door open, snuck up behind Nate, tranquilized him, and dragged him back out. The whole thing took about thirty seconds.

Chris was oblivious to all this happening sixty feet or so behind him. When the deliveryman handed him the clipboard and pen to sign for the flowers, he took them without hesitation, and a well-placed dart knocked him out.

The deliveryman caught the slumping guard and laid him down quietly, out of sight behind the receptionist's desk. Then, the team leader went quickly to the front door and gave a quick hand signal to the rest of the team outside.

Logan smiled and turned to Nathan.

"Two down," he announced. "But the place isn't clear yet. They're sweeping for more hostiles, and to find where the other two friendlies are. Sit tight, it shouldn't be much longer. And Martinez is in position. If our bad guy shows himself in that window, we'll be able to take him out."

"Delta to Tango."

"Go Tango."

"In hall. Voices from my left. Checking it out."

"Roger that, Tango."

The team leader went to the headmaster's office, bent down to the keyhole, and listened to Stacy pleading.

"Mr. Wallace."

A glare but no answer.

"Mr. Wallace. Please," Stacy implored, tears coming to her eyes. "I've slowed the bleeding, but it won't stop. I need more towels or bandages or something. Please."

"Oh, all right," Mr. Wallace said tersely. "I'll be right back. Just so you don't try anything, though..."

He unplugged his desk phone, dropped it in the floor, and stomped on it until it broke. Then he pocketed Brad's cell phone.

The rescue team leader hustled silently from the door and took cover behind the receptionist's desk, where Chris continued his involuntary slumber.

Mr. Wallace came out of his office, locked the door, and headed upstairs with the gun plainly visible in his right hand.

"Tango to Delta."

"Go Tango."

"The other friendlies locked in an office. Armed hostile just went upstairs. Extracting?"

"Roger that, Tango, and take out the hostile."

"Ten-four, Delta. Switching to lethal."

The SWAT team stayed where they were and watched Wallace come back down the stairs with towels under his left arm. He transferred the gun from his right to his left hand, pulled the key out of his right front pocket, and opened the door. As he started to enter the room, the team converged.

Wallace saw movement from the corner of his eye and spun fast toward the team leader, raising and firing his gun as he did so. The shot went wide, and the echo of gunfire filled and reverberated through the main hall.

In response, he was met with two silenced rounds to the left chest. The team pushed him forward and into the room, closing the door behind them. They gave the thumbs-up sign to Stacy and Brad, then motioned for silence.

Two took positions on either side of the door while the third tactical officer, who had also had training as a medic, checked Wallace for a pulse, then went to Brad and began checking his wound.

The fourth radioed in as quietly as possible.

"Delta."

"Go Tango."

"Third hostile down, one to go. One of the friendlies was shot in lower leg. Doc's checking him out now."

"Roger that, Tango. Hold position for now. Martinez sighting up the fourth hostile. Sit tight."

Across the hall, Mikel stopped mid-sentence when he heard the shot, and quickly went to the door, locking it.

"It seems your white knight brought some friends to rescue you," he said with derision, turning back to face her.

What he saw stopped him in his tracks.

Bella, his love, his angel, was backing away from him toward the window. She was pointing his own gun at him and although she wore a confident expression it was undermined by the way her entire frame was trembling.

The mild shock faded from his face and was replaced by a smile that was pure evil.

"You're pointing my own gun at me," he said conversationally, beginning to ease across the room toward her.

"Damn right I am," Bella replied. "You make my flesh crawl."

"Oh, I don't know," he said, making his voice soothing and calm. "Maybe you'll feel differently once you submit to me."

"Like hell I will," Bella answered. "You've touched me all you're going to."

He laughed. "Angel, I can see your hands shaking. Be honest. You've never even held a gun until now, have you? I really don't think you have it in you anyway."

His pace toward her increased slightly.

"And you will be mine, make no mistake about it. If it's by force the first few times, so be it. I find it more exciting when a woman struggles."

"I can and will shoot you if you don't stop moving," Bella announced.

"Come on, Bella, I dare you. I don't think you have the guts," he sneered, moving just a little closer now.

Her back was now pressed against the windows. He was ten feet away and closing.

"Logan? Friendly just came into view at the window again. She backed toward it this time though. I think she's in trouble, boss," Martinez radioed.

At this bit of news Nathan immediately raised his binoculars again to watch Bella.

Logan answered, "Roger. If you get a clear shot at the suspect, take it. Don't kill him unless you have to; we want him alive."

"Roger that."

Bella was out of room to move. Left or right was out of the question; no way would she get past him to the door before he got to her.

She took a deep breath and tried her best to remember the little bit that Nathan had shown her so far about firing a weapon.

She raised it a little higher, and said, "Please stop. I don't want to kill you, Mikel. But I will."

He paused, looking at her speculatively for a moment.

"No, dear heart, I think you're bluffing," he answered teasingly, and moved to within three feet of her.

As he leaned forward and down to grab for her, he was hit by two different rounds—one from Martinez' high-powered rifle, which entered just below his right collarbone as it was intended to, and the other from a now screaming Bella, who fired blindly three times and struck him once dead center in the chest.

At the first shot, SWAT was on the move from across the hallway. They busted down the office door to find Bella holding the still-smoking gun limply at her side, tears streaming down her face.

Mikel laid crumpled at her feet.

"Tango to Delta. All clear here. Hostile down. Call for EMS."

"Roger Tango. We're coming in."

The SWAT team leader walked over to Bella and gently pried the gun from her hand.

"Are Stacy and Brad okay? Brad got shot," she said softly, still looking down at Mikel.

"Yes, ma'am, we know. But he's going to be just fine. Let's get you and your friends out of here, okay?" he told her kindly.

She raised her head to look at him, and he saw the mixture of relief and anger in her eyes.

"Sure. One thing first."

She kicked Mikel as hard as she could in the balls.

"*Now* we can go," she announced, then she walked out of the building and into Nathan's arms.

Several hours later, Nathan and Bella walked hand in hand toward the elevators to leave the hospital.

Brad's surgery to repair his shattered left knee had gone smoothly. While he had a long course of physical therapy ahead and would never be able to push too hard on it, the doctors expected pretty much a full recovery. He and Stacy planned on coming to Virginia for a visit as soon as he was able to travel comfortably.

Nate, Chris, and Tommy remembered nothing of what had happened. Bella had told the authorities onsite everything Mikel had said about the serum. Once his laptop was destroyed, the serum seemed to go dormant in its hosts with no ill effects.

The team managed to access his workrooms, recovering another computer that contained videos and detailed notes regarding his experiments. FBI techs were combing through everything else on the hard drive, but what they already had was enough to put Mikel Metzger away for at least two lifetimes.

Max had found the coded pages in Adolf's private office. He was already in route back to Langley with the documents, and to coordinate a memorial service for Manfred sometime within the next week.

Bella and Nathan had also talked with the surgeons that had worked on Mikel. Complications during surgery had put him in a coma.

"Currently he's in a vegetative state, with only minimal brain activity," the neurosurgeon, Hightower, had informed them. "There's a very small chance he could regain consciousness; anything is possible. The human body has remarkable self-restoring capabilities. But it's been my experience that patients usually don't come out of that state. He's been settled into our long-term care ward on the fourth floor."

"In the event that he did wake up, what would happen?" Nathan had asked.

"In the remote chance that he regained both consciousness and an ability to have any sort of normal brain function," the doctor replied, "we would rehabilitate him, just as with any other patient, then turn him over to the authorities to stand trial."

"Fair enough, Doc," Nathan had said, shaking the man's hand. "I'll be keeping in touch to check on him from time to time."

"Sure thing, Agent Thomas, call me here or at my office anytime."

They'd said their goodbyes to the busy neurosurgeon and walked side by side to the bank of elevators to wait for a ride down to the hospital's first floor.

"Are you sure you're up for the drive?" he asked her. "Because if you're not, we can ship your stuff home, and we can fly instead. Just say the word."

"I like the idea of getting to take a leisurely drive with you cross-country," Bella smiled up at him as they entered the elevator. "Kinda romantic."

"I agree," Nathan said as he pressed the button they needed. "I just want to make sure you're comfortable, that's all."

"The thing that matters most is that I'm with you," she said, snuggling close.

Chapter Nine

One week later, only two days before Christmas, Bella sat in her grandfather's favorite chair facing the fireplace, wrapped up in her grandmother's robe. A solitary tear traced down her cheek as she stared at the flames. The temperature in the house was fine; the chill that had descended in her soul was the problem.

The day had just been brutal. She'd been simply overwhelmed by the number of well-wishers coming up to her to share their special memories of her grandfather. The emotional battering it dealt her to get through not just the memorial service but even retreating to the house to eat and reminisce with everyone who'd loved Manfred had exhausted her. It seemed to last a lifetime, but finally the house was empty and quiet.

"Here, baby," Nathan said, offering her a cup. "This will help."

Bella managed a wan smile and took the cup from him.

"It smells really good," she said, breathing in the rising steam. "What's in it?"

"Tea, with honey and lemon. And a dash of whiskey," Nathan said, sitting in the other armchair.

"Whiskey?"

"Yes, whiskey. Well, it's more like a generous helping than a dash. Honey, you're exhausted. I know how rough today was for you. I was thinking you'd probably want hot tea, and to soak in the tub, then get some sleep."

"How'd you know about the tub soak thing?"

"I have three sisters, remember? And growing up we all shared the upstairs bathroom. I learned early that when girls get upset, they head for a bubble bath. I also learned," he leaned forward with a smile, "that the quickest way to get into trouble with sisters is to leave the seat up in the middle of the night."

Bella laughed.

That's better, he thought.

Bella took a long sip of her tea, flashing those hypnotic blue eyes at him over the rim. She swallowed, set the cup on the little side table between their chairs, and said, "The bubble bath sounds great. But," she said, standing up, "only if you join me."

"Absolutely," Nathan replied, reaching for her hand.

When they reached the bathroom, he glanced at the old-fashioned clawfoot tub, and said, "I don't think we'll both fit

in there. But if you want, I'll stay and talk to you while you soak. Your call."

She nodded.

He rubbed her shoulders as she soaked in the tub, noticed her head drooping more and more.

"Bella," he said gently.

No response.

"Bella," Nathan said again, just a bit louder.

"Hmm?" she managed.

"Let's get you out of the tub, and we'll get some sleep. We could both use it."

"M-hmm."

He helped her step safely out onto the floor mat and wrapped a bath towel around her slender frame.

"I'll be right back, okay? Let me go around and get the lights turned off."

"Okay," Bella said, yawning. "Meet you on the pillows."

Nathan went downstairs and peeked into the kitchen. *God bless those women,* he thought, referring to Stacy, Bella's best friend, and Ms. Robbins, the widow neighbor. *They put all the food away so Bella wouldn't have to deal with it.* Stacy and Brad were staying here with Bella while in Manassas and had already gone to bed for the night; Brad's knee was acting up from a recent injury, and he'd finally had to take a Vicodin.

Nathan switched off the kitchen light and continued to make his way through the ground floor, making sure doors were locked and lights extinguished. His cell phone rang just as he was headed back up the stairs.

"Thomas," he said.

"Nathan? Max. Just checking on things. How is she?"

"Exhausted, which is not surprising. It's been a hard day for all of us."

"Agreed. Hey, I didn't want to burden her with this today, but Manfred's lawyer wants us at his office tomorrow for the reading of the will. Two-thirty."

"We'll see you there. And Max?"

"Yeah?"

"I know he was your best friend. I don't think I've taken the time to tell you yet – I am really, really sorry for your loss, man."

Silence for a bit, then, "Thanks, Nathan. See you tomorrow afternoon."

Nathan turned off his phone and climbed the stairs.

He paused at the bedroom door and just watched her for a moment. She was already sleeping. He marveled again at finding the woman of his dreams, and the way it had happened.

I went to Vegas to take a break, that's all, he mused. *Just a little relaxation before work picked up. And I met the love of my life.*

The recollection made him smile as he crossed the room.

Nathan changed into his pajamas as quietly as possible and gently slid under the covers. Bella stirred in her sleep, feeling the warmth of him next to her, and instinctively moved closer. He wrapped his arms around her and heard her sigh. Closing his eyes, he rested his head against hers and drifted into sleep.

"Hey Abby," Paula said as she put her purse in her locker. "What's it like tonight?"

Abby laughed. "You're kidding, right? Quiet. What else?"

"You on tomorrow?"

"Nope. Believe it or not, I managed to swing two days off in a row. See you Monday."

"Good night, Abby."

Paula checked her uniform one last time in the mirror before leaving the ladies' break room to head to her station. Picking up the first clipboard, she looked at Miriam, the other night nurse on duty.

"Any changes anywhere?"

"Only one," Miriam replied. "New one in four-oh-four. I don't think she'll be with us long."

"How so?"

"She's pretty bad off. Sad, too. She's only nineteen. Car accident."

Paula sighed. "Breaks your heart."

Miriam nodded. "I know. We'll just keep her comfortable, I guess."

"I'll start down at the other end."

"Sure thing."

Paula grabbed the first four charts and headed to the end of the hallway to room four-thirty. She went into the first three rooms in turn and took vital signs, making notes on each patient's chart. Although her patients were comatose, Paula believed they could still hear and sense some of what was happening around them. So, she talked to them as she worked. *I believe in miracles* she had told co-workers previously. *I know that someday, if it's meant to be, one of them will respond.*

But none had yet. Not in the three and a half years she'd been working this floor.

She finished her first three and headed toward room four-two-five and her favorite patient. She had a special place in her heart for this one. The first time she saw him, she had fallen hopelessly in love.

Paula knew it was foolhardy, being in love with an unconscious man who might never wake up, but she couldn't help how she felt. So as much as she could, she took a little extra time with him. She prayed that if a miracle happened on the fourth floor this holiday season, that he was the one it happened to.

But it wasn't happening tonight. His vitals remained unchanged, pupils still fixed, monitors still reflecting a bare minimum of brain-wave activity. The only sound in the room besides the chirp of machines and her voice was the rasp of the respirator. She sighed as she made her notes on the chart, then went to his side and leaned down close to his ear.

"I'll be back to check on you later," she whispered, and kissed his cheek. "I love you."

She left the room as quietly as possible, heading back to the nurse's station to drop off the completed charts and pick up the next four.

A knock on the door woke Nathan up.

"Yes?" he called out blearily.

"Hey guys," Stacy said. "Breakfast is ready, if you're interested."

"Thanks, Stace," Bella replied. "We'll be down in a bit." To Nathan, she said, "How did you sleep?"

"Like a rock," he mumbled. "Seems like only five minutes, but it's..." he grimaced as he looked at the alarm clock. "Seriously? We got eight hours? It sure doesn't feel like it."

Bella kissed him.

"You'll be happier once we eat. Stacy makes the best omelets on the planet."

They headed down the stairs hand in hand. Brad was already at the table drinking coffee with Max Jones, and Stacy was finishing up at the stove. She pointed to a plate at the end of the table with her spatula.

"Yours is there, Bel. Extra done, with ham and cheese."

"Extra done?" Nathan asked as he sat by Max and reached for the coffeepot.

"Not shiny. At all. To anyone else, they'd be burnt. But that's how Bella likes them. Oh, and cooked on both sides, too, *before* you fill it and fold it. Right, Bel?"

"Absolutely." Bella sat and lowered her head down toward the plate, savoring the aroma.

"Bacon's on a plate in the middle, and here come the biscuits," Stacy announced, placing a towel-covered bowl on the table and taking the seat next to her husband.

For a time, the only sounds heard were the clinking of forks against plates, an occasional 'please pass', and noises of contentment. When the meal was finished, they all pitched in to help with clean-up before moving to the living room.

"So, what's on tap for today?" Brad asked.

"Well, we have the will reading this afternoon. And at some point, Nathan and I need to check status on the case, make sure everything's being closed out," Max replied succinctly.

He turned to Nathan and continued, "Though it may be a long, long while before any sort of trial happens. Have we heard anything on Mikel Metzger?"

"Last report said no change, still in a coma," Nathan said earnestly. "And personally, I'm totally okay with that. I want him to pay for killing Manfred, but he's much less of a threat to anyone the way he is right now."

After a lull developed in the conversation, Max leaned forward and gazed at his goddaughter intently.

"Bella, will you still be starting the spring semester in Arizona?"

"I've decided to come home, Uncle Max. I'm going to transfer to the University of Virginia. Why?"

"Is that so? Good to hear. I have a proposal for you."

Bella arched an eyebrow.

"And that is?"

"Come work for me," Max said simply. "I find myself in need of someone who can teach French, Russian, and German to our students at the Academy. And you, my dear, speak all of those. You're even better at them than Manfred was – he used to say so himself..."

Then his face clouded for a moment, and he murmured, "God, I miss that old man."

"As do I, Uncle Max," Bella said softly, squeezing his hand. "As do I."

***

Paula crept back into room four-two-five in the few minutes before her shift ended, to spend a few more moments with the man she loved. She talked to him softly and stroked his cheek, hoping against hope that he would respond somehow – a blink, a shudder, something, anything. But there was nothing, just like always. Every day, for almost three weeks now. She knew it was probably futile. She sighed, told him she'd be back tomorrow, kissed his cheek once again, and left.

***

The reading of the will started off as expected; as Bella was Manfred's only living relative, she received everything except a small sum of money that Manfred left for Max – *just in case he manages to outlive me,* Manfred had written.

But the old man had made a change very recently that surprised everyone.

The lawyer cleared his throat and read aloud, *"To Nathan Thomas, I leave a token of my esteem. He'll know what to do with it."*

The lawyer handed a small box to Nathan. Puzzled, Nathan opened it, then smiled, closed it again, and tucked it into his pocket.

"Hey Mr. Conner, how are you today?" Faith Thomas called out as she approached her front door. Mr. Conner was a very sweet old gentleman that lived just across the way from her.

"Doing well, dear, how are you? Got any big plans for the holidays? I have a single nephew coming into town any day now, I could hook you up, just say the word," he announced, beaming at her.

"I appreciate that, Mr. Conner, but I'm good," she laughed. "See you later. Merry Christmas."

As she slid her key into the lock, she could hear her phone ringing.

"I'm coming, I'm coming," Faith muttered to herself as she raced into her living room. She reached the phone short of breath.

"Hello?"

"Geez, took you long enough," was the smartass reply on the other end. "Are you getting old, or what?"

"Love you, too, baby brother," she said with a chuckle. "What's up?"

"Checking in to see what your plans are for New Year's Eve."

She glanced around her lonely townhouse.

"Oh, you know, the usual rager," she answered sarcastically. "What'd you have in mind?"

"Well..." Nathan paused. "Um... I was wondering if it'd be all right if I brought Bella down to meet you."

"Sure. I've been dying to meet this girl you've been going on and on about," Faith exclaimed.

"Awesome. We're gonna drive down, should be at your place by Thursday afternoon."

"Sounds like a plan. Hey, you want me to get Jandy and her brood over here, so Bella can run the gauntlet all at once?"

"Hell, yes," Nathan replied. "What about Sarah?"

"She's stuck in Cali, working through the holidays."

"Won't be the same without her," Nathan answered. "We'll have to catch her another time."

"I'm really looking forward to seeing you, little bro," Faith told him.

"Me, too. Love you. Catch you later?"

"You got it. Love you. too. 'Bye."

Faith smiled a moment, then dialed and waited.

"Yo, big sister, you and yours have been requested to join the fun New Years' Eve..."

Faith had just gotten home from work on Thursday when she noticed a man knocking repeatedly on Mr. Conner's townhouse door.

"Can I help you?" she offered.

The man turned and crossed the street to her vehicle.

"Sorry to bother you, miss, but I'm looking for Jack Conner. Have you seen him?"

"I'm sorry, I haven't lately," she replied, frowning. "Come to think of it, I've not seen him since Monday. I just figured he was traveling again. I know he doesn't have any family locally."

"I'm an old friend of his," the man said with a warm smile and friendly green eyes as he held out his hand.

"Max Jones."

She shook it. "Nice to meet you."

"He and I were supposed to get together today, but I haven't been able to reach him. If you see him before I do, would you please ask him to call me?"

"Um, sure. Happy to," she said. Then concerned, she added, "You think he's all right? He's a really sweet man."

Max paused. "I'm sure he's traveling. Anyway, thanks for your help. And Happy New Year."

He walked back across the street.

Just then, Faith realized she'd forgotten to swing by and get groceries for tomorrow night.

No way am I going to try shopping on New Year's Eve. Dammit.

Sighing, Faith climbed back into her car and drove away.

"Max Jones," she mused. "Interesting character. I hope Mr. Conner's all right."

———

Max worried as he went back to his car.

Not like Jack to not return calls, he thought. *Not like him at all. Especially when it's about a new code to crack.*

He knew how much Jack loved cryptography.

"Keeps me young," Jack had said once with a twinkle in his eye.

Something was not right. He could have gotten into the town-house with no issues. Max had been extremely well trained. But that would have been overstepping, and he'd also been trained to be discreet.

He placed a call to the local police department, asked them to come perform a welfare check on one Jack Conner, and waited for them to arrive.

———

Ninety minutes later, pulling onto her street with enough groceries to feed a small army, Faith was amazed at the number of red and blue lights up and down her block. She saw Max standing on the curb talking to an officer.

Rushing across the street, she asked, "Mr. Jones? What's wrong?"

Then, she hugged herself as she saw the stark, impersonal black zipped bag on its gurney being brought out of Mr. Conner's home.

"Oh," she gasped. "Oh, no."

Max came over to her.

"Something didn't feel right, so I called and asked the police to come check on him. I've known him for twenty years, and he has never not returned a call. Medical examiner said it looks like he had a heart attack sometime this morning."

Faith stammered, trying to think.

"I know he had a nephew, he mentioned him once, but I don't know his name or any way to contact him."

Max patted her hand.

"It's all right. I found his lawyer's number and reached out to him. He should have all the contact info to make the notifications."

Unsure what else to do, to say, Faith made her goodbyes, and with a solemn heart, returned to her car to carry bags into her house.

"You look nervous already," Nathan remarked, as they took the highway exit leading to Pantego, Texas.

"I am," Bella admitted. I'm meeting two of your three sisters. I was an only child, remember? I have no idea what to expect."

He laughed.

"Well, it's noisy when we all get together, no question. Jandy and her husband Tony have two kids. God, they've got to be like, nineteen and twenty now, I think."

At Bella's puzzled glance, he said, "Jandy's the oldest, she's forty-four, then Faith, she'll be thirty-six in June, then Sarah, who just turned thirty, then me."

"And you'll be twenty-seven next summer," she exclaimed. "That's quite a gap from oldest to youngest."

"Tell me about it," Nathan said. "And I'm the only boy, so double spoiled."

He grinned mischievously.

"Every single one of them lost their damn minds when I went into law enforcement. They worry, even though it is a family tradition."

"What do they do?" Bella asked.

"Sarah's a freelance marketing consultant. Landed a huge gig out in San Francisco, but the deadlines she's dealing with means she's missing this get-together. Faith is an accountant, and Jandy is a fashion designer."

"So, you and Tony get along?"

"Yep, absolutely. It was nice when he and Jandy got together. Finally had another male around to help balance things out. You'll get a kick out of him, he's funny as hell."

He drove ten minutes more, then parallel parked on a quiet side street lined with pretty trees.

"Well, here we are," he announced, gesturing out of her window. "And, baby, no need at all to be nervous. You're awesome, and they are going to love you."

He got out, walked around and opened her door for her, picked up their luggage in one hand and grabbed her hand in the other.

"You ready?" he asked.

Bella smiled. "You bet."

As the clock at the nurse's station chimed midnight, Paula made an extra swing into room four-two-five, crept close, and lowered her face to his.

"Happy New Year, baby," she whispered, and kissed him on the cheek before straightening up and quietly continuing her rounds.

Don't go! Mikel ranted inside his subconscious. But it was like being encased in mist, like floating both outside and inside himself. He could hear everything, see everything. External sights and sounds penetrated downward into the abyss that surrounded him. But no matter how hard he tried, he couldn't move, couldn't respond, couldn't make them see that he was here, *I'm right here, dammit!*

Had Paula stayed a few more minutes, she would have seen the single tear streaking slowly down the cheek she had kissed.

It was after two in the morning. Faith, Bella and Nathan were still up and having a grand old time. Nathan's sisters and brother-in-law had taken to her immediately. Bella couldn't remember the last time she had laughed so much. All had taken turns regaling her with stories from Nathan's childhood.

But Tony and Jandy had to cut their visit short. Tony's work as a paramedic up in Denton meant extra shifts this time of year. By now, Jandy was probably asleep, and Tony would be on duty. Lauren and Jordan, their kids, both had to work and hadn't been able to come at all.

Bella smiled to herself as she listened to Faith and Nathan go back and forth good naturedly about his last Yahtzee roll.

"It was three," Nathan persisted.

"Whatever, dude, it was four," Faith stated, teasingly.

So, this is what having a brother or sister is like, she thought. *Pretty damn cool.*

"Hey, you two, I'm gonna use the ladies' room right quick," Bella told them, and headed upstairs.

Nathan watched her go then turned to look at his sister. "So," he asked, "What do you think?"

"She's amazing, and perfect for you," Faith replied sincerely. "Never seen you happier, little bro."

Nathan noticed the wistful look in her eye.

"Topic change," he intoned. "Faith, how are you doing? Really?"

Faith sipped her tea.

"You know what? I'm good. I'm moving past it."

"Come on now, I know that tone," he chided.

"It's hard. You know? I just never, ever expected that from him. Never saw it coming."

"He didn't fight the divorce?"

She looked directly at her brother.

"Nathan, the first words out of his mouth when he realized I'd caught him weren't 'I'm sorry', 'I love you', or not even 'I made a mistake' or 'It's not what it looks like'. You know what he said to me? He said, '*I don't want to be married anymore*'."

"And knowing you, you probably said '*wish granted*'," Nathan patted her hand. "Faith, I am so sorry."

"Bygones," she said tersely, and he could see her stuffing it down. "I'm better off. Truly. Anyway, your lovely girlfriend is about to come back. We really like her, Nathan, and I know Sarah will feel the same way, too. I just hope we didn't scare her too much. You did warn her we're a noisy bunch, right?"

Bella came down the stairs and caught the last question.

"Yes, there was a hundred percent transparency," she quipped, grinning. "Hey, I've had a blast tonight, but I can tell the road trip is catching up with me, so I'm turning in."

Faith glanced at her watch.

"Jesus, it's almost three already. Haven't stayed up like this in a long time. I need to get to sleep, too. I have to say, one of the better New Year's Eves I've had in a while though."

She got up and came around the table to hug Bella again, then Nathan.

"You guys got everything you need?"

Nathan nodded.

"Yep, we're good. I noticed you have extra blankets in the closet, so, yeah, I think we're set."

He turned to Bella.

"Ready, hon?"

"Yep," Bella confirmed, then took his hand, and they walked up and into the second bedroom.

Faith went around the bottom floor and turned off the lights, made sure the front door was locked, and headed upstairs to her room as well to face yet another round of sleeping alone in a huge and empty bed.

Happy New Year 2010, she thought as she drifted off. *Please God, let it be kinder than 2009.*

Chapter Ten

HE TOOK a break from swinging the sledgehammer and paused the music in his earbuds, sweat pouring down his chiseled torso.

"Pretty good progress," Rick Conner told himself. He took another swig of water and pulled out his bandanna to wipe his face.

The past eight weeks had been pretty much a blur. Once he'd gotten the call Uncle Jack was gone, time had seemed to somehow accelerate and slow down simultaneously. His arrival in Pantego had been solemn and quiet, and he'd thrown himself straight into the work to deal with the grief.

Across the room, his cell phone rang. He strode to it, checked the number, and cursed.

"Get a clue, whoever you are," he muttered, swiping right to disconnect. He didn't make a habit of answering unknown numbers.

Now Rick took a moment, scanned the space, compared it to the blueprints in his head.

"Pretty much on schedule,' he said to himself. "Should be able to open on time."

He was beyond ready to get this project done, so he could enjoy the results. Grinning, he took another sip of water, picked up the sledgehammer, and was about to continue carving out his vision.

His phone rang again, but this time, he recognized the number.

"Hey, Stan," he said.

"Great news Rick. We have multiple offers on the townhouse – all above asking price."

"That's awesome," Rick replied. "Meet up tonight and go over them?"

"Sure thing," Stan said. "I'll be by around six. With any luck, you can have that whole deal done by the end of the month."

He ended the call, put his earbuds back in, restarted Drowning Pool's *Tear Away* on his iPod, and went back to work.

Life had decided to cut the group some slack in 2010, it seemed. After the harrowing and heartbreaking way 2009 had wound down, they were all due.

Bella's first semester at the University of Virginia was going well, and Max had again extended his offer to come join his team, but Bella was determined to finish her degree first. The money Manfred and Rose had left her meant she could keep up with the beautiful old house, live just fine, and focus on her classes, so she opted to jump right into the new semester with a full course load.

Stacy and Brad had made the move to California. Brad had started at his new job a bit later than planned due to his unforeseen injury, but he was already making a name for himself in the firm. Stacy's dream of attending Cal Tech had launched with the spring semester, and whenever she and Bella spoke, Bella could tell Stacy was in her element there.

Nathan was still carefully outlining the formal case against Mikel Metzger in the increasingly unlikely event he regained consciousness and could stand trial. He and Bella were about to make a trip to California in March during spring break, not only to see Stacy and Brad, but so Sarah and Bella could finally meet.

Max Jones, however, was becoming increasingly frustrated. In reviewing Jack Conner's background again, he'd discovered more about the nephew that Jack had mentioned to Faith. That nephew piqued his interest in a big way. Rick Conner had built a twenty-year career as an officer in the Navy. As a cryptologist. With the highest security clearance anyone could have. And he'd just retired from active service back in October, so he was now a free agent.

I bet he's as good as Jack was at codebreaking, maybe even better, Max thought and grinned. *And if he'd ever answer his damn phone, I could find out. Man, I want him on my team.*

He was done trying to reach out by phone. Another trip to Pantego lay ahead. He called and booked a flight for the following week.

Max stood in front of Jack Conner's old townhouse, looking to his right down the street. *Ah, there it is, I see it.*

The lawyer had mentioned that if Rick wasn't home, he could probably be found at the other building Jack had left him. Max crossed the street and strolled the two blocks down. As he got closer, the whir of an electrical saw and a small dumpster just outside the front door told him he'd found the right place.

Stepping inside, he glanced around and could see right away that some serious time and effort had already been put into the place. Movement ahead and to his left suggested that following the whine of the saw would produce the best results. As he walked further into the space, Max saw a man looking to be early forties – at most – setting down the saw to take a drink. The man noticed him almost immediately, eying him warily as Max approached.

"You must be Rick Conner," Max grinned and stuck his hand out.

"I am," Rick replied with a level voice and stare that gave nothing away, extending his hand also.

They shook.

"And you are...?"

"Max Jones," came the reply. "I worked with your Uncle Jack for twenty years. I've been trying to reach you for a while now. You're hard to get ahold of."

"Well, you found me," Rick said nonchalantly. "What can I do for you?"

"Rick," Max began, "how do you feel about puzzles?"

Rick's eyes lit up. He grinned broadly. "Love 'em. Whatcha got?"

Max read him in.

March became April, then May, and still no perceptible change from the patient in room four-two-five. Paula's heart died a little each shift. She knew every other week there was a routine call that came in from the East Coast checking his status, but no visitors, ever, and he had no next of kin or friends listed at all in his charts. It made her so sad. She continued to spend as much time as she reasonably could with him; it was her way of making up for the fact that the rest of the world seemed to have forgotten him completely.

Faith sighed to herself as she idly flipped channels at six-thirty on a Saturday night, after a long week of crunching numbers.

"Figures," she muttered to herself. "No help finding a distraction here."

But she needed to. If she spent one more Saturday night like this, she might just have to pull her hair out. A year of these kinds of Saturday nights was beginning to weigh heavily.

On the way home from work one day she'd noticed a new bookstore had opened a couple of blocks away. Maybe she could burn some time there, find something to add to her growing collection. Faith had found long ago that she enjoyed seeking out new literary treasures almost as much as reading them. She loved the feel of books in her hand, losing herself in endless possibilities, unraveling mysteries happening worlds away from the solitude of her couch.

Grabbing her phone and purse, she took a deep breath, locked her front door behind her, and nervously stepped out of her self-imposed exile.

At the corner, there was only a pause for the light to change, and she was able to continue her quest. She could see the little sign dangling from its chains looming larger, announcing her destination.

"*Book Keepers*", she read aloud. "How clever."

Grinning, she stepped over the threshold into heaven.

Books.

Racks and racks of them, from floor to ceiling around the perimeter of the store, and an interminable number of standalone shelves as far as she could see, bursting with pages upon pages.

She stepped forward about ten paces, closed her eyes briefly, sighed contentedly, taking in the sounds and smells as well as the sight. Faith already loved everything about this place, and she'd just gotten here.

Lost in her reverie, she almost jumped out of her skin when someone gently cleared his throat and said, "Welcome to Book Keepers. I'm Rick Conner, may I help you find something special?"

Bella and Nathan settled in for a night of TV bingeing. They'd discovered several favorite shows they had in common, but both were typically so busy during the week that the routine had become take-out and catching up on recorded episodes on Saturday nights.

She sighed happily as she arranged the nest for their standing date-night plans. She had a fresh drink, amazing Chinese food, and the love of her life snuggled in with her. *It honestly couldn't get any better than this,* she thought contentedly, as they queued up the season six finale of "Grey's Anatomy".

Faith and Rick stood silent for a few moments, maintaining eye contact, watching and being watched, completely baffled by the idea of each other. Rick cleared his throat again, and that seemed to break the spell.

"I've got spy thrillers and murder mysteries over here, by author," he managed, gesturing to the right. "Next sections down the right side are sci-fi, romance, and the other fictional genres. Left side is all the nonfiction, biographies, and so on."

Faith chuckled.

"Makes perfect sense to me. Our creative selves are right brain driven, so this layout is spot on."

Now it was Rick's turn to be momentarily dumbstruck. He gaped, blinking.

"That is *exactly* why I set the store up this way; you're the first person to notice."

The moment was broken by the telephone at the front register ringing.

"I'll be right back," he said as he hustled to answer it.

As her eyes roamed the titles to her left, she noticed that he had all thirty-seven of J.D. Robb's "In Death" series written to date, stocked and available for purchase – her absolute hands-down favorite series of all time.

What?

She'd never even seen them all offered in one brick and mortar place. And, she realized, he had arranged them in chronological order rather than just lining them up alphabetically as other stores did. She was a huge fan and collector, books one through thirty-two in her possession already, so his presentation pleasantly surprised her.

Well, she mused, *got the big three-six coming up. At least I know where I can buy myself presents now.*

Faith started to pivot around to check the titles to her right, and her focus failed her as, once again, she was looking into Rick's eyes.

An involuntary shriek escaped her.

"Sorry if I startled you," he said, beginning to grin.

"Damn, you're quiet," she muttered, hand on heart. "Do you always sneak up on people?"

"Only when I see they obviously have a favorite author in common with me," his grin grew as he pointed to the set she'd just been looking at. "My favorite series ever. J.D. Robb rocks. I've read them all at least once. It never gets old."

"No spoilers!" Faith laughed and mimed covering her ears. "I've only gotten a bit over halfway through them. But yes, the ones I own I have read at least once, too."

She ran a loving hand lightly across the spines.

"I was just admiring the way you organized them. Every other bookstore I've been in insists on displaying them in alphabetical order. It's maddening. Don't they know there's a reading sequence involved here?"

"I know, right?" Rick exclaimed. "You can't read book one, then skip ahead to book twenty-three, you won't know what the hell's going on."

"Yes! Someone besides me gets it!" she smiled in triumph.

"You have a great smile and an even better laugh," he said softly. "Miss...?"

"Faith."

She extended her hand.

"Faith," he repeated, clasping her hand in his. "Beautiful name for a beautiful woman. It is Miss, isn't it? Not Mrs.?"

The question caught her off guard.

"I'm not married. Not anymore," she added, and couldn't manage to hold back a brief frown. "You?"

"Was," he said, and his eyes lost their spark for a moment. "Not anymore."

By mutual agreement, they took a break. Bella and Nathan hauled their food containers to the kitchen.

"God, baby, did you see that?" Bella asked, referring to the episode they'd just seen. "Did you see that plot twist coming? Because I did not."

"I know, right? What the hell are they thinking, knocking off Reed *and* Charles?"

Bella laughed. "Exactly."

Her phone rang. Absentmindedly, she scooped it up, noticing Stacy's name on the caller ID.

"Hey, Stace, what's up?"

"Hey Bel," Stacy replied. "Not interrupting date night, I hope?"

"You've got excellent timing," Bella responded. "We were just taking a break."

"Oh, okay. Good. Bel, I've got some news."

"Uh-oh. What's going on?"

"Not bad news, good news. Nathan nearby?"

"Standing right here. Why?" Bella's confusion came through in her voice.

Stacy laughed. "Put me on speaker, I want to include him, too."

Puzzled, Bella did as Stacy asked. "Okay, you're on speaker, go ahead."

"We are, too," Brad said. "Hi there."

"We wanted you guys to be the first to know," Stacy almost shouted it. "We're pregnant!"

Bella squealed loudly. "Oh my God, guys, that's awesome. Congratulations!"

She beamed at Nathan, happy tears beginning to form. Then, she took the phone off speaker mode and started peppering her best friend with questions.

"How far along are you? What's the due date? What'd the doctor say? Everything going all right?"

"Bella, calm down," Stacy laughed. "Although I do think it's cool that you're as excited as we are."

Bella found herself pacing as she talked, and she knew Stacy probably was, too.

"I hadn't been feeling that great the last two months or so," Stacy began. "Tired, cranky. Figured it was just school-related stress. Then, about two weeks ago, the morning sickness kicked in. Hard. So, I went and bought a test. Bella, it wasn't even the whole five minutes they tell you to wait for results, and that thing was showing up positive in a big way."

Bella closed her eyes, pacing, living vicariously through Stacy.

"So," Stacy continued, "I scheduled a trip to my doctor, had the appointment today. And she confirmed it. She's saying a due date of around November twelfth."

Bella grinned so big she was sure Stacy could feel it through the phone. "My money's on November eighth."

"I thought about that," Stacy replied. "How cool would it be for my best friend and my child to have the same birthday?"

Chapter Eleven

Max frowned slightly as he read Rick's email.

"*Not a Fibonacci,*" Rick had confirmed. "*My gut says this is more old-fashioned, more straightforward than a mathematical sequence. If we can locate the cipher key, we can crack this thing wide open. If you will send me all the data you have on Adolf Werner, I'll keep working it.*"

Max leaned back, considered for a moment.

What the hell, he thought. *If anyone can crack it, it'll be a Conner.*

He fired off a missive to his unit secretary to make a complete copy of the Werner/Metzger files and overnight them to Texas.

The next afternoon, Rick stared thoughtfully at the thick sheaf of data that had arrived via courier just before he closed the store.

"Man," he muttered. "That's quite a stack."

Max had honored Rick's request; he'd sent a copy of every single scrap of paper he had pertaining to the mysterious coded document, and the man in whose possession it had been discovered.

He organized the data in piles, almost without thinking, as his focus reached and pivoted back around to his favorite thing to ponder lately – Faith. Just her name alone made him smile. Rick hadn't gotten much rest lately. He had replayed their chance meeting and subsequent dinner date again and again in his head. When he closed his eyes to try to court sleep, Faith's face came immediately into view.

Be honest, he told himself. *Been forever since you've felt this way.*

She'd been seriously hurt before. He could tell. He knew it might take a long while to convince her to trust again.

He sighed. No point in thinking about that again right now.

Rick reached for the first subset of pages, leaned back comfortably, and began to read.

Another shift, same set of hopeless circumstances, Paula thought as she prepared to leave for work. She shook her head violently, almost as a defense mechanism to ward off that kind of thinking; it achieved precisely nothing. It was her and Abby on the ward together tonight, so at least there was that.

The young lady in four-oh-four had passed – in her opinion, mercifully – the previous night. It had been hard to witness that slender frame slowly withering away like that. The raw anguish of the girl's parents and little brother had washed over Paula like a rogue wave when the end came, and the decision to turn off the machines was carried out. She'd held their hands and cried with them.

Paula showed her badge at the gate, then made her way to her usual parking spot. Putting the car in park, she leaned her head down so it rested on the steering wheel, then said her usual prayer.

Please, God, if you can hear me, let the miracle happen tonight.

She remained with her eyes closed for a few moments, then sighed, grabbed her purse, and headed to the building to get clocked in.

When they met for dinner, Faith asked, "How was your week?"

"Well," Rick answered, "pretty interesting. Met a guy a while back named Max Jones. He used to be—"

"He came back?" Faith interrupted.

"You know him?"

"Kind of," she said. "He was looking for your Uncle Jack the day before New Year's Eve. Saw me on the street and asked me if I'd seen him lately. Said they were supposed to meet but your uncle wasn't answering his phone."

"Yeah," Rick said. "Uncle Jack always tried to answer, even if it was just to say, 'I can't talk, I'll call you back'. And he never failed to return a call."

"Anyway, long story short, Mr. Jones is the one that sensed something was wrong, called the police, and had them check it out, and that's how they found him. Oh, and, sorry I interrupted you."

Rick grinned.

"You're forgiven. So, you must be the 'attractive younger woman' Max was referring to when he told me that exact sequence of events. Small world."

Faith blushed.

Their conversation was paused as their food arrived and was placed neatly before them. After the waiter refilled their iced teas and left, Rick leaned over and inhaled. "Hmm. Smells and looks fabulous."

"Best part is that it tastes just as good."

"As I was saying," Rick resumed, "Max came down, oh, around the end of February, I guess. Introduced himself, said he used to work with my Uncle Jack, and was wondering if I'd be interested in a little consulting work since Jack was gone."

"Really? What kind?"

"Solving puzzles."

"How weird. Why would he ask you that?"

"Remember when I told you I was retired Navy? Well, I was active service for twenty years as a cryptology technician."

"That is seriously cool '007' sounding type stuff," Faith stated. "But what the hell would you need codebreaking skills for in the civilian world?"

Rick leaned in closer.

"It's not for the civilian sector," he whispered.

"Oh," she said, then her eyes widened as understanding dawned. "Ohhh..."

"Yeah," Rick grinned, and took another bite. "Anyway, it's classified, I can't share more than that, but suffice it to say it's damn interesting work. I got all the relevant files sent to me this week. A lot of stuff to dig into. I live for this kind of thing. And I get to put everything I learned from my Navy career to good use."

"Wait, aren't you going to get into trouble for even telling me this much?" she asked, panicked.

"No," Rick chuckled. "Besides, I trust you completely."

Paula was approaching the end of her shift and, as usual, opted to spend the last few minutes of it with the patient in four-two-five. She approached the bed and talked to him for a few minutes about how her week had been, how beautiful the weather had been lately, various normal everyday things, as she usually did. Then, as usual, she leaned over to kiss him goodbye, telling him she loved him.

His machine beeped differently than she had ever heard it beep before.

She whirled, confused, to look at the display.

Now she heard a new noise behind her. Turning back toward the bed slowly, she was shocked and amazed to see his head turned toward her, eyes open, looking at her intently for a moment before he closed them again.

That didn't just happen, she told herself. *The machines would have erupted. That was a fluke.*

She told herself she'd imagined it, that she'd desired that exact thing for so long that her mind had begun to play tricks on her. Trembling, she hurried to the door and stepped out.

Mikel opened his eyes again long enough to watch her go, then slipped into sleep once more.

Bella came awake screaming in terror, swinging blindly.

"What?" Nathan asked, turning on the lamp next to the bed. He could see she was very pale, glassy eyed, and sweating. He reached for her, pulled her close to him.

"Baby, it's okay. I'm here. Just a bad dream, baby, it's over now."

Slowly, her breathing settled to normal as she clung to him, breathing in his scent.

"It was a bad one this time," she whispered, shivering all over. "Really bad."

He knew just what to do to help her relax.

"Come on baby," he said. "Let's go soak it out."

He gently got out of bed with her in his arms and made his way to the tub.

The only change they'd made to the grand old house since Bella had inherited it was to remove the clawfoot bath and install a Jacuzzi-style outfit big enough to hold them both. Sitting her down softly in her makeup chair, he ran a hot bath, adding a lavender oil to the water. Then he held her hand for support as she climbed in first. He got in behind her, leaned back, pulled her back against him, and turned on the jets.

She sighed, and he could feel her muscles already relaxing, always a good sign. She sometimes talked out the nightmare with him, but not always.

At least they're less and less frequent, thank God, he noted as he closed his eyes and kissed her hair.

They stayed that way for a time. Nathan knew Bella would sleep through the rest of the night when her head drooped back against his shoulder.

He turned off the jets, nimbly got them both out and dried off, then they returned to their bed. She immediately flung an arm and leg over him, put her ear to his chest so she could hear his heartbeat as she slept, and was out.

Bella awoke well before her alarm the next morning, which irritated her. Her head felt fuzzy, and it was in agony. She stretched, reached over, then realized Nathan wasn't in bed with her. Confused, she grabbed her robe and put it on as she went downstairs to find him.

She found him in the kitchen, pacing while talking on the phone with his full-blown 'work mode' face on.

Oh, not good at five in the morning, she thought as she crossed in front of him to the counter.

Then again, five a.m. pretty much sucks outright all by itself, in my opinion, she rationalized, and grinned a bit.

As she reached for a cup to make herself some tea, he paused his conversation, gave her a blank look, and went into the living room to talk further. Her eyebrows raised as she watched him retreat.

What the hell? He's never done that before. What's going on?

Trying to put it in the back of her mind, she busied herself with making her tea, reaching up in the cabinet for an Excedrin while she waited for the kettle to come to a boil. Her headache was getting worse. Or maybe it was the sudden wave of foreboding she was feeling. Either way, something had to give.

Excedrin would at least solve one of them.

She made her tea, sat at the kitchen table, and was taking her fifth sip when Nathan returned to the room. He poured himself coffee, sat at the table next to her, and ran his hands through his hair, obviously agitated about something.

Bella became very, very still.

"Nathan. What is it?" she asked in a small voice. Part of her somewhere deep inside already knew the answer.

He lifted his eyes to hers, a storm swirling in them, and took her hand.

"He's awake."

Bella flinched, closing her eyes as if she'd been struck.

"I have to go to Arizona," he said. "That was Max on the phone; they called him at four-thirty this morning. I have to see for myself, talk to the doctors."

"I know, baby," she said simply. "I can't. I just can't, not this soon."

"I wasn't going to ask you to, Bella," he stated very softly. "Never even considered asking you to do that. I know how hard that would be on you."

She smiled at him, although the headache was now at a screaming point, and her eyes were welling with tears.

"Okay," she managed, though her voice shook.

"I'll be back as quick as I can, honey. And he's not getting out. He's not going anywhere. I promise, Bella. He will never have the chance to hurt you ever again."

He lifted her hand to his lips, kissing it.

"When do you have to leave?"

"Max said he'd be here within the hour, and he's already scheduled our flight out. Bella, do you want me to get Ms. Robbins to stay with you until I get back? I might have to be gone overnight."

"No. I can manage," she said, a little calmer. "I have a full slate this week to keep me occupied, and like you said, he's still in custody."

They went together back to the bedroom, where Nathan packed a small overnight bag and checked, then secured, his sidearm.

"Come on, walk me down," he gestured.

They traveled back down to the front door. He held her more tightly than ever before.

"I'll try my damnedest to be back tonight. Okay?"

"Okay. Nathan, please don't worry about me, I'm good, okay?"

"I love you, Bella," he said, as he heard the crunch of car tires in the driveway.

"I love you, too, Nathan," she responded, giving him a long, tender kiss before watching him climb in beside Max and drive away.

The flight occurred without incident, and within fifteen minutes, Nathan and Max were in an agency car, headed toward Mikel's current residence. As they pulled into the hospital, Nathan showed his badge, and they were cleared to priority parking.

"Doc said to meet him over at his office in the professional building," Max pointed out the three-story structure that sat about five-hundred yards across the street from the main hospital building. "He's expecting us."

Nathan took a deep breath, held it for a moment, then released.

"Let's go see what's up," he stated.

They left the car and walked inside, then followed signs and took the elevator to the third floor. A young woman in a business suit met them as they stepped off the elevator.

"Director Jones? Agent Thomas?" she asked.

Receiving nods as her response, she continued.

"I'm Anna, Dr. Hightower's office manager. We've been expecting you. Dr. Hightower had an emergency consult that came in about a half-hour ago. I expect him back shortly. He asked me to show you to the conference room. Right this way, please."

They followed her down the hallway, and she paused, indicating a door to her left.

"There's coffee and bottled water on the credenza, and restrooms are just down this hall to the right. Please make yourselves comfortable, and if you need anything, just pick up the phone and dial extension two."

Anna stayed until they were seated comfortably, then returned to her station.

Nathan got up and went to the window. From here, the six-story hospital loomed just slightly off to the left. He already knew exactly where the long-term care ward was. Subconsciously, he clenched and unclenched his fists as he relived last fall's nightmare, when the woman he loved was almost taken from him.

He imagined calmly strolling to room four-two-five, locking the door quietly behind him, moving to the bed, placing his hands around the throat, and squeezing, squeezing...

Max joined him at the window. He had felt the tension growing within Nathan from all the way across the room. Now he laid a hand on Nathan's shoulder, as a father would his son.

"I know it's a gut-kick to be back here," Max said. "I get it. Truly. But when Dr. Hightower gets here you'll have to push aside the personal and focus on the job. Believe me, I'm feeling it, too."

Nathan's gut loosened a little.

"You're right, I know you are," he muttered apologetically. "And I'm probably going to hell for this, but part of me is pissed he woke up. Beautifully built criminal case aside, he was much less to worry about when he was in that freaking coma," he finished with bitterness.

"I agree," Max said simply, squeezing his shoulder before returning to his seat.

A few moments later, a very tired Dr. Hightower entered the room.

"Gentlemen." He walked forward with his hand extended in greeting. They shook, and the neurosurgeon and Nathan joined Max at the table.

"Well, where to begin," Hightower mused as he took his glasses off and rubbed his eyes. "I was paged about three this morning with an urgent code. I didn't realize it was about Mikel Metzger until I got here. I immediately went to the fourth floor to see for myself. He was awake, alert, though he wouldn't speak to me. My current assumption is that he remained mute by choice, not because of any neurological defect."

He got up, retrieved a bottle of water, and sat again.

"Why do you say that, Doctor?" Nathan inquired.

"Because his vital signs were all normal. And I ordered another full round of scans of his head. Gentlemen, it's the damnedest thing I've ever seen in my entire career. No brain damage, zero. It's like the trauma and coma never even happened. I fully expected there to be some residual damage at the very least. Quite frankly, I'm shocked he came out of the coma at all. Previous scans done, my entire thirty years of experience up until this case, had led me to believe what I told you months ago, which was that the chances of him coming back from a vegetative state were slim."

"Is he able to be remanded into Federal custody at this time?" Max asked.

"We'll keep him here another six weeks, at least. He's developed some minor infection from the gunshot wound to the chest that's been lingering. The thoracic surgeon ordered one more round of different, more aggressive antibiotics to try to address that. If they don't work, Dr. Ford will have to go back in. That would, of course, delay things.

"Aside from that," Hightower continued, "we need to work on rebuilding his muscle strength. We routinely do some rudimentary physical therapy with our long-term care patients, to keep the larger joints from freezing and so on due to immobility. But he'll need more intensive work than that to overcome lying still for months."

Hightower took a long, long drink.

"After that," he concluded, "once those hurdles are cleared, I see no reason why he wouldn't be able to be transported to whatever facility you choose."

Nathan leaned forward.

"Please tell me he's being properly monitored and restrained. He's not just dangerous, Dr. Hightower. He's evil."

The doctor waved his hand. "We have full restraints on him and armed guards on the door. But even without them, his muscle tone currently is such that – trust me – he's not going anywhere under his own power right now."

They all rose and shook hands again.

"I've not had a chance to update my notes on this case," Hightower said. "Been a little hectic today."

He grimaced as his pager went off yet again.

"But as soon as I do, I'll forward you all copies of everything in his patient file, and I'll ask Dr. Ford to do the same."

Hightower led the way out the door to the elevator.

"If you'll excuse me, gentlemen, I need to see what this last page is about." He headed to his office.

Nathan and Max rode down in silence, absorbing what they'd just heard.

"Nathan, are you thinking what I'm thinking?"

"Yeah," Nathan said. "I am. Put Federal guards on this, not just local. I think Hightower is among the best in his field, but he has no clue about what security measures are really needed here. I think he's underestimated his patient's strength. And I don't think FCI will work, either. It's good, but it's only medium security."

His features hardened.

"We're going to need to put him in a max security facility when he leaves here."

Chapter Twelve

BELLA ONLY HALF-LISTENED through her lecture classes. Her mind kept drifting away, and not to a happy place. Somehow, she managed to get through the day, but she still felt uneasy, unsettled, unprepared.

I know, she told herself. *I need to go practice. That will help.*

Swinging by her house, she went to her side of the bed, pulled out the Walther PPK .22 Nathan had bought her. She unloaded the magazine, made sure the chamber was empty, and stripped it apart to clean it as he'd shown her. She'd found she liked the smell of gun oil, the attention to detail required as she carefully cleaned each piece, then reassembled. She'd also learned that if you were a good enough shot, a .22 round could be just as deadly as a bigger one.

She attached the trigger guard, loaded the gun and ammo into their carrying case, got back into her car, and drove to Quantico. With a wave to Barney, one of the front-gate guards she'd known for years, she parked and walked toward the stately gray building housing the gun range.

"Hey Bella, how are you?" It was Mark manning the range this afternoon.

"I'm good, Mark," she replied. "You?"

"Yep," he answered, checking his log. "Number ten's open, that all right?"

"Great," she said. "Thanks."

He handed her the requisite ear and eye protection, then checked her case to make sure what she'd brought in was within guidelines and had been transported safely. Once he confirmed she'd already put in the earplugs, he pressed the buzzer for her to enter through the door at the end of the room and motioned her through.

She made her way to lane ten, nodding in recognition to several of the other lane's occupants as she passed.

Upon reaching the lane, she set her case in front of her. She got out her oversized earmuff-style headphones and put them on. She'd discovered through multiple trips here that the little plug inserts weren't quite enough to prevent a headache following target practice.

She swiveled behind her to select a target to aim for. *Hmm. Standard bullseye again?* She considered.

Nope. I think, for what might be coming at some point, I want to use the silhouette this time.

She shuddered a bit at the scenario that thought had implied, then straightened her shoulders and selected a silhouette target anyway. Turning back, she affixed it in place with the clips, then pressed the button to move it away from her to the three-yard mark.

Now she unpacked her weapon. Taking care to keep the muzzle pointed down range, she took off the trigger guard, then set the gun on the little shelf in front of her. Bella opened her box of ammunition, picked up the magazine, loaded ten live rounds to start. She picked the gun up in her right hand, slid the magazine in with her left until it clicked into place. Last, she pulled back the slide, then let it travel forward, which chambered the first round.

This first set would be done right-handed, her naturally dominant side. She stepped up, took aim using the Weaver stance, right index finger on the trigger, head angled on a vertical axis to the right slightly to compensate for being left-eye dominant, and fired the first three shots, aiming for mid-torso. The next three shots she aimed for center of the head, followed by four more shots mid-torso again.

The slide stayed back after the last shot, indicating the gun was empty. She sat it down on the shelf, pressed the button to return the target to her so she could view the results.

"Not too shabby," she told herself, noting that the head cluster could have been tighter but were still grouped together well, up and to the left of center. The mid-torso shots were, too, although also not as centered as she'd have liked. Her right-handed attempts in each target area had all landed in a radius a playing card or two would cover.

She moved her target back out to the three-yard mark, which equaled nine feet, dropped the empty magazine, added ten more rounds, clicked it home again.

"Now," she said aloud, "left-handed."

She switched her grip the opposite of the previous setup, so that now her left hand controlled the weapon, and her right hand provided the support. Sizing up her target again, she fired, the same pattern of three mid-torso, three head, last four mid-torso. Then, setting her empty weapon down carefully, she once again brought the target back to her for reviewing.

"Much, much better," she studied appreciatively. "Now we're talking."

And Bella was right. For someone who'd done everything right-handed her whole life, she was a much more accurate shot as a lefty. It made her grin to see her left-handed efforts were not only dead center of each area she'd aimed for, but that each was grouped so tightly she could place a quarter over the holes and completely cover them up.

She repeated the whole process again, first right-handed, then left-handed, with her target moved out to six yards away, or eighteen feet, then again at eight yards away, which equaled twenty-four feet. As the distance increased, she did see a natural decline in the group-ings, but she expected to.

She double-checked her firearm was devoid of rounds, released the magazine, put the trigger lock back on, and packed up her bag. Taking her target down, she headed off the range.

She walked over to Mark, handed him the safety glasses back, took her earmuffs off and plugs out, opened her case for him to confirm that once again her weapon was properly secured for transport.

"How'd you do?" he asked.

"Take a look," she said, and offered the silhouette.

"Nice groupings," Mark acknowledged as he pointed to the left-handed attempts.

"Yeah." She grinned. "As a southpaw, no less. Gotta love that opposite-eye-dominant thing."

He grinned back. "See you later, Bella."

"'Bye, Mark. Take care."

She felt much more in control and self-confident as she drove home.

They'd just landed when his cell phone rang. "Thomas," he answered.

"Hey, it's Mitch. You back yet?"

"About to walk off the plane as we speak. What's going on?"

"I was able to retrieve and restore some deleted files on the Metzger computer," Mitch explained. "You're going to want to see these."

"On my way," Nathan said. "Should be there in about twenty minutes."

Hanging up, he turned to Max.

"I need to swing by the office. Mitch found something."

Rick blinked, frowned, re-read the last few passages of the report in his hand. His antenna quivered. He reached over and waded through the stack of papers he'd already reviewed until he found what he was looking for. It was the inventory sheet of all the items confiscated from Adolf Werner's office suite and safe. He held both documents side by side.

Re-reading the report, then scanning the list, he smiled like a predator whose prey had been cornered.

There. Right there in black and white.

Yes, he thought in triumph. *Hell yes. I think I just figured it out.*

Only one way to know for sure.

He went downstairs, flipped on the light, traveled through the non-fiction section until he found what he sought. Grabbing the volume, he turned off the lights again and retreated upstairs to put his theory to the test.

God, I love this codebreaking stuff, he grinned as he poured a fresh cup of coffee

If his hunch was right, it was going to be a very long and revealing night.

"Holy shit," Nathan breathed, starting to see red. "Holy fucking shit."

"Yeah," Mitch muttered, clearly uncomfortable with what he'd found and had to disclose. "I knew you'd want to know about this."

What they were talking about were all the Bella-related files Adolf had only thought he'd permanently deleted from Mikel's computers. Mitch, computer genius and Bureau legend, had managed to restore them all.

There were just over a thousand of them.

Pictures. Videos. Word documents, hundreds of pages' worth. Entry after disturbingly graphic entry in some sort of vile homage to her. What he was willing to do for her. Most troubling from Nathan's vantage point as her boyfriend was what Mikel wanted to do with and *to* her.

Mitch and Nathan had only read one or two so far, but that had been plenty disturbing enough to witness, and they'd stopped.

"I realized he was probably obsessed with her, but sweet Jesus," Nathan remarked, trembling slightly with rage. "I never figured anything close to this level."

Mitch fidgeted.

"Nathan. For the record, for the case, someone will have to review all this." He gestured in the direction of the screen. "Every single file, every single word, to make sure that what needs to be included in state's evidence at trial is."

He cleared his throat and continued.

"As the head of the computer lab, I can assign it to one of my techs, or I can keep this one. It's at my discretion. And in my opinion, the one person I think should definitely *not* review any more of this is you."

Mitch saw Nathan's jaw clench.

"Nathan," he said gently. "If you insist on this, you run a risk of seeing things, reading things, hearing things you won't be able to wipe out of your memory. You're in a committed relationship with the focus of all... this," Mitch faltered, not quite sure how best to refer to the river of disgusting and twisted things he'd uncovered. "The best way I can think of to protect her from knowing about it all is to minimize how much *you* know about it all."

"Thanks, Mitch, I know you're looking out for me, and I appreciate it."

"There's more, Nathan. I've been in the Bureau over twenty years now, so let me give you some advice. You're up to your neck right in the middle of this thing, both personally and professionally. It's not uncommon at all for higher-ups to reassign the case in that situation. In fact, it's standard practice. Because if the agent loses objectivity, can't stay impersonal, they can't do the job. I think you're shaping up to be a hell of an agent. But kid, I'm surprised as hell you're still even active primary on this case at all. At some point, you'll have to choose whether to react as a Federal Agent or as Bella's boyfriend. You won't be able to balance both successfully and do either one justice. That's just human nature."

"Mitch is right, you know," the Assistant Director said from the doorway, and walked slowly over to join them. "As a matter of fact, I've been looking for you, Nathan, to talk about that very thing."

Nathan sat in one of the visitors' chairs in the Assistant Director's office. His direct supervisor, the man heading the BAU, occupied the other. Both men sat quietly as the AD spoke.

"Nathan, this move isn't a negative reflection on you or your work, at all. You know that. Your files, methods, research, on all this have been exemplary. But it was a gray area already to leave you on this case, given that Mikel Metzger stalked, then took hostage and attempted to kill, your girlfriend. This new data that's come to light pushes this whole deal from gray right over into the no-go section."

The AD went on.

"We need to have a one-hundred percent airtight case here. We've overwhelmingly solid physical evidence that cannot be refuted; the defense attorneys won't even bother to try. What they *will* try is to discredit how the evidence was found, and the investigators who collected it. They will look for any sign, any chance to start a witch hunt for hidden agendas or ulterior motives for framing their client – whether any exists or not. Reasonable doubt, Nathan, remember that. That's all they need to prove. If you stay involved in this case as an agent, in *any* capacity, it presents them a big juicy bone to go after and tear to shreds to try to get this guy acquitted of multiple murders."

It burned a hole in his gut.

Nathan knew they were right; of course, they were. His continued involvement in this case would likely result in the exact scenario the AD had just predicted. He damn sure didn't have to like it, though.

Nathan looked at his boss, then at the AD, eyes blazing.

"What about Bella?" he said, with much less emotion than he felt. "Is there a better approach to take that increases her odds of not having to testify at all for any of it?"

The AD inclined his head to Steve Brown, Nathan's supervisor.

"Two completely separate cases," Steve indicated. "The six deaths committed in conjunction with the Institute and its research, that's a stand-alone case. Brendan Jones's murder ties back to the six, manner of death is identical, so we roll him and Adolf's death into that case too. We pursue that one first, take it to the grand jury first. Bella's nowhere near being involved in that piece. In that scenario she was just another employee at the Institute.

"After that, we pursue the second case, for Manfred's murder and the stalking and assault on Bella. And in the second one," Steve admitted, "you need to prepare yourself and her that she'll probably be subpoenaed to testify. No way around it. She had a front-row seat for Manfred's death, she got a good enough look to give one hell of a description to the police sketch artist. At some point, the defense will try their best to get her to the stand to try to shake her testimony."

"We don't like it, either, Nathan," the AD said calmly, noting the distress on his agent's face. "But that's the reality here."

"I know," Nathan stated. "And for the record, I do completely get why I'm being reassigned. Steve," he said, glancing to his right, "give me whatever caseload you want, I'm not picky."

Then he turned his gaze forward again, looked at the AD.

"May I speak freely for a moment, sir?"

"Absolutely, Agent Thomas."

"Sir, I really, really hope you guys nail him and he's caged for the rest of his natural life. For the past five months, I've held Bella when she wakes up sobbing and screaming and fighting for her life all over again. And it cuts me to the core, every time. But now, I don't have to choose between reacting like an agent or as her boyfriend anymore."

He stood.

"So, I'll tell you both now, face to face and on the record, that if he ever gets loose and comes for her, I can and certainly will put that bastard down like the rabid dog he is, without thinking twice about it."

The AD kept a neutral tone and expression. He wanted to say, "Amen, son," but couldn't. So instead, he replied with, "Noted. Good evening, gentlemen."

Nathan nodded once, turned on his heel, and headed home.

———

Rick stood up, stretched, yawned, and paced a bit to loosen up his cramped leg muscles.

He'd done it.

He hadn't finished decoding all of it yet. Not by a long shot. But what he'd found so far confirmed his hunch had been dead on.

Smiling, he walked to his computer, typed out an email to Max, and hit send.

He checked the time. Almost nine p.m. He'd go a little further tonight, then pack it in. He had all day tomorrow to keep working on it.

———

Max drove a solemn and quiet Nathan back toward his house. He knew exactly what had happened; he'd been in this business too long not to. But he waited patiently.

"I'm off the case," Nathan finally said.

"I figured as much," Max replied. "You get why, don't you?"

"I do," Nathan said earnestly. "And to be honest, I'm glad. Those things Mitch found. Some of the things Mikel wrote about her. Max, I read a couple of them without thinking it through first. Just working my case, you know. But they were bad. Really bad. Twisted, sick. As soon as I read those things, I knew. I knew that if I had any opportunity at all, I'd kill him without hesitation, and to hell with my badge and the case both."

"I know," Max said. "I wouldn't hesitate to either. For Bella, and for Manfred. So, it's probably best we're out of this from the official side of things."

Nathan lined out the rest of the conversation he'd had, about Bella and testifying.

"Hopefully, it won't come to that," Max observed. "I mean, the FBI could certainly bring a case against him for Manfred, since among other things he was a contracted Federal employee and therefore falls in their jurisdiction. And I want to see justice done for him, as my oldest friend. But as Bella's godfather, I want it to just go away, to spare her that risk of having to relive it all in open court."

He paused.

"I tell you this now, Nathan. I would rather see Mikel Metzger only get charged for the first set of crimes, and forgo vengeance for my friend, if it means Bella has a better chance to heal in peace. She has a lot of living yet to do, as do you. I don't want either of you to suffer longer from this just to try and settle a score."

"That means a lot, Max."

"What are you going to tell her?"

"The truth. Well, most of it, anyway. I don't want to mention the files that were found. No good can come from her knowing about that part of it."

Max pulled over to the curb close to the house for a moment, so he could turn and look at Nathan.

"Son," he said gently, "how do you plan to keep that a secret? I can see it on your face as plain as day. Bella's one of the smartest people I've ever known, and she's also in love with you. If it's so easy for me to spot, she'll have no trouble at all seeing it. So how are you going to do this?"

Nathan sighed heavily as he ran his hands through his hair.

"I'm still not sure, Max. I just know in my gut that telling her what we found is going to wound her even more. She already wakes up screaming sometimes as it is."

"Well, Nathan," Max pondered. "You can be truthful without being overly truthful. What I mean is, tell her additional evidence was found. That while you don't know precisely what it was, your higher-ups do. And they felt that leaving you on this investigation could open the case up to accusations by the defense that some evidence gathered was tainted or planted, due to your personal connection to some of the people involved. It's not really a lie, Nathan. That is exactly why they pulled you. You truly don't know the full scope of those files. And by your own admission, you don't want to."

Nathan tilted his head and considered Max's words. "That could work. I hate holding back from her, but I really feel I need to not share everything this time."

"I know, believe me." Max patted his shoulder. "But in our line of work, sometimes omission is more merciful."

They continued down the street and pulled into the driveway. Nathan could see Bella standing at the door.

"Night, Nathan," Max said. "I'll see you later."

He watched as Nathan climbed the steps, then gathered Bella in for a hug. Waving to them both, he backed out of the driveway and started home. His phone buzzed, and he pulled over to check it.

He smiled.

"Hot damn," he said. "Conner broke it."

He typed and sent his reply.

Rick heard the ping of incoming mail as he continued to work. He opened his phone and read.

Great news. I knew you could crack it. I'll be at your place at seven p.m. tomorrow.

Rick looked at his progress and checked how much further he had to go.

"That could still work," he noted, and whistled to himself as he went back to it.

As soon as they were inside, Bella said, "Something happened, something big. You look exhausted, and worried. What's going on, baby?"

Nathan led her to the couch and sat down.

"I'm off the Metzger case. It's been reassigned. I meet with Steve on Wednesday afternoon to get up to speed on my new cases."

"What?" Bella rose up in indignation. "How dare they? You've busted your ass on this thing."

Chapter Thirteen

BELLA PACED FURIOUSLY BACK and forth before she noticed how quiet Nathan was.

"Oh," she said as she realized what was happening. "They reassigned it because you and I are together, didn't they?"

"Kind of."

She sat again and took his hand. "I'm not following."

"They were able to retrieve a bunch of deleted files from Mikel's computer. Over a thousand of them. I don't know all the contents. I just know that the AD felt removing me from the case would negate any ability for his defense team to attack any aspect of how the evidence against him was found or gathered."

"So those files that were found pertain to me."

"My presumption is yes."

"And if you stay on the case, any part of it, they're worried someone might accuse you of framing him or whatever, as revenge for those files."

"That's it in a nutshell."

"Hm." Bella sat, mulling it all over. "Makes sense. I mean, from what I know so far, the evidence against him for those murders is rock-solid, gathered by Arizona PD and the FBI teams, not you personally. But I can see where if something involving me has popped up, his lawyers would take that and try to discredit everything else with it. Including you."

She leaned into him and sighed. "Are you okay with all this?"

"I actually am," Nathan said truthfully. "It means I don't have to worry about which side to look at all this from, Federal agent or boyfriend. I can just concentrate on being there for you."

"Arizona. How did that part go?"

He exhaled heavily. "Long or short version?"

"Your choice, just fill me in."

"Well, he's awake and lucid. Hightower says tests show no sign whatsoever of any residual brain damage. Which means he'll be mentally fit to stand trial. We've put our agents on watch at the hospital, including right outside his room. They want to get him completely healed up before they turn him over, and he won't be going to FCI."

"Because it's only a medium security facility, and if anyone needs to be in max, it's him," Bella finished for him.

"That, right there. That's one of the many, many reasons I love you," he said sincerely, kissing her. "You get it."

"Thanks," she said. "Nathan? Will I have to testify?"

He paused a moment.

"They're planning on splitting all this into two cases. First case, all the murders relating to the research project, Brendan since he was killed in the same manner, and Adolf. That case doesn't touch you, no testifying at all. That will be submitted to the grand jury for indictment any day now."

They both breathed a sigh of relief on that one.

"Second case they're putting together to possibly pursue," Nathan proceeded cautiously, "is your grandfather's murder, kidnapping, and attempted murder on you."

She blanched.

"If that one goes forward, I'll definitely have to testify. No way around it. Without me, they won't be able to even put Mikel at the scene."

"I know. But baby, I don't want you to go through that. It's not right that he won't directly pay, on record, for taking your grandfather, for hurting you. But it's worth way more to me that you're okay and that you stay okay. My advice, Bella, is we watch from a safe distance as they crucify him in the first case, take our comfort in justice that way."

She stared at him for what seemed like an eternity.

"I don't know what to do," she said finally. "I don't. Part of me wants to hold my head high, march into court, tell the world what a cruel bastard he is, make him pay for taking Granpa from me."

Nathan nodded understanding.

"But part of me is scared shitless at the thought of having to be in the same room with him, watching me with those dead, gray eyes." She shuddered at the thought. "He already invades my dreams. You know that. I'm afraid testifying will make that worse."

Nathan pulled her close.

"Bella, there's no need to choose right this minute. The way Steve and the AD were talking, they wouldn't even *present* the second case to the grand jury until after sentencing is completed on the first case. Which means we have anywhere from six months onward to make that decision."

Nathan paused, then added, "And I hope you know that you never have to face anything alone ever again. You know that, right?"

"I know."

"I want to show you something," he announced suddenly. "Wait right here, okay?"

A confused Bella nodded, and Nathan quickly left the room to retrieve the little box Manfred had willed to him. When he came back and sat beside her again, he gently said, "I think it's time you see exactly what's in here."

Then, he opened the box and turned it toward her.

"Those are their wedding rings," Bella said immediately, tears coming to her eyes. "And my grandmother's engagement ring he gave her in 1954. She used to let me wear it sometimes when I was little and played dress up."

It was exquisite – a delicate silver ring, adorned with a small, tear-shaped sapphire, surrounded by little diamonds.

Tucked into the box was a handwritten note.

"Bella and Nathan – I hope your love stays as magical as mine and Rose's did – Manfred."

Nathan carefully removed the sapphire ring from its cradle and took one knee in front of Bella.

"Bella Amsel, will you marry me?"

"Yes," she whispered, and smiled as he slipped the ring onto her finger.

Paula grabbed the first four charts, as usual, and headed to the end of the hall to work back toward the nurse's station. She walked along, distracted, flipping through charts, and nearly screamed when she saw movement in the hall almost right next to her.

"You all right?" the man asked.

Hand on heart, she stopped for a minute to regain her composure. "You scared the hell out of me. Usually on this floor, nothing moves that's not dressed in nurse's scrubs."

He chuckled. "Sorry about that, ma'am."

"Why are you here, exactly?"

"Guess they didn't fill you in yet. He's awake," he said, jerking his thumb backward at the door. "Until he gets transferred out of here, we're standing watch, more for everyone else's safety than for his."

"He's awake? When? How?"

He held his hands up and replied, "Whoa, slow down. I have no idea about when, or anything. I'm just on watch here."

"Sorry," she said. "It's just that almost never happens. Usually, when people leave this floor, it's to go be buried."

She paused, her mind racing.

"Anyway, I'd better get started on rounds."

She walked swiftly away to room four-thirty, went in, and closed the door.

She had to sit down because she was shaking so hard. Her love was awake. She almost couldn't wrap her head around it. Her prayers had been answered. Finally.

He was under guard now, Federal agents, not local. She'd noticed the man's badge and gun.

That meant he'd done something very, very wrong. Maybe several somethings. Paula never watched the news. It made her too sad. As a result, she didn't know all he'd been accused of. She honestly had no clue about who she'd fallen in love with.

Oh, sweet Lord. What had he done that would require armed watchmen?

Put it away right now, honey, get hold of yourself. You still have a job to do.

She took several cleansing breaths and refocused her mind. She took four-thirty's vitals, made notes in his chart, administered the dosages as written, noted the date, time, and her initials. Then, she took another deep breath and left to head back toward her favorite patient and his keeper.

She smiled politely at the man that had startled her before, moved into the room, and shut the door.

Mikel lifted his head and stared at her.

Slowly, cautiously, she approached, noticing the new additions to his setup. Full restraints, a piece of hospital equipment never used on this floor before in her almost four years here that she could recall. The handcuffs around both wrists and ankles that connected him to the metal bed frame, however, were by no means typical hospital equipment.

Baby. What the hell did you do? she thought.

Paula cleared her throat. "Hi," she said. "I'm Paula."

"I know your voice," Mikel said, and watched her as she drew closer. He noted her light-brown hair and jade-green eyes. She didn't look more than twenty-five, twenty-six years old, at the most. Young. Malleable.

"You do?"

"You spoke to me," he replied.

"You could hear me?" Paula asked, astonished.

"Every word. You talked to me about your day, the weather."

He gazed intently at her.

"Yes, that's right. I did."

"You kissed me. Told me you love me."

Now she stammered, blushed, unsure what to say, and like a predator whose prey had been run to ground, he knew he had her.

"Did you mean it?" Mikel asked her.

She lowered her eyes.

"Yes," she whispered. "I did."

Rick was making excellent strides. He'd gotten a little over twenty-five double-sided pages done so far, he estimated. A little over double that left to go, give or take. Now he rubbed his eyes and took a break from decoding to review the roughly fifty decoded ones so far.

Teaching himself to speed read all those years ago had paid off several times over in his career, and ordinarily, this would have been no exception.

Unfortunately, the code turned to German once the cipher was applied. He knew a handful of phrases, in several languages, but beyond that, he was going to have difficulty translating from German to English without assistance.

Fuck.

The clock struck one a.m. Tuesday morning.

He hesitated, considering.

Part of him really wanted to keep going, but part of him knew he needed to get some decent sleep and start fresh in the morning.

He scooped up both the coded and decoded pages and the book, took them into his bedroom, and locked them in the safe. Then he sent Max another email before he set his alarm for six a.m.

In Manassas, Max was unable to sleep, so he reviewed Rick's email as soon as it arrived. He chuckled, typed a reply, and went back to his book.

Rick woke just before his alarm went off. He started the coffeepot to begin another very long day of transcription, then picked up his phone from its charging station and read Max's reply:

Dear boy, don't worry, we have all the cool toys. I'll be there at seven p.m. tonight as agreed and will bring the perfect thing to deal with the second part.

"Sweet," Rick grinned, and headed for the shower.

Tuesday started off calmly enough at Faith's place of employment, but by lunchtime it was over the top. An intern had opened an innocent-looking email attachment that launched a ransomware virus straight into the company's mainframe. All the files on the server were now either encrypted or missing altogether. The entire company was at a standstill. All hell was breaking loose.

Fortunately for her, she'd asked for and received permission Monday afternoon to back up all accounting files onto a large-capacity portable thumb drive. Her company's third-party IT team had been having other issues with the outdated server already, and she'd gotten tired of hearing 'server's down again.' The most recent versions she had of everything she needed were only a half-day old.

My being frustrated with our equipment and our service provider wound up being a good thing, she mused. *Who'd have thought?*

So, at noon on a Tuesday, she unexpectedly found herself home. Since the mainframe was corrupted, remoting in wasn't possible because it was unsafe. She'd cleared it with the President to continue to work from home, keeping everything on her personal computer so that when the crisis was finally over and the all-clear given, the accounting files could be restored from a current timeframe and a virus-free location.

Not that there would be much work. All her files were pretty much current already. Much of what she did daily hinged on inventory coming in, sales going out, the ebb and flow and balancing of daily activity. And right now, they were dead in the water. Until the company was fully functional again, she'd have some free time.

Christ knows how long that's gonna be, she thought to herself.

There would be a lot of catchup work to do once it all went back to normal. If they were lucky, they'd only lose a couple of weeks of business. Worst case scenario, it could break them completely if they couldn't repair the damage.

She had to admit, it had her worried. There was a good possibility they wouldn't be able to bounce back from this.

She sighed.

Well, the upside is Book Keepers was closed today. Maybe I can go spend some time with Rick.

She pulled out her phone and sent another "Contact Us" message when she realized they still hadn't exchanged phone numbers yet. Then she went up to change into jeans and a t-shirt.

"Hey honey," Bella called out. "Didn't you say you had to meet Steve tomorrow afternoon?"

"Yeah," Nathan hollered back. "But he called and pushed it out to Monday. Why?"

"Hmm. Anything else you have workwise between now and then?"

"No. Why?"

"Well," she announced, "My last final of the semester we had the option of taking online. I just finished it. So, if you're not busy, and I'm not busy, maybe we could, you know, be not busy together."

She batted her eyes at him as he rounded the corner.

"You know, like maybe a romantic getaway somewhere."

"Bella Amsel, I like your style," he exclaimed as he swept her up into his arms.

Rick had heard his bookstore email chime. He opened and read it, smiled, and answered. Then he'd gone back to his desk. But now, he found himself watching the clock and grinning maniacally, willing it to move faster. After about twenty-five minutes, Rick could no longer contain himself and made for the lift.

He arrived at Book Keepers' front door almost as Faith did. He turned the key and let her in.

"Hi," he said. Then framed her face and kissed her passionately.

"Hi yourself," she threw back, then rattled the bag. "Hungry?"

"Famished," he said.

They returned to the lift and headed up, then into the kitchen.

"So, how are you home in the middle of a Tuesday?" he asked her as they unpacked the food.

"Well..." Faith muttered, and filled him in.

"Wow, that sucks," he commiserated.

"Truly," she agreed. "To be honest, it's got me worried, Rick. We're a regional company. Not a lot of loose capital just lying around idle as a cushion to ride this kind of thing out. No freaking telling how much damage that virus caused to our entire history of files, not to mention loss of current and future business while they try to deal with it all."

She sighed.

"I love it there. I just hope it survives and I have a 'there' to go back to."

"Baby, it'll all work out," he told her, patting her hand. "By the way, I missed you."

"Aw," Faith said, leaning over to peck his cheek, "I missed you, too."

They ate their sandwiches and fries, then moved to the living room. Faith's eyes widened when she saw the papers stacked on his desk and on the coffee table.

"Wow, hon," she marveled. "Whatcha got going here?"

"Remember when I told you about Max?"

"Ah, yes, puzzle solving."

"Yep, and it's a doozy. I figured out the cipher key and was able to start decoding pages. Problem is, they're in fucking German. I know how to order a beer in German, and that's about it."

"Really?" Faith's eyebrows peaked. "I took a year of it in high school, but that was ages ago. I don't remember much of it at all. As it turns out, there's not much call in my career to use it."

"Well, I let Max know it's got another layer to it, and he's coming down tonight. Says he's bringing something with him that can solve the German-to-English piece," Rick grinned wickedly and added, "But don't tell him I told you that."

"Let's do this. I don't want to get you into trouble. Seriously," she said, when he grinned again. "So, if I need to go now, tell me. If you want me to stay and hang out while you handle this, I can do that, too."

"Well, he said he'd be here at seven. It's one now. I have about..." He glanced at his desk, calculating. "Well, a lot left. I estimated around a hundred double-sided pages. It took me from six a.m. to one a.m. to get about thirty of that decoded yesterday. Today, so far, I've done another ten, maybe?"

"Let me help you," Faith offered. "It will go faster with two. It's not like I'm going to stumble upon any big secret, I remember just about as much German as you do. So, show me what you're doing and let me help. I pinkie swear to tell no one."

"You know what? I'll take the help," he said. "It's fun, just time consuming. But we'll need another cipher key, so we aren't passing this one back and forth. Let me go grab another copy."

Rick went downstairs and returned in short order with another book.

"Okay, here's what we're doing," he said as he picked up a coded page and showed it to her. "See the series?"

"Numbers, slash marks, and spaces," she noted. "Let me guess. Page number, line number, character position? And space between means space between the letters you're forming? Like, where one word ends and the next begins?"

"Jesus Christ, you're a natural," he managed, blown away by her. "I love your mind, Faith. You're one hell of an accountant and you'd have made one hell of a CTT."

It was her turn to grin wickedly.

"Well, hell, let's get started. I'm gonna grab us some tea."

She sauntered off to his kitchen, stopping at the doorway to intentionally throw a sultry look his way, before laughing and stepping out of sight.

He watched her go.

I love that woman, he realized, and his heart fluttered. *Hopelessly, completely in love with that woman.*

She came back, handed him a glass, and noticed the look on his face.

"What?"

"Nothing," he said, handing her the twenty double-sided pages from the bottom of the stack, a pen, and a blank writing tablet. "Where do you want to set up?"

She looked around at the stacks in the living room area and thought a second.

"Well, to be able to see your handsome self, somewhere in here. But if I'm expected to focus, I'm better off at your kitchen table. Plenty of space to work."

"Kitchen table is probably best," he admitted, then pulled her closer. "But first..."

He pulled her closer and kissed her tenderly.

As they parted, she breathed, "Baby, you keep doing that and we'll never get this project of yours done. But as soon as it is, you owe me a candlelight dinner."

She kissed him again, then nibbled his bottom lip.

"You're on."

Chapter Fourteen

Paula had no idea what to do.

She'd gone over her first ever conversation with Mikel time and time again. He'd given nothing away as to what he thought or how he felt. After she answered his questions, he'd just stared at her for a long moment, then laid his head back and let her do her normal routine of checking vitals. He didn't say another word to her as she'd left his room, and she'd been too uncomfortable with the guard at the door to return at shift's end like she always had before.

Where did things go from here? She honestly didn't know.

***

Dr. Hightower had finally been able to update his notes to Mikel's records and had forwarded them to the Bureau to Nathan's attention.

He saw them, overcame his urge to review them, and passed them on to Steve. He'd also emailed the good doctor to let him know that Steve was the one all future correspondence needed to happen with.

Then, after checking that all loose ends involving being pulled off the case were tied, he'd gone to Steve and told him he was taking the rest of the week off and would be back Monday.

He and Bella packed two overnight bags and climbed into her truck.

"Where to, my love? I'm all yours."

"When you have to be back?"

"I meet with Steve at three p.m. Monday."

"Well," Bella suggested, "what do you think about making a trip back to where we met?"

"Vegas?"

"Yep."

"I could be persuaded. I already know I'm going to be with the hottest woman there."

She laughed.

"I was hoping you'd agree, because I already booked our flight and hotel. Our flight leaves in about two hours."

"Well, then," he smiled at her. "Guess we'd better get going."

<hr>

At five p.m. Faith finally had to stand and stretch. She glanced at her watch.

Four hours, already? Jesus.

She had to admit; Rick was right. It was time consuming, but a hell of a lot of fun watching the mystery get solved letter by letter, row by row. She'd already completed twelve of her twenty assigned double-sided pages.

She walked out to the living room.

"How it's going out here?" she asked him.

Rick counted and said, "I knocked out another ten or twelve so far. You?"

"Twelve little double-sided bastards conquered, eight to go," she reported, rolling her shoulders to work out the kinks.

"Nice." He nodded in approval.

"I'm taking five," she said, heading to the bathroom for a break. As she did, the accountant in her calculated her current productivity rate.

Let's see, four hours, twelve two-sided pages done, so twenty-four pages total, so six pages an hour. Not bad. Not bad at all.

Coming back into the living room she told Rick, "I should be down to the last couple of pages by the time Max gets here. I'd like to stay and see this through. What's Max going to do, shoot me?"

He laughed.

"I don't think he would. If you want to stay, great. If he's upset that you're involved, I'll smooth it over."

"You know, there is one good thing about all this," she quipped. "The dude that wrote the coded pages had really big handwriting. Think how much this would suck if he'd written really, really tiny, and it *still* came out to one-hundred double-sided pages."

"I know, right?" Rick said. "I thought the same damn thing about eleven o'clock last night."

They smiled at each other.

"Okay, break's over. Back I go," she announced.

The next two hours flew by. She heard Rick's phone ring, and him answer, just as she finished page eighteen of her assigned twenty.

"Showtime," he warned her, and went down to let Max in.

Bella and Nathan strolled hand-in-hand down the Strip, people watching and enjoying the evening air. They stopped in front of the Bellagio just in time to witness the next scheduled fountain show, choreographed to music.

"That was really pretty," she remarked. "I didn't get to see that the last time I was here."

"If you like that, come with me to Venetian," Nathan told her. "They have an actual canal, with gondolas."

"Really?" she asked. "That sounds awesome."

So, they experienced the gondolas at Venetian, and the bustle of New York New York's casino floor. After that, they retraced their steps to the row of slots where they met. Fortuitously, the two machines they'd played back then were unoccupied.

"Think we'll get lucky again?" Bella asked.

"I already did, finding you," Nathan replied softly, and kissed her.

Max not only wasn't upset, but he also wasn't surprised, which in turn surprised Rick and Faith.

"What?" he said, looking back at them. "Rick, did Faith not tell you her brother's an FBI agent? Nathan Thomas. I know him well. Great kid. I wasn't worried about Faith here."

"Oh," Faith exclaimed. "So, *you're* the 'Max' Nathan mentioned doing some work with in Arizona and Virginia. Small world."

"Yes, I am. And I was wondering when the universe would shift just enough for you and Rick here to meet," he pronounced, and kissed Faith's cheek. "Nice to see you again, dear. For the record, some of the best codebreakers I've known are accountants. It's the attention to detail."

"But wait," Faith interjected, completely confused. "I never even told you my name the one time I met you. So how do you know Nathan Thomas is my brother?"

"My dear," Max chuckled. "Nathan is dating my goddaughter. Her grandfather Manfred and I made it a point to know all about him, including who and where his relatives are, the moment they started dating."

He smiled as her jaw dropped.

"Besides, you and he have the same eyes. Now," he continued, "let me show you what I've brought."

He unpacked the oversized rolling bag he'd brought, pulling out a laptop and portable scanner.

"Nice," Rick said, checking the gear.

"Wait until you see what it can do," Max told him with a twinkle in his eyes.

He plugged it all in, connected the scanner to the laptop, then turned it all on.

"Watch," he instructed. Grabbing the first five decoded pages, he placed them in the scanner's intake tray. The machine pulled them all through in rapid succession.

"Now for the fun part," Max told them, and pressed a few buttons.

Watching the screen, Faith and Rick marveled as, with a few keystrokes, the computer seemed to effortlessly switch what they were looking at from German to English in a heartbeat.

"Now, it's not actually physically overwriting what was scanned," he explained. "It's just converting it in the background into the translated new document, which it's then presenting the results of. We get done here, we'll have a complete copy of the pages in *German* saved in this laptop, and a complete copy of those pages translated into *English* saved in this laptop. No need to tell it to 'save as', or anything else. You tell it 'whatever I give you, make a copy of it in such and such language', and it's all automatic. Pretty damn cool huh?"

"That is..." Rick started.

"Cool as hell," Faith finished.

Max roared with laughter.

"Damned if you two aren't perfect together. Now, bring me the pages, in order, so I can keep feeding this thing."

Rick handed Max more decoded pages, beginning with number six, while Faith returned to the kitchen to finish up her last one. Within twenty minutes, all but two of Rick's and Faith's pages remained to be scanned in.

Max helped himself to some coffee while Rick and Faith finished up the decoding part. As he waited to be able to feed in the remaining pages, he asked, "So, how did you crack the code?"

Rick grinned as he worked. "Well, I waded through that mountain of paper you sent, and read Manfred's report and your main summary. Then, I compared those two with the inventory list of things confiscated from his office."

He paused to write down what he'd found and began looking up the final one.

"When I saw that an autographed "Mein Kampf" was on the list, I skimmed the reports again, and it hit me. Someone with ties close enough to Ernst Kaltenbrunner to refer to him as 'Uncle' had to be pretty damn steeped in Nazi lore to also have a signed copy of that book in his possession."

Rick paused again and looked up at Max.

"So, I played a hunch that the book was the cipher key. And I was right."

"Impressive, Rick," Max beamed approvingly. "Jack would have been proud."

Rick's last two pages were done, so he handed them over and went to check on Faith's progress. She met him at the kitchen door with the finished product, and they walked back over to Max together. Another twenty minutes passed, and finally, all pages had been decoded and scanned in.

Max scrolled up to the top of the converted document and began to skim them as Rick moved to the bar to pour drinks for the three of them.

"Max, what will you have?"

"Scotch, neat," came the distracted reply.

Holy shit, Max thought, the light dawning on him as he began to slow down and truly read what they'd converted over into English. *Am I understanding this correctly?*

"Hey, Rick."

"What?" Rick said as he began to make his and Faith's amaretto sours.

"Rick."

Now he could hear the steel edge that had crept into Max's voice, so he set down the mixer and turned toward Max as Max slowly lifted his head to stare back.

Faith heard it too, as she came out of the bathroom.

"What's wrong, Max?"

"Do you know what this is?" Max inquired.

"No, but somehow I have a feeling you're going to tell us it's big trouble," Rick answered seriously.

"This isn't just some random Nazi propaganda. It's a set of blueprints to resurrect the whole damn Reich," Max verbalized and sat back, dumbstruck.

Silence reigned for a long moment before Faith spoke up.

"Guys, is it just me, or is that an extremely dangerous document that multiple groups of extremists would kill to possess?"

Max looked at her solemnly. "Young lady, that's an excellent summation, and completely accurate." He stood and began packing his equipment back into his bag.

"I'm afraid that Scotch will have to wait until another time, Rick. I have to get back to Langley with this, tonight."

Rick handed Max the original coded pages, then asked, "What about all my copies of your other files? You want them loaded up with you tonight, or should I overnight them back to your office?"

Max turned to Faith. "I would presume an accountant for so many years would have her own personal office shredder?"

Faith grinned. "You assume correctly, and it's an industrial-strength, highly rated one. Quality matters."

"It does indeed, Faith," Max took her hand. "By the way, I enjoyed your being here and helping. Would you be interested in further puzzle solving alongside your young man here?" he asked, pointed toward Rick.

Faith pretended to consider for a moment, then smiled.

"I think he and I make a great team. And yes, I am up for more adventures, should you decide you need more codebreaking consultants."

They walked Max and his oversized bag back to his car, standing there on the sidewalk until he was out of sight.

Bella sighed and leaned her head on Nathan's shoulder as they stood on their hotel balcony viewing the night atmosphere only found in Vegas.

"This is even better than the first time I was here," she stated contentedly.

"It is?" he asked, eyes sparkling with humor.

"Of course," Bella grinned mischievously. "I have a surprise for you."

"Oh?" Nathan's eyebrow raised as he followed her back to the room, and his look turned to puzzlement as she reached into the inner pocket of the bag she'd packed and pulled out a little box.

Then his lips curved into an incredulous smile.

"Wanna go get married? Twenty-four-hour chapels, no waiting."

"Are you sure you don't want a big fancy church thing, Bella?"

She took his hand. "Nathan, if everything that's happened the past two years has taught me anything at all, it's to never, ever take a single day for granted. I don't want to wait to marry you. I don't need a big fancy church thing. I have you. That's what I want."

He pulled her into his arms.

"And I have you, and that's all I want or need. So, yes. Let's get married. Tonight."

Nathan was beginning to realize that the love of his life could be much sneakier than he thought. An arranged open horse carriage ride later, they stood in a chapel reciting vows to each other, with Stacy and Brad looking on as witnesses. Bella had called them and asked them to come be part of the ceremony.

It was, all of it, a happy surprise, and he realized he'd never been so proud and humbled at the same time as when the pastor pronounced them husband and wife, then told him he could kiss his bride.

As they turned to go back down the aisle, Stacy barreled toward them both, arms outstretched. Brad followed behind a bit more sedately, aiding his still healing left knee with a fashionable cane. But he, too, enveloped each of them in a bear hug when he got close enough.

They returned to Fiamma's, where they'd had their first ever meal together, and enjoyed an excellent encore meal complete with tiramisu with Stacy and Brad as company.

"Stacy, you're glowing," Bella remarked, beaming at her best friend. "Truly. Expecting agrees with you."

The mom-to-be smiled back and started to speak, then trailed off.

"What's wrong?" Bella leaned forward, concerned.

"Oh, wow," Stacy said. "Bella, feel this."

She grabbed Bella's hand, held it to her belly.

Bella lit up.

"The baby's moving," she managed, and she and Stacy both looked around the table with happy tears starting to brim over.

Once he got off the plane, Max had called his boss, the Deputy Director for Analysis, at home, and arranged to meet at the office. They happened to pull into the lot at the same time, walking all the way into the building together without a word.

Once settled into his office, the DD gestured to the side table. "Would you like a drink, Max?"

"For this, sir, we might both need one," Max said solemnly.

Receiving a nod in the affirmative, he poured out two glasses of Scotch, handed one to his supervisor, and took a seat in one of the visitors' chairs across the desk. Pulling the laptop out of his bag, he fired it up, then opened the file he wanted to share and slid the computer across for the DD to read.

Max nursed his drink and waited patiently. He knew the moment the DD grasped the significance of what he was reading – the sharp intake of breath gave it away.

Pausing and picking up his drink, the DD muttered, "Well, well," and sipped thoughtfully.

"My thoughts exactly," Max quipped, without humor. "Sir, I'd bet money that Adolf decoded the pages himself at some point, prior to burying them in the Wall. I'm positive he would not have gone through that much effort and risk to hide them without knowing exactly what they were. What I can't be certain of is what he did with the translated pages. Keep them? Burn them?"

"I've read your entire file on this case, so I know that any previously decoded pages were not found anywhere at Metzger Institute."

"That's correct, sir."

"Sounds like it may be time to press our Brazilian friends a bit harder to let us look around his personal complex on Lake Manaca-puru, as well as the company's locations in Manaus and Macapa."

"Agreed. One more thing, sir. We have no idea what he may or may not have shared with his son Mikel. My presumption is that Adolf read him in completely, and that Mikel therefore has full knowledge of these exact contents, if not actual decoded pages stashed somewhere at the Institute that we didn't recover."

The DD mulled it for a moment.

"Then I guess we'd better hedge our bets and search the Institute again, too. Get some sleep, Max. Fly out there tomorrow."

She paced back and forth, back and forth in her little apartment. Paula wanted to see Mikel again as soon as possible, but she wasn't scheduled to work for the next four days. With round-the-clock armed men outside his door, she sure as hell didn't plan on showing up outside of her working hours. It would raise too many questions, and she knew in her heart her actions so far were *already* questionable where the patient in room four-twenty-five was concerned. If she'd ever been caught kissing him, she'd have been fired at the very least, and possibly have her nursing credentials pulled, too.

The very thought made her palms sweaty.

But she wanted to know. She needed to know. If her feelings for him weren't reciprocated in any way, it would be so much better to find out now rather than later.

And if he didn't, well...

She stopped pacing for a moment as it hit her.

She'd honestly never thought this whole scenario out past him possibly waking up. She had no idea, at all, what to expect or hope for now. Hollywood always made it seem like love at first sight was a foregone conclusion in these situations.

But she'd worked the coma ward long enough to know that Hollywood seldom got it right.

Oh, my God, I'm going to have to come right out and ask him, Paula realized, and the thought of being so brazen, so forward, shook her. *I don't have the luxury of time here.* She'd overhead other staffers talking about him, about how in as little as six weeks, he could be sent away, and she'd never see him again.

I can't, I just can't, she panicked in her head.

You're going to have to, if you want to know where things stand, her inner self cried back. *You love him. You know it. You've never felt this way, about anyone, ever. Don't you owe it to yourself to find out if there's a chance to be happy here?*

The man Paula loved was thinking of her, too, although not quite in the same way. Dr. Hightower's assessment had been spot-on. Not a damn thing wrong with Mikel's brain. Now he used the only tool available to him presently and schemed.

First, build back my leg strength, he prioritized. On that score, Nathan had not been right. He'd lost some muscle tone and control, no question. That would take a bit of time. Fortunately, he'd been in such excellent shape when he'd been shot.

Still can't believe my angel shot me, I really didn't think she'd do it—

No. He would not allow himself to go there right now. *Stay focused!*

His physique had been such that although he did have some rehab ahead, it shouldn't take long.

Second goal, obviously, is to get the hell out of here. No question there. *Third, get to the stash.* Mikel had replicated his entire laptop's contents, all his research, the complete nanotechnology program, onto a couple of hard drives and secreted them away in the desert. No one would ever find them but him. He just had to get there.

Which brought his mind back to that silly little nurse who said she loved him. *What was her name again?*

He smiled wolfishly.

"That's right. Paula," he murmured. She'd be an extremely handy tool to complete steps two and three once he was ready.

He also realized she was probably one of those heavily burdened by a conscience. *Well. That wouldn't be difficult to maneuver around.* He knew exactly what to say, to do, to keep her compliant for however long was necessary.

After that, well, casualties in his quest to get his angel back were to be expected.

Chapter Fifteen

"Good morning, Mr. Thomas," Bella purred in Nathan's ear as she ran her hands down his chest.

"Mmm. Good morning, *Mrs. Thomas*," he replied. "Care for some more celebrating?"

"I thought you'd never ask," she said teasingly, kissing him and shifting position to cover his body with hers.

The ring of Bella's cell phone derailed her wicked plans. She reluctantly got to her feet, strode over, picked it up, and answered.

"Dammit, Brad, this'd better be good," she stated, only half-teasing.

Nathan watched her, a smirk on his face, until he saw her body language change abruptly. Now she was blindly reaching behind her for the edge of the chair, and he could see her trying not to cry.

"Ok, we'll be right there, see you as soon as we can." She hung up the phone.

"Honey, what's wrong?"

"Stacy started bleeding. They're on the way to the ER right now."

Without a word Nathan sprang out of bed and hurried to get dressed like she was, so he could take her to her best friend's side.

They raced to the hospital, hands held tightly, silent worry filling the car.

She leapt out as they got to the patient drop-off area; he parked while she went in to find Brad. Nathan joined them in a few minutes.

Brad looked gray and sick with worry. "They took her back just now," he managed, and rubbed his hands over his face.

"What happened?" she asked.

"I don't know." Brad shrugged his shoulders, shook his head. "Everything was fine last night when we went to bed. I was reading the paper, letting her sleep in a bit this morning. She woke up about a half-hour ago, and when she pulled the covers back to get out of bed, she noticed the blood."

"Was she hurting at all?" Bella asked.

"Not that she mentioned," Brad said. "But you know how high a pain tolerance she has, Bel. It would have to hurt bad enough to almost kill anyone else for her to even mention it. This pregnancy's been hard on her up until the last three weeks or so. Really bad morning sickness around the clock, feet swelling, the works. She's been happier lately since some of that let up. Now this."

A nurse came out into the waiting area.

"For Stacy?" she inquired, pointing at them. Seeing them nod, she motioned for the three of them to follow her and led them to another smaller waiting room.

"She's being checked out right now, and the doc will be by here to speak to you in just a moment," she said soothingly, then walked away with the brisk pace that most people associate with many emergency room personnel.

It seemed like forever but was only a few minutes more, and the doctor came to join them. She held out her hand to Brad.

"You must be the dad-to-be," she said. "Nice to meet you. I'm Dr. McCune. Have a seat guys, and let's talk about some things."

Seeing the panic rise on Brad's face, she patted his knee.

"Okay, just breathe, Dad. The baby is fine," she began, and Brad slumped his shoulders in relief.

"Oh, thank God," he managed.

"But," Dr. McCune continued, "in my professional opinion, Stacy needs to greatly reduce her activity level. I believe this baby will get here and be fine. But to help make sure that happens, Mom needs to be on bedrest, at least until she's within three weeks of delivery. There's a chance the baby could try to make his or her appearance too soon. We can mitigate that risk with bedrest. If we can get past the thirty-seven-week mark, the baby's lungs should be developed enough at that point to be out of immediate danger. Obviously, the longer we're able to go, the better. Most of a baby's weight isn't added on until the last week or two of pregnancy. One week may make the difference between making a mandatory trip to the NICU, or not."

"What's the NICU?" Nathan asked.

"Neonatal Intensive Care Unit," the doctor explained. "Any baby weighing less than five pounds five ounces automatically goes to NICU, because underweight babies have more immediate health risks, usually from being born prematurely. So, the more weight the baby can put on before it's born, the better."

"Good to know," Bella said. "Anything we can do to help?"

"Just be there for Mom," she said. "Stacy strikes me as extremely active, so bedrest for so long is going to be a real challenge for her."

She turned to look at Brad.

"She mentioned she's attending Cal Tech. Great school. You'll need to see if she can take her next set of classes online. She most definitely will not be able to hike around all over campus. If online or independent study isn't possible..." she trailed off.

She didn't need to say more. Everyone there knew Stacy well enough to know that if leaving school for a while meant her baby would be born healthy, the choice would be a no-brainer.

"Can we see her?" Brad asked anxiously.

"Of course." Dr. McCune beamed. "Follow me."

Mikel had shored up most of his escape plan details at this point. He knew what day it would be; the irony of that choice had made him smile. He just needed some assistance to pull it off. And he already had the perfect candidate in mind. The next time she was on shift, they needed to have a little talk.

The door to his room opened, and he glanced up hopefully, then set his mask carefully back to neutral. It was Abby, not Paula. He'd have to wait a little more.

"PT time," she announced cheerfully as she entered the room, two very strong-looking orderlies following behind her. "But first, vitals."

She ran the standard drill, making notes, checked under his chest bandage to see how well the new round of antibiotics was working, then nodded in approval.

"Looks much better," she told him. "Dr. Ford will be pleased to hear about that. It means no more surgery."

He remained quiet, watching her work, silently summing up the two beefy guys with her. He knew he could probably take out all three with little to no effort and no noise – Adolf had trained him well. But for now, it was much more advantageous to pretend to be more atrophied than he really was. He allowed them to remove all the restraints and manhandle him into the wheelchair for the trip down the hall to the physical therapy unit.

The sooner Paula comes back, the sooner I'm out of here, he told himself, and ground his teeth as he put on a convincing show of having trouble lifting his left foot to take a step. *Cannot possibly happen quickly enough.*

***

"It's not even a question," Stacy said. "I'm taking a medical leave from school. I was already thinking about taking the summer off. Now I'll just extend that to next spring. No way in hell am I going to put our child at risk."

"I know, baby," Brad told her, holding her hand.

"Look at it this way," Bella offered. "You've been telling me how much you want to catch up on your fun reading. Now's your chance."

Stacy grinned. "I did say that, didn't I?"

She sighed, tracing her hands lovingly over her belly.

"And I can easily fly out and see you as often as you want. I know Brad's got that conference in Arizona coming up in July. I'd be happy to come stay with you while he's traveling."

"Me too, as long as I don't catch any new cases," Nathan joined in.

"Yeah," Stacy answered, squeezing Bella's hand. "That'd be nice, guys. Thanks."

"So, are they turning you loose today, or keeping you here?"

"Dr. McCune said she'd be back with release papers shortly. She doesn't think flying back is a good idea, changes in altitude and pressure and so on. Luckily for us, we drove here. It's only about a four-hour trip by car back home to Pasadena."

Bella and Nathan stayed with them until Stacy was signed out and safely buckled into the front passenger seat of Brad's car. Bella leaned through the window and kissed her check.

"Love you, girl. We'll be out to hang with you in about four weeks, okay? Call me as much as you need to."

"Love you, too," Stacy said, and she and Brad waved goodbye and started home.

Nathan wrapped his arm around Bella as they walked to their rental car. "What would you like to do next?" he asked. "It's Wednesday morning. I don't have to be back until Monday at three, remember?"

"I know," she said. "Want to go check out the Hoover Dam? It's under an hour from here."

"You got it, baby." He grinned and kissed her as they headed out on their mini adventure.

He was finally back in his room. Shackled and restrained again, but alone so he could finally think and plan some more. He'd asked the nurse to please turn on the television set – and had grinned darkly at the thought that someone who'd furnished the coma ward had been optimistic enough to put TVs in rooms occupied by those who would most likely not rebound from their situation.

Mikel watched the screen until at last he saw the in-house advertising banner scroll across the bottom that indicated exactly which facility he was in.

Okay, good. He thought. *If memory serves, it's among the oldest facilities in the city.* Which would mean more weak points to exploit to cover his escape.

He longed for a laptop to be able to further his planning. But until Paula came back around, it would all have to wait. He already knew she was the only one he'd be able to trust.

Patience, he told himself. *What's a few more weeks after losing six months of your life?*

The Hoover Dam was *huge* in real life. All the pictures they'd ever seen really did not do it justice. Bella and Nathan were taking it all in when his phone rang.

"Thomas," he said, then, "Hey, Faith. What's up?"

"Nathan, my company needs some help."

She quickly walked him through what had happened.

"I know the perfect guy to talk to," he responded immediately. "Let me make a call and get back to you, okay?"

"Okay. Thanks, bro. I love you."

Nathan dialed the direct number to Mitch's desk at the Bureau. "Mitch. Hey, bud. What's up? Need your brain," he began.

Once Nathan had read him in, Mitch said, "Absolutely, we can help. It sounds very similar to another case we dealt with about six weeks ago. Pass on my number, have them reach out as soon as possible. There's still a chance to salvage their stuff."

Nathan rang Faith back, passed on Mitch's desk number. "Have your boss call him right now, Faith. Mitch thinks he can still fix the damage, but he'd have to move quickly."

"Oh my God, Nathan, I owe you huge for this. Love you. Gotta go."

Faith called her boss back and passed on the data. She could hear the renewed hope in his voice.

"Keep me posted, sir," she said. "You're welcome, sir. Bye." As she hung up the phone, she felt renewed hope within herself.

I was scared to death for Nathan's safety when he went into law enforcement, she mused. *But man, am I glad he did.*

Frustrated didn't even begin to describe it.

Max had brought a very skilled team and some extremely sensitive equipment with him back to the Metzger Institute in Arizona. They'd combed the entire grounds, from the roof tiles all the way down to the last floor tile on Sub-Level Three.

Nothing.

He knew something had been missed. He knew it. He'd been doing this work for way too many years for his gut to feel this strongly about something and be wrong. But nothing had surfaced so far.

Maybe not in the Institute, but close enough nearby to be easily retrieved, he pondered. It would make sense.

The problem with that theory was, it could literally be anywhere. The Institute was outside of any city or town, surrounded by the desert. Someone could search out there for years and never find anything at all without knowing precisely where to go and look.

His fist clenched, pounded lightly on the armrest in time with his thoughts as the team and their toys settled back into the private transport to return to Langley.

Dammit. Dammit. DAMMIT.

Bella and Nathan were on a hot streak.

They'd returned from Hoover Dam, grabbed a bite, and now had returned to the casino floor. She'd taken up station again at the machine she'd been on when they met – and was up almost four-hundred dollars.

Nathan's machine right beside her wasn't cooperating, so he'd moved to the next row over and was having better luck there; he was ahead by about three hundred. The way the machines were laid out, they were sitting back-to-back in the same aisle.

A man walked up to Bella, introduced himself, and tried to make small talk. Bella was polite but focused on her machine, hoping he'd get the hint and leave. When he asked her to join him for drinks, she made damn sure her wedding rings were clearly visible as she said no and announced she was happily married. She even called out to Nathan to ask how his machine was playing right in front of the guy, so that he'd realize her husband was in the vicinity. But the man just kept going, ignoring her polite refusals, Sand getting more and more suggestive as he went.

Bella knew all too well that Nathan could hear every word, and that it was probably making his blood boil that some idiot was so blatantly continuing to hit on his wife. She also knew that Nathan knew she could handle herself and was opting to remain quiet and let her try to do so first.

But the guy just wouldn't leave her alone, and she sensed the moment Nathan was about to get up and get in the man's face. At that point Bella abruptly pressed the "Call Attendant" button on her machine to help attract casino personnel her direction.

Then she stood on her chair, raised her hands, and let loose on the man. She didn't curse or scream. She didn't need to.

What she *did* do, in a very calm but extremely loud voice, was announce to everyone within earshot that this gentleman was being rude and aggressive, that she was happily married and that she'd told him so, that he'd refused to get it through his head that she wasn't interested in him at all, and could someone please bring security and get this man to leave her alone?

Her chosen method of addressing the problem worked very well. A crowd started to gather as people stopped to listen to the young lady standing on her chair like she was directing traffic. Crowds on casino floors always drew security's attention, so two menacing-looking types arrived quickly. One of them reached for the man and pulled him away from Bella.

"Come on, Barney, you've been warned about this before. You're not even supposed to be in here. How'd you sneak in this time?"

To Bella, he said, "Ma'am, I am so sorry he bothered you. We'll take care of it."

They escorted him away toward the casino's front entrance.

"Nice job, baby," Nathan said, holding her hand as she stepped back down off the chair. "No violence, no mess, no profanity, just asshole exits stage left."

She beamed. "And effective," she noted, as she received a small round of applause and a 'you *go*, girl' from the crowd that had witnessed the exchange.

The onlookers dispersed, and Bella and Nathan continued their evening undisturbed for a time. About a half-hour later, another gentleman came over, showed them his casino ID card, and introduced himself.

"My name is Darrell, and I'm head of Guest Relations here. Security told me what happened. I'm so sorry you were harassed like that. We'd like to make it up to you."

"It wasn't your fault another patron was a jerk," she pointed out.

"It is when he's on the no-entry list and manages to get past us and into the casino," Darrell said evenly. "Again, we'd like to make it up to you. Are you guests here at the hotel?"

"We are," Bella said. "We're here until Sunday."

"Excellent," Darrell replied. "Let us do this for you. What's the room number?"

"Four-oh-two," Nathan said.

Darrell handed them two new key cards.

"Please allow us to upgrade you, at no charge, to one of our honeymoon suites on the top floor. Also, please accept this voucher for a free spa session, on us. Your new room, Suite B, is ready for your arrival whenever you'd like to move your things, and you can just leave the keycards for four-oh-two in the old room."

"You don't have to do that," Bella said sincerely. "But it's appreciated."

"I watched the video playback," Darrell confided, and grinned. "Most women would have decked that guy. But the way you handled it? Elegant. Made a scene without making a scene, you know? Nicely done."

He shook their hands.

"So, enjoy the rest of your stay with us, and good luck." Darrell continued his trip through the casino floor.

"Honeymoon suite, huh?" Nathan put his arm around her waist, eyes twinkling. "Want to go move our stuff, check out the new digs?"

"Certainly," she said, and hit the Cash Out button on her lucky machine.

They went back to the old room, packed up, then took the elevator up as high as it would go. When the doors opened, the difference in ambience was immediately obvious.

Soft, thick, luxurious carpet stretched before them in a whirl of blues and grays. Well-kept and very fresh flower arrangements lined the hall, perched on mahogany tables. Reaching the far end, they found it.

"Honeymoon Suite B," Nathan pointed at the door. Using his keycard, he opened the door, and Bella started to walk through.

"Wait," he exclaimed, then scooped her into his arms, bag and all.

"I want to do this right," he said, kissing her, then carried her over the threshold.

"I could get used to this," Stacy said as Brad brought dinner to her.

"Added benefit is, I get to spoil you some," he winked at her as he set the tray down carefully.

The ride home had been uneventful, which pleased them both.

Now she frowned as she cut a piece of pork chop off to bite into. "I know taking the time will delay my degree," she started.

"It will," he agreed. "But it's worth it."

"Oh, I know that," she waved her fork. "But this whole episode kind of underlined for me that we haven't talked about a plan for after the baby gets here."

She sighed, chewing thoughtfully.

"I mean, I have a double major, hon. Chemistry and Math. I want to go into research of some sort. Not teaching, I don't think I'd have the patience for it. But I also don't want to be one of those moms that works all the time and never sees her kid. I don't know what to do."

She burst into tears.

"Baby," Brad murmured as he sat on the bed and put his arm around her. "We'll figure it out. Plenty of parents manage to balance work and family just fine. And you don't have to do this by yourself. I've already talked to my firm about telecommuting, so I can be home more to help with the baby."

"You have?" She sniffled. "You'd do that for me?"

"Yes," he replied, and kissed her hair. "I have. And we're a team, Stacy. I did it for *us*."

"What did they say about it?"

"They're extremely supportive. Stacy, most of the upper management at my firm have families and very busy personal lives. They totally get what it means to need to try to have a healthy balance.

That's one of the reasons I applied there, in addition to their stellar reputation in the industry. There are not many facets of my job I can't do from that desk right in there," he revealed and pointed toward the living room.

"Really?"

"Really," Brad confirmed. "And the few things I would have to be onsite for are just not that frequent. Helping new clients get onboarded may require travel, and some quarter and year-end closings may, too. But other than that, I can do it all here. Not only are they supportive, honey, they're encouraging it. They've even ordered me a portable scanner and fax machine to install here."

"*Really?*"

"Really, Stace."

"Wow. Honey, you work for some great people."

"I really do," he agreed. "Now. I know you want to go into research, and I support your goals one-hundred and ten percent. So please don't think you have to sacrifice your career because we've started our family. We can do both, together. Okay?"

"Okay," she managed. "Brad, I love you. So much."

"I love you too, Stacy," he answered. "And you're going to be one hell of a good mom *and* one hell of a researcher. You just wait and see."

Chapter Sixteen

Still no Paula today.

Dammit.

Mikel's impatience was starting to rise. He willed himself back to calm, continued working through the plan he'd constructed, checking for frailties. Lots of little things had to happen just right, or escape wouldn't be possible. For instance, how to get access to certain levels of the building. He figured Paula would have an electronic keycard, but she wouldn't automatically have access to everything.

Why would she? What need would a nurse have to go to the basement?

Unless the morgue was down there, he realized.

Then it would be plausible. *Hm.*

He'd have to find out for sure. If that was the setup here, and he thought it probably was, there'd be no need to alter Paula's access levels.

He smiled wolfishly. It was beginning to gel nicely in his head.

He just needed to see Paula.

Paula had just gotten out of the shower when her phone rang. It was Miriam.

"Hey Miriam, what's up?"

"Paula. Thank God I reached you. I'm supposed to be on at eleven tonight, but Andrea's sick, running a one-hundred-and-three fever. I can't go in. Can you cover me?"

Andrea was Miriam's eight-year-old, and a recent kidney transplant recipient, so any fever was a cause for concern.

"Happy to," Paula said, and meant it. She'd not been enjoying the idea of four days off in a row.

"You're the best. Thanks. I owe you. I'll call in and let them know you're taking the shift."

"No problem. Tell Andrea I said I hope she feels better."

Paula pulled on a scrub set, wrestled her hair back into a ponytail, packed a lunch, grabbed her bag, and headed into work.

Max and the DD had met in the office again and were sipping glasses of Scotch as Max revealed the fruitless results at the Metzger Institute. Then the DD shared his findings.

"Everything we've been able to find out points to Adolf becoming a Brazilian citizen back in the 1970s. As you know, although we do have friendly relations with Brazil, they're extremely protective of their own. They've gone so far as to refuse extradition requests from us, even though an agreement exists, when it comes to their citizens."

"So," he continued, swirling the liquid in his glass, "that means any trip down there is unsanctioned, to avoid causing political tension. If you go down there to check out Metzger's various holdings, you'll have to do so as a civilian. No Company gear, no backup."

"Understood," Max replied and finished his drink. "I thought that might be the case, and I've adjusted accordingly for it."

The DD grinned. "That's why you're one of my favorites, Max," he said bluntly. "You never, ever get rattled and you never look at just one possibility or one approach. Good luck, don't get caught, and come see me when you get back."

———

Paula stepped back into Mikel's room for the first time in three days. He watched her quietly approach and could plainly see she was very nervous. He decided to take control of the conversation from the start.

"Could you come here, please? Bring a chair, sit down. I'd like to talk to you."

She nodded, pale and frightened, like she was about to be chastised, or worse. But she did as he asked.

Bring it, he told himself. *Sell this. Your ticket to freedom depends on her cooperating.*

He made a show of struggling valiantly to lift his restrained hand to reach hers. Now she smiled, offered hers, watching his face, relaxing a little.

"Baby," he said softly, slowly. "I am so glad to see you. I missed you so much."

He continued to spin the web of deceit he'd trap her in, to lie, to woo, to manipulate. He laid out for her a fantasy tale picture of riding off into the sunset and living happily ever after. He could see by the happy tears brimming in her eyes that she'd fallen for it, hook line and sinker.

Mikel rejoiced on the inside.

"Now, my love, come closer," he beckoned, and when she complied, he kissed her passionately, completing his entrapment of her heart. After a long while, he pulled his lips back from hers.

"Here's what we need to do for us to be together forever," he began.

———

Nathan and Bella were enjoying being totally spoiled in their honeymoon suite. The view out on their private balcony was spectacular, complete with a beautiful table and chairs for fine dining al fresco. They'd taken advantage of it, eating a three-course meal under the stars the previous night.

And the bed. Oh, dear Lord. The bed. It was huge, the biggest bed either of them had ever seen, with the softest, most luxurious sheets ever. It was like floating on air but with perfect support in every way.

They'd tested it. They'd jumped on it like little kids. They'd had pillow fights, started to wrestle. Then the mood had turned, and they'd spent the rest of their night making earnest love on it as husband and wife. After, they slept, and woke peaceful and refreshed.

Now they were enjoying the wickedly big tub, complete with lighting effects, a built-in surround sound system, and with so many jets she'd lost count. The tub in Honeymoon Suite B was so large Bella believed they'd have had no trouble swimming laps if the mood struck them.

"Another mimosa?" Nathan asked.

"No, I'm good for now," she smiled and sunk further down, letting the jets work their magic. "You want to do the spa today, or later in the week before we leave?'

"Your call, baby," he murmured, eyes closed. "I'm just enjoying the moment."

"You know," she thought out aloud. "We haven't told Max or any of your family that we got married. We probably ought to share that news at some point. Hopefully, they won't be mad."

Nathan's eyes flew open.

"My sisters' feelings will probably be hurt at first," he admitted. "I am the baby, after all. But they love you. I'm pretty sure they'll forgive us. Eventually."

He frowned. "Maybe."

"Maybe we can make it up to them somehow," she offered. "Like maybe another small ceremony over the summer?"

"Yeah," he brightened as an idea came to him. "You know, technically, we could just do that, and not tell them we're already married. I bet we could talk Stacy and Brad into keeping our secret."

"Nathan Thomas, I'm surprised at you," Bella said, laughing. "You would omit that really big fact on purpose, just to avoid any fallout?"

"You've never seen my sisters in high gear." He grinned at her. "But I have. It's horrifying."

"Well, we'll have to talk that one out some more," she said sincerely. "I don't like keeping secrets. Well, not *usually*," she corrected when she saw his eyebrow go up. She'd known he was about to point out that this entire trip to Vegas they were on had been a complete surprise to him.

He roared with laughter.

"You knew exactly what I was about to say, didn't you?"

"Yes, I did."

He pulled her in close for a kiss.

"Like I've said before, Bella. We're fated."

———

Paula steeled her nerves and returned to Mikel's room toward the end of her shift.

"Forgot to add a readout note in his chart," she explained to the agent, holding up his chart, then went inside his room.

Moving quickly to his side, she kissed him and spoke in a low voice.

"I have to go soon, my shift's about over. But I wrote down the list, and I'll do it like we planned. Okay?"

"Okay," he said, trying his best to plaster an *I-love-you-so-much* look on his face.

Evidently, he was successful, as her eyes lit with pleasure and surprise, and she kissed him deeply again before she left.

She's so lovely – and gullible.

He smiled to himself.

This is going to be so easy it's almost anticlimactic.

Four weeks later, the United States was working its way toward July Fourth weekend. Bella and Nathan were winding down the week in Pasadena. Brad had been at a conference in Phoenix all week but was scheduled back Friday night; they expected him home anytime now. They'd flown out to keep Stacy company while Brad traveled, as promised. Stacy's baby bump seemed to have doubled in size since they last saw her.

Stacy laughed when Bella said, "Wow," as they'd arrived.

"Yeah, I'm probably a little heavy on food these days. But it doesn't seem to be traveling anywhere but to the kid."

They'd had a great visit through the week. Stacy was in high spirits. She filled Bella in on the changes to Brad's work schedule.

"That's awesome, Stace," Bella told her sincerely. "I always knew Brad was a good one."

"He *so* is." Stacy sighed and smiled. "I'm so lucky, Bel, I have a great husband, great best friend, and I'm going to have a perfect baby here before we know it."

Her hands lovingly traced the baby's current location.

Brad came rushing through the door.

"Hey, man," Nathan started to say, then saw the look on Brad's face as he turned on the TV and started flipping channels.

"Dude, I heard about this right after I landed, you're going to want to see this," Brad said, just as Nathan's phone began to ring.

"Thomas," he answered, then listened while his eyes were riveted to a TV screen that was now filled with scenes of evening sky, smoke, fire, chaos, and ruin.

"Yes, sir, on my way," he said abruptly, and hung up.

By this time, Bella had helped Stacy up and into the living room.

"What's wrong, Nathan?" Bella asked, not liking the look on his face.

The men turned to look at their wives.

Nathan paused.

"Something happened in Phoenix, at the hospital. Initial reports are some sort of massive explosion. Steve called just now, and he asked me to get to the scene right away."

"Why you?" she demanded. "Mikel Metzger's not your case anymore."

"I just got assigned to assist in the investigation into the explosion itself," he said. "I'm the only BAU member that isn't working something else right now."

He strode over to her, took her hands.

"I have to go there, babe."

"I know. Let's haul it to the airport. I'll fly home as planned, and you can change your ticket for Phoenix."

It had really been very simple. He'd asked her to bring only two extra things to his room that shift – a tiny lockpick, nestled unseen in her pulled-back ponytail, and a digital wristwatch. She'd obeyed, undone his left side hospital restraints, then handed him the lockpick so he could work off the handcuffs binding his right arm and leg to the bed.

Child's play. He was loose in under sixty seconds.

Then, as discussed, she'd cried out, right on cue.

The agent who'd rushed in to defend her hadn't had a chance at all. Mikel came from behind the door, grabbed, twisted, and broke the man's neck. He was dead before he hit the floor.

Paula's eyes grew huge, but she said nothing. They moved the agent's body to Mikel's bed, then covered and angled the dead man so he looked like he was sleeping soundly.

She covered Mikel with a sheet once he'd gotten on the gurney she'd grabbed from the hallway. Then, she waited, timing it until she knew Abby would be at the other end of the floor making rounds. As silently as possible, Paula pushed the gurney into the elevator and pressed the button for the basement, where the morgue was located, just as Mikel thought it would be. The elevator ride seemed to take forever.

The next part they'd also planned. Upon reaching the basement, Paula was to push the gurney over to the morgue doors, then exit the building, get her car, and drive around to the side street nearest the morgue entrance, and wait for him to join her. Mikel didn't want her to know the exact next steps. Otherwise, she'd have tried to stop him.

And she'd done as he asked. Once he heard the exit door shut behind her, he'd leapt off the gurney and worked his way into the maintenance and boiler room areas with frightening ease. He located the pipes carrying oxygen throughout the hospital, and as he'd suspected, they were highly vulnerable.

He'd smiled.

Rummaging through the assorted collection of cleaning supplies and chemicals nearby, he found everything he needed for a rudimentary but still very effective incendiary device.

Ten minutes later, he was in Paula's car, concealed by blankets in her back seat, and they were driving away. Twenty minutes after that, when the digital wristwatch he'd used as the detonator counted down to zero, he and his accomplice were well clear of the area.

At two minutes past seven, on a hectic Friday night of July Fourth weekend, the deep, throaty rumbling began from deep in the bowels of the hospital. The entire structure seemed to shudder as if struck, its exterior walls at ground level bulging as if the building had drawn in one massively huge breath.

A single beat of stillness, nowhere near enough time for its occupants to react, much less run. Then the rumbling was a deafening roar, a horrifying exhale upward and outward, spewing an onslaught of stone, glass, metal, fire, flesh, and bone.

The hospital had ceased to exist by three minutes past seven.

Nathan arrived on the scene around eleven p.m., roughly four hours after the blast had occurred. He found the fire chief, introduced himself, and was quickly brought up to speed.

"It looks like something maybe started in the lower levels but spread out quickly to the upper floors as well," the fire chief explained. "The combined force and fire weakened the structure, so what didn't explode collapsed under its own weight right as we got here. All six above-ground levels came down."

He stopped, mopped his face. "I've never seen anything like this, man. Ever."

Nathan's mouth set in a grim line. His jaw tightened, and he was silent for a moment.

"Chief. I know it's early yet, but any idea at all how many people might have been inside when this thing blew?"

"Hundreds, Agent Thomas," the chief said bleakly, his voice starting to break. "Hundreds, maybe more."

"I can answer that," a man said, striding toward them. "I'm Tom Brindler, the Chief of Surgery here. When I heard about this, I activated our Emergency Management Team, and they got me this."

He handed a list over to Nathan.

"That's everyone who was a patient here as of tonight, who had signed in to be seen in the ER tonight but not discharged yet, and who worked here that was on shift or on call tonight. That list alone is four-hundred and fifty-two people. There's no way to know how many visitors were here seeing their loved ones..." The doctor stared at the destruction and trailed off, one silent tear tracing down his cheek, but he didn't notice, or didn't care.

"We set up triage across the parking lot, over there," he pointed toward the professional building. "But so far, no survivors to treat yet."

"Thank you, Dr. Brindler. I'm so sorry," Nathan said with heart-felt sincerity.

"Find out who did this, Agent Thomas. Find out who decided they had the right to take so many good people."

He straightened, and with visible effort composed himself. "I need to keep reaching out to my staff who were on call tonight. I may be able to mark some of those names off your list as 'safe'," he said. "At least, I hope I can."

"Mark me as 'safe', Tom," Dr. Hightower said as he approached. He looked haggard, haunted.

Dr. Brindler grabbed and hugged him.

"Jay. You weren't in there. Thank God."

"Nope," Hightower sighed. "I got paged around six-twenty, so I would have been. I'd have been right in the middle of that some-where. But my car battery was dead, had to get a jump start, and that put me about a half-hour behind. I pulled into the professional building lot right as it blew. Tom, our brand-new CAT scan machine we installed up on the fourth floor last month landed about five feet from my car." He pointed behind him, still amazed it hadn't crushed him.

"Jesus," Brindler said. "That thing weighs over two tons."

Nathan looked at what was left of the hospital, then toward the professional building lot where the equipment had landed.

He and the fire chief came to the same estimation at the same time.

"Around four-hundred yards, give or take," the fire chief stated. "A lot of force needed to move that thing that far."

Nathan nodded in agreement with the rough math.

Jesus.

Hightower ran his hands through his hair, eyes glossy with remembrance, and shock.

"I dodged the damn thing, got my car stopped, and I ran toward the building, shouting to see if I could find anyone, help anyone. No one answered. No one."

The fire chief's radio squawked.

"Go ahead," he called back, then listened. "Roger that, proceed with caution, all units."

He turned back to Nathan and the doctors.

"All the biggest hot spots are out now. Time to look for survivors. We're bringing in heavy equipment to lift some of the big pieces, and search and rescue teams, including dogs. More searchlights will go up all the way around the perimeter."

"I've called the Red Cross, and they're on their way, too," Brindler said. "We're going to need support, food and water for the emergency workers. It's going to be a long, long next few days."

Bella made it back to Manassas without incident, raced to turn on her television the moment she made it through her front door. The hospital blast was the lead story on CNN. Her eyes welled with tears as the announcer confirmed at least four-hundred and fifty-two people, probably more, had been inside when the incident occurred.

She grabbed her phone, texted her husband.

I love you, Nathan. You be damn careful and text me when you're able.

Then she sat alone, watching the screen with horrified grief at the events unfolding, like millions of other viewers at that same moment.

Max had just completed the last leg of the flight back from Manaus. Despite his best efforts, he'd had no luck at all being able to access anything Metzger related, by legitimate means or otherwise.

He found his car in remote parking, began the drive home, flipped on his radio, and heard the announcement about the suspected terrorist attack in Phoenix. He found a lot to pull into just outside the airport and parked, listening in disbelief. He knew there was no way in hell he could get officially involved.

But he also felt deep in his core that the facility holding Mikel Metzger being bombed was no coincidence at all. His professional and personal antennae were pinging, pinging *hard*, screaming to him that Mikel had something directly to do with this chaos.

He also knew they'd never be able to prove it.

Chapter Seventeen

Mikel and Paula had reached his promised land.

Two miles away from the Institute, he'd had her take a sharp left onto a barely visible track. One mile down, he had her stop. He walked southwest five-hundred feet, located the three mesquite trees, and began to dig with the shovel he'd asked her to have waiting in the trunk.

Three feet down, he could feel the resistance of metal against metal. He reached down and retrieved what he'd hidden – a fireproof strongbox. It held portable drives containing a complete backup of all his research and files, vials of the serum and two extra syringes modified to inject it with, a full set of alternate identity documents – social security card, driver's license, birth certificate – and a hundred-thousand dollars in cash.

Triumphantly, he returned to the car and directed her the rest of the way to the Institute. There was no guard to take on, no police presence to sneak past; in the authorities' minds, there wasn't need for any, with Adolf dead and Mikel in a hospital ward and soon to be in federal prison. So, the feds had cleaned the place out, then locked it all up, posted 'No Trespassing' signs, and left. The front gate was now secured with not one but several thick long chains and serious looking locks.

Mikel wasn't discouraged by that at all. He'd helped design this place, and he knew very well that appearances could be deceiving. There was one entry he'd added to the building that even Adolf hadn't known about, and Mikel had never had cause to use it.

Until tonight.

He directed Paula around the right side of the exterior wall. There was a little outcropping that seemed to occur there naturally. But there was nothing natural about it. He felt around until his fingers found the indention just underneath a stone that peeked out. He pressed it hard, and the mechanism he'd built swung to life, parting the seemingly solid set of rocks to reveal the very first step of a staircase leading down into pitch black.

Mikel retrieved a flashlight he'd stashed in the formation's interior, held his hand out to her.

"Shall we?"

The search and rescue effort moved painfully slowly due to all the twisted and mangled debris piles. Twelve hours in, fifty-eight bodies had been recovered, but no one alive had been found at all, and best estimates were that only about one-tenth of the site had been gone over so far.

There was a whooping cry of joy and proof of a miracle. The northeast elevator had gone straight down its shaft as designed, and luckily nothing had caved in on top of it. Firemen had worked their way to the elevator car's roof and, wrenching open the emergency escape hatch, looked down at five terrified but hopeful faces and one tiny bundle wrapped in pink sleeping soundly in her mother's arms.

It was the Tanners, a young mom and dad headed home from the fifth-floor maternity ward with their second child and her four-year-old big brother. The other two survivors were two nurses, an OB nurse named Violet who was escorting them out to their car, and Abby, Paula's co-worker, who'd caught an extremely lucky break when she'd realized just before seven p.m. that she needed to go down to the dispensary on the second floor. She'd pressed the elevator button, joined the group from the maternity ward, the doors had closed, and they were almost to the second floor when all hell had broken loose.

The group was battered and bruised, but not seriously hurt despite the elevator plummeting another floor so fast. The cables and brakes had held just enough to keep the force of impact very light under the circumstances.

They were liberated in short order, and cheers and applause went up all over the site as they emerged alive and free. Violet and Abby immediately headed over to the triage area to check in and help however they could. With renewed optimism that perhaps other survivors would still be found, the search-and-rescue teams resumed their efforts.

By day three, that hope had faded.

By day seven, it was gone completely.

Of the four-hundred and fifty-two confirmed occupants listed, only twelve people – six in the elevator and six on call but not onsite – had been marked as 'safe'. Almost three-hundred bodies had been recovered by the end of week one. Although recovery efforts would continue for another four weeks until the entire site was cleared, the remaining people were now listed as 'missing – presumed dead.'

Mikel Metzger and Paula were two of those names.

Well before their status on the list of the missing was updated, Paula was no longer in her right mind. Mikel had seen to that right away.

Once they'd descended into the abyss and come out into Sub-Level Three, he'd changed out of his hospital gown and into the clothes he'd asked her to bring for him. He'd also stealthily loaded a serum vial into one of the syringes and placed it out of sight but within reach of the bed in the room he'd led her to.

"What now?" she asked him shyly.

"This," he'd said, and swept her into the most passionate kiss she'd ever experienced.

He played it to the hilt, caressing her, teasing her, rendering her completely relaxed and off guard.

"It's…. it's my first time," she whispered shyly.

Mikel smiled and murmured against her mouth, "I'll be gentle, sweetheart."

At first, he added in his head.

Mikel could tell she was so lost in the adrenaline of the moment that she failed to feel his right hand let go of her right hip. As he sent her screaming over the edge toward her first orgasm ever, he pressed the syringe to the back of her neck and infected her with the serum.

Now she could be completely controlled. And he found over the next week that it was very exciting to be able to program her in advance to be compliant to his commands or to struggle against them, depending on his mood. He'd very effectively taken her body and mind hostage, to use as his whims directed.

Not that he'd ever been driven by sex, really.

But, he thought, *why waste an opportunity, when you could completely control the outcome like a god?*

She flinched now, drawing back as he reached for her again. He frowned, tapped a few keys to set the proper mood, and got started.

Bella and Nathan's duly recorded marriage license arrived in the mail Friday morning, July ninth. It beat Nathan Thomas to his home by two days.

He'd spent almost all those nine days since his arrival on scene helping at first to collect evidence and search for survivors, and then to help collect the dead. Steve Brown, the head of BAU, had arrived on the evening of the eighth day to relieve him. He took one look at Nathan and sent him home for a mandatory five days off. He also reminded Nathan that counseling services were available to his agents for good reason – to help them deal with scenes like this one. Nathan merely nodded, headed for the airport, home, and Bella.

When he walked through their front door, Bella rushed him like a wave. They clung together in the hallway for a long while. No words were spoken. None needed to be. She'd known the second she'd seen his face that he'd been deeply scarred by what he'd seen, possibly permanently. So, she followed her intuition, held him close, and comforted him as best she could.

Then she took his hand, and without a word led him upstairs, drew a hot bath, settled them both into it. When she reached for him, he moved over to her, held on again, and cried like a child in her arms, finally allowing the heaviness, the pure horror he'd had to stifle to do the job he'd been asked to do, to surface.

Later, they climbed into bed. He laid his head on her chest, wrapping his arms around her. She stroked his hair until he was able to relax enough to finally sleep.

Then, only then, once she knew he would finally get some peace, she closed her eyes and joined him there.

It was the first week of August 2010. Recovery efforts at the hospital had ended, and site cleanup began in earnest.

For the BAU team it was particularly frustrating because not a single shred of evidence that had been found pointed to any sort of suspect at all. For a while, it was theorized that the whole thing had simply been a tragic accident. It was a few tiny slivers of what used to be a digital watch that pointed to something more sinister.

But they were charred, no DNA or fingerprint retrieval possible at all. BAU had no choice but to suspend active participation in the case until and unless new data surfaced pointing to someone they could chase.

Bella had offered to listen, but Nathan had refused to share with her his experiences at the site. He'd done a few sessions with a Bureau-sanctioned counselor, then called it good, determined to move on. She felt it was a wedge between them, but she didn't how to fix it. So, she respected his wishes on the matter and kept her concern to herself.

Mikel and Paula drove lazily up the California coastline into Oregon. He'd changed his appearance to match his new identity. He'd made her dye her hair black and wear contacts that altered her eye color from their gorgeous natural green to a cornflower blue. To anyone who saw them, they looked like any other beautiful Californian couple, quickly noticed then just as quickly forgotten.

He was fascinated at just how much she resembled Bella once the transformation was complete.

He'd also adjusted the way he dealt with her. After an ill-conceived attempt to escape on her part a few weeks back, he'd turned the nanotechnology coursing through her system on, and he'd left it on. No further attempts to part ways with him after that. Besides, he'd never had it activated in a host for long stretches at a time, so Paula was now a walking experiment; it would be interesting to see if any side effects occurred from such prolonged exposure.

Mikel was very pleased with the way things had gone so far. They'd already had successful mission-related stops in Ely Nevada, then Bakersfield, Sacramento, and Chico while in California. Next stops would be in Oregon – Medford, he'd decided, would do nicely, then Salem – before swinging east and then south again for just a bit.

He knew the authorities would piece it all together at some point; the game wouldn't be as much fun if they didn't. And if they proved to be too incompetent to figure it out, well then, he'd just have to hand them some clues, wouldn't he?

Mikel smiled.

"Good girl," he told Paula, like she was a well-trained pet. Which, thanks to nanotech, she pretty much was.

Paula beamed.

"Thanks, baby." Then she bent back over, staging the girl's body as instructed at two a.m. in a rest area off a highway just north of Sutherlin, Oregon.

"Don't forget the picture," he reminded her.

"Got it."

A new Polaroid joined the souvenir stash in the glovebox as they drove away toward Salem.

They traveled another forty-five minutes before finding a little dive motel that rented by the hour, sheets extra. She paid cash for the room and went in. He joined her about ten minutes later, taking care to not be seen from the motel's office.

With a few keys tapped, he set her programming for sexually aggressive, then leaned back and enjoyed himself thoroughly while she did all the work.

"Terrifying," the shaken teenagers told the Oregon state trooper. "We've never seen a dead body before."

It was just after three in the morning. Two high school kids out way past curfew had decided that since they were in big trouble anyway for being late, they might as well at least enjoy themselves and finally 'do it' after dating for two whole weeks. They'd pulled into the deserted rest area and had started to make out. The girl had happened to glance over as they paused to maneuver to the roomier back seat, because a flicker of light that hadn't been there before caught her eye.

Then she screamed as she saw the body, lying faceup about thirty feet from their car, now clearly visible under the floodlight that had finally come on all the way.

The young woman they'd discovered would eventually be identified as a nineteen-year-old resident of Medford Oregon named Lily.

Bella answered her front door to find Max standing there.

"Uncle Max!" she cried, hugging him. "It's good to see you."

"Good to see you too, girly," he beamed at her. "Can I come in?"

"Absolutely. Nathan's not here right now though."

"Actually, I came to see you."

"You did?" she asked as they went to the kitchen. "Hey, want some coffee?"

"Yes please," Max answered as he sat at the table.

"Whatcha got?"

"Well, mainly I wanted to check on him, see how he's doing. I know the hospital site was rough on everyone who worked it, even the seasoned guys. With that being his first ever mass casualty scene," he nodded thanks as Bella handed him coffee, "I've been a bit concerned about him."

She let out a sigh.

"Me too, Max. I've told him several times that I'm here to listen, and he flat refuses to share with me. I know he went to some sessions with a Bureau counselor, but he only did two or three to get Steve off his back about it, then he stopped going."

She frowned into her tea.

"I don't even think he's aware of it, but lately he must be having horrible dreams, Max. Bolting upright in bed and just screaming with what sure sounds like grief. But he's not awake."

"Night terrors," Max told her, taking her hand for comfort.

"Sounds like night terrors. Big traumatic environments like what he experienced those nine days can trigger them and PTSD both. Bella, you have *got* to convince him to keep seeing the counselor. He won't ever be able to forget what he saw. Those things will always stay with him. But he needs to learn how to live with it before it consumes him professionally and personally. Working scenes like that one will make or break you. I'm speaking from experience here, dear. Sometimes, no matter how much we want to think it will, just stuffing it and not dealing with it does nothing to solve any of it."

"I'll try my best," Bella nodded her head. "But I have a feeling I'm going to need your help here, too. Maybe between the two of us, we can get him some help to deal with this. Will you please talk to him as well?"

"Happily, dear." Max patted her cheek. "You two are my family, you know."

"Speaking of family – Faith and Rick. I think it's great."

Max laughed.

"Me, too. Nathan filled me in when you two got back. I'm sorry I missed the big moment. Rick invited me but I had a work-related obligation that couldn't be moved."

Bella's eyes twinkled. "Which is Uncle Max-speak for spy-catching detail?"

"Something like that," he quipped, his eyes twinkling back.

She grinned. "Any luck?"

"Nice try. Now, inquisitive child, let's talk school. How's it going?"

"Well," she said, "let's see. I started UV back in January, took a full load in spring, took summer I off, about to wrap summer II. When school starts in September, I'll officially be a senior, target date to be done is next May."

"Have you thought more about what you want to do once you've got it done?"

"Actually, yes. I think I'll take you up on your offer, Uncle Max. I think teaching at Quantico and Langley is a great way to go."

He smiled. "I was sure hoping you would say that to me."

"I thought you'd be pleased. I've mulled it over ever since you mentioned it, and the more I have, the more it appeals to me. And it doesn't mean I can't tutor kids on the side at some point if I want."

"No, you should still have room for that too, if you'd like."

He set down his cup.

"And when's the wedding again?'

"We went with... Wait, what? How did you know that? I mean, I told you we eloped, but I never said anything about another ceremony."

Max roared.

"Dear child, I've met one of Nathan's sisters already. And from what I've heard, they are all very close. If the other two are anything like her, only another ceremony with them all present will placate their not being present for the first one. He is the baby, after all," he finished, exactly mimicking Nathan's earlier words to her. "Or did you two opt to not tell them about the first one?"

"Well..." Bella hesitated. "I wanted to, but Nathan's a little scared of them sometimes, I think. He said he would rather keep news of the first one off their radar completely. I don't like deceiving them, but Max, you should have seen his face when I mentioned telling them. Nathan looked like a deer in headlights."

She giggled.

"I looked like a deer in headlights about what?" Nathan asked as he came into the kitchen. He kissed Bella, and said, "Hey Max, how's it going?"

"About telling your sisters we had eloped," Bella answered.

"Well, yeah," Nathan admitted freely with a grin. "You two have never seen them when they get mad. I have. It's scary stuff. No need to poke that bear unless we have no choice."

He poured himself some coffee, brought the pot over to the table to top off Max's cup, and sat.

Bella turned back to Max.

"To answer your question, we chose a simple ceremony here in the backyard, and it will be at four p.m. on Saturday, October the twenty-third. That's about ten weeks out."

Max immediately pulled out his phone and marked the event on his calendar, then tucked it back into his pocket.

"I will most definitely be here."

"I sure hope so." She smiled softly. "Because I'd really like you to walk me down the aisle."

At just about nine p.m. on an ordinary Tuesday night, Mandy was headed home. She'd worked her shift at the zoo, then gone to dinner with some co-workers. The commute from Mayfield to the zoo in downtown Boise sucked, but she couldn't afford to move closer in yet. The bubbly twenty-year-old probably could have found something closer to home, but she loved her job, especially tending to the baby animals.

So, she gritted her teeth, endured the road time, and prayed daily that her ancient Suzuki Sidekick held up for one more trip. Another piece of her life she couldn't afford to upgrade yet.

She took her exit off Interstate 84 toward her house, turned left, and had just started up the road toward Sheep Creek. The Sidekick lurched suddenly, rattled violently, and let loose. Smoke billowed, accompanied by a pungent odor indicative of terminal issues in a combustion engine.

"Dammit!" she yelled, flinging open the door and slamming it behind her in frustration. She stalked around to the front of her car, started to open the hood, then thought better of it when she realized there was nothing she could accomplish. The cell phone she'd forgotten to charge wasn't any help either.

"Hey, you need a lift?" said a voice beside her.

Startled, Mandy looked up and into the car that had pulled up beside her. She saw a young woman, maybe mid-twenties, with raven-black hair and blue eyes like hers, watching her with a friendly smile.

"Um, sure," Mandy said. "I don't think this thing is going much further. Let me grab my purse."

She walked back around to the driver's side of her car, leaned in through the window to grab her purse, and grabbed her keys too, more out of habit than functionality at this point. When she straightened back up and turned around, she was met with a rag of chloroform to the face.

Her body was found two days later, a colorful scarf tied much too tightly around her slender neck, and her picture had joined the glovebox souvenir set as Mikel and Paula's nondescript beige sedan continued toward Helena, Montana.

Over the next month, they would add four more pictures as they continued along the course Mikel had charted in advance.

Chapter Eighteen

STACY AND BRAD were discussing travel for the wedding.

"No way we can drive that, honey. You'd miss a ton of work," she said firmly. "That leaves flying."

"Stace, what about the baby?" he asked. "You've been on bedrest the last three months for a reason. I don't have any idea if flying is safe for you or not."

"Look." She took his hand. "The doctor said I'd have to do the bedrest thing until I got to thirty-seven weeks, right?"

"Right," Brad agreed.

"Okay, so, if the due date is around November twelfth, three weeks earlier is right at thirty-seven weeks along, honey. And the doctor told us before that the due date isn't set in stone. She said she thought *no later* than November twelfth, but probably sooner, right?"

"Right," he agreed again.

"So, this is doable," Stacy announced. "We can't drive it, and no way in hell am I missing this ceremony. That means we're flying."

"I don't like it. I think it poses a risk. Not just to the baby, but to you."

Now she patted his cheek. "Brad, I love you, and I love that you worry about me. But everything is going to be just fine."

She smiled and kissed him.

While others were discussing travel plans to join the happy couple on their big day, Bella and Nathan were suffering, both alone and together, through their first big fight.

It had been long overdue. Ever since he'd set foot at the horrifying bomb scene on July Fourth weekend, he'd become more and more distant, snappish, and short-tempered.

What tipped the tension into the boiling point was completely unrelated and completely minor in the grand scheme of things – running out of coffee.

Nathan had snatched the empty can and flung it across the kitchen in frustration, narrowly missing her as she'd walked into the room. She'd been studying all morning, researching for a paper she was writing that would count as a third of her grade in Advanced Russian. Her headache was raging, and she'd been heading for the Excedrin when she'd found herself dodging missiles.

Bella had had enough.

"What the hell?" she demanded.

"What?" he snarled back.

"Oh, hell no," she said, tired of walking on eggshells around him. "Don't fucking snarl at me like that. What is your problem?"

"Nothing," he snapped.

Bella exploded. "Bullshit. Something is seriously wrong with you lately. You don't eat much anymore, and you drink coffee like they're going to stop selling it..."

"Not a goddamn thing wrong with that," he interrupted.

"*Shut up and listen!*" she yelled, shocking him into being quiet for a moment. "You don't sleep worth a damn anymore, and you won't talk to me. I can't help you with whatever is wrong if you won't fucking let me. And now you're gonna throw shit around the house? Seriously?"

Bella looked at him defiantly, hands on her hips.

"I love you, Nathan Thomas. But I'm tired of feeling like I have to watch everything I say and do so I don't set you off."

"Then don't. I'm going out."

He slammed the front door hard behind him.

She sat at the kitchen table, her soul raw, and began to cry.

He was gone for four hours, just driving around aimlessly, trying to get through his anger at her that he knew was misplaced.

Finally, the mad began to wear off.

Taking a chance, he headed home. He let himself in quietly and walked toward the study, where Bella had been trying and failing to get back into a rhythm with the paper she had to finish.

He saw her – *really* saw her – for the first time in weeks. He saw not just the anger, but the hurt and the fear and the worry. It cleared the cloud in his head that he'd been living under.

His shoulders drooped as his temper was replaced with remorse and humility.

"Bella, I'm so sorry," he said sincerely.

He turned, went into the kitchen, and sat at the table, holding his face in his hands.

She'd looked up at him just before he spoke, and seeing the man she loved shattered broke Bella's heart and canceled out her anger. She got up and followed him.

"We're a team, baby," she said softly as she sat beside him. "I can't be there for you if you don't let me in."

"I see them in my head, Bel. Twenty-four-seven. They never go away. I see the face of every dead body I helped pull out of the rubble. Some of them were little kids. Really little kids. And I still see them."

Nathan's shoulders hitched.

"I close my eyes, try to sleep, and I'm right back there."

She wrapped her arms around him.

"Nathan, you don't have to go through this by yourself. And you really can't keep all this inside. You need to start working through this somehow. With me, with the counselor, whatever. But baby, you gotta do it. Carrying this is killing you."

"I know," he managed against her shoulder. "I know."

Stacy took the phone off speaker mode, said goodbye, and set the phone down.

"See? I told you," she said triumphantly. "The doctor gave the green light to fly up for the wedding."

"Okay," Brad exhaled. "I guess it's a go then. I'm still nervous about it, for the record, but doc says it should be fine, so…"

"Oh, honey. You worry too much."

She kissed him.

Over the next two weeks, Nathan did daily sessions with the counselor and found that with each session, he was able to sleep a little bit better. He knew he would never be able to completely forget what he'd seen, but he'd begun the journey to make peace with it all. He also resolved to not shut Bella out anymore.

He was at his office, working a cold case file, when she knocked on his doorframe.

"Got a second?" she asked.

"Hi, honey," he said, and stretched. "Perfect timing. Just about to go to lunch. Want to come?"

"Yep," Bella said. "I timed that pretty good."

"As always," he replied, kissing her as they started to leave the building.

"So, what sounds good?"

"What's a good celebration meal?" she asked in return, her eyes glowing.

He was confused. "What are we celebrating?"

"This." She pulled a little stick out of her pocket.

He took it and looked at it, but it didn't register at first what it was. He looked over at her, completely puzzled.

"Huh?"

She laughed.

"Two lines."

It dawned.

"This... this is a positive pregnancy test..."

"Yep."

"We're... we're having a baby? Are you sure?"

"It's the third one I've taken in three days."

"Really?"

"Really. And I just came from the doctor's appointment that also confirmed it. Due date, roughly, is around mid-March."

Nathan whooped with joy, scooped her into his arms, and swung her around.

"We're having a baby!" he shouted.

Alesha had surprised them both.

They had gotten into Cedar City, Utah, around six p.m. and had been driving around looking for a suitable candidate. Malls, gas stations, and grocery stores were usually good places to spot what they were looking for, and Cedar City had been no exception. They had spotted Alesha at the Chevron.

They followed her home a little way outside of town, making sure to keep a reasonable distance, then waited until nightfall. No one else had come or left. Around ten p.m. they noticed lights being turned out through the old farmhouse. Once all was dark, they waited another thirty minutes, then approached the back door.

Mikel wasn't that surprised to find it unlocked; in an area like this, crime just didn't happen.

Until now.

Easing their way into the house, he made sure Paula took point, as usual, and that only he had on gloves, as usual.

Paula snuck quietly down the hallway until she reached its end. To her right, a bathroom. To her left, the bedroom. She could make out a lone silhouette on the bed that was centered on the west wall. Paula entered the room. Mikel lingered in the hallway and watched her move around to the left side of the bed to intercept her target. Each of them realized too late that the woman was still wide awake.

Alesha shrieked in surprise, then shocked the hell out of both Mikel and Paula by emitting a warrior's yell, jumping out of bed, and attacking like lightning. Her first swipe with her left hand at Paula created long gashes down Paula's face and neck. Her right hand then came around balled into a fist and landed squarely on the bridge of Paula's nose, breaking it. Blood spurted as Paula screamed and stumbled backward.

Mikel stepped through the doorway, left arm extended, and tasered Alesha before she could do more damage to his pet. He then reached over, flipped on the light, and cast a glance around the room. He saw trophy after trophy – for boxing.

Huh, he thought, eyebrows raised. *If it wasn't vital that my DNA and fingerprints shouldn't be found here, I'd engage. Might have been fun to see what she can do.*

Alesha was out cold, face-down on the carpet next to her bed. She had hit her head on the nightstand on her way to the floor. Paula was conscious, bleeding, in pain, and pissed. Mikel pulled zip ties out of Paula's bag and secured Alesha's hands behind her, taking care to only touch her with his gloved hands.

Paula shoved him out of the way, grabbed the nearest trophy, and rained down blows on Alesha's head and torso, punctuating her speech with each one.

"Fucking. Bitch. Broke my *fucking. Nose.*"

Over and over, she swung her arm back as far as it would go, then brought the blunt object forward with as much fury and strength as she could. Blood was cast onto the ceiling and walls with each motion. She stopped after a few minutes, completely exhausted. Then she threw down the trophy at what was left of Alesha, glowered at Mikel, and left the room.

Mikel grinned, then called out to her.

"Didn't you forget something?"

Paula returned and rolled the body enough to get at least a profile Polaroid to add to the others. Then she stalked across the hall to the bathroom to try to get her nose to stop bleeding.

Which was fine with him.

As a matter of fact, the more she touches and leaves traces of herself, the better, he thought smugly.

Tiffany, a petite twenty-two-year-old from Trinidad, Colorado, encountered the traveling killers a week after Alesha got some shots in. She was much less of a threat than Alesha had been.

Thanks to Paula's still bruised and battered face, Tiffany believed her when Paula knocked frantically on her door, asking to use the phone to call for a ride to escape her abusive husband. She paid for her altruism with her life, and her death state was captured for posterity and joined the rest.

The next stop, nine days later, was Bismarck, North Dakota. Fifteen-year-old Rachel, walking home from school alone, never arrived. Her mother, frantic with worry but telling herself she was overreacting, finally called police at nine p.m.

Her body was found two days later, her beautiful sky-blue eyes now murky with death.

Three days after that, Mikel and Paula were within one-hundred and fifty miles of their next destination, Johnson City, Kansas. Fatigued, they stopped at a motel for the night.

Mikel had noticed a change in Paula. Maybe it was the nanotech finally starting to get a bit twitchy from operating continuously. He found he had to power Paula all the way down more and more frequently. He also noticed that his commands took a bit longer to be obeyed.

Glitch in the matrix, he thought, with no emotion. *Sometimes experiments have unforeseen complications.*

His only concern was, could she last long enough to make the final few stops? He really didn't want to have to break in a new pet this late in the game.

Speaking of which, his opponents were a severe disappointment. Not a single agency had, to his knowledge, linked any of it together.

As long as this mission trip has been, you'd think someone out there would have thought to check for similar murder cases, he muttered internally with disgust.

Ah, well, almost time to have the pet send off a package, he decided gleefully, watching Paula as she slept.

And he knew exactly who it should be delivered to.

Rick paused the television to go answer the door. He brought back a visitor with him into the living room.

"Max," Faith exclaimed, shuffling over to hug him. "What a nice surprise!"

He hugged her back with one arm, then extended the flowers he'd brought her. "For you, my dear."

"Thanks, Max, they're lovely," she said. "Let me go get these into a vase."

"I'll get it down," Rick offered. "I put it on the top shelf."

They all walked companionably into the kitchen.

"Max, you're just in time for lemon bars and coffee," she offered.

"That sounds wonderful." He beamed.

"So, how have you been?" Rick asked as they got comfortable around the table.

"Not bad," Max answered, and sipped his coffee thoughtfully. "Not as much progress as I'd like on some things at work. But overall, not bad."

"What brings you down?" Faith inquired.

"Couple of things, actually. I wanted to come and check on you, see how you both were doing."

"Wonderful."

They talked a bit more, just catching up.

"Bella's asked me to walk her down the aisle," Max told them.

"Aw, how sweet," Faith replied, patting his hand.

"Yes. It means a great deal to me." He grinned. "And at my age, it's not often you get to have a pretty young lady on your arm."

They laughed.

"I have to ask – whatever happened with the document we decoded?" Rick began. "I mean, hopefully you can tell us."

"Yes, yes," Max waved his hand. "I trusted you to decode it, so no point in locking you out of what came after."

He filled them in on the trip back to the Metzger Institute in detail. The Brazil trip, given that it wasn't sanctioned and therefore didn't technically happen, he was less forthcoming about.

"That must be so frustrating," Faith said. "I mean, from every-thing I read in the files and heard about Adolf and Mikel so far, it would be a no-brainer that Adolf *told* Mikel the whole thing, at the very least. I would expect there to be a translated hard copy somewhere."

"I agree," Max responded. "But if another translated copy does exist, like we think, I have no clue where it was hidden." Another sip of coffee, and he continued. "I also think that hospital explosion was no accident, and that Mikel had something to do with it. But I can't prove it. Not yet anyway. Technically, it's in the FBI's side of my world. Strictly speaking, I can't be involved with that piece at all."

"They never found his remains?"

"No. He is one of the many that were originally labeled 'missing – presumed dead'. It's my understanding that list has shortened quite a bit; they used DNA testing to identify roughly a hundred of the people on that list whose remains were only partially recovered. And they aren't done testing them all yet."

The three sat in silence for a moment.

"You know," Rick suggested, "I wonder if anyone's thought to check out video."

"Of the hospital?"

"Actually, I was thinking the parking lots. I saw on the news coverage that the professional building lot was in proximity. Right, Max?"

"Yes, it is. Go on."

"Well," Rick's brow furrowed in thought. "Could they not check the footage for that day to see if the cameras in that lot, or the hospital lot, captured people coming or going, maybe cars left in the lot, that they could also link back to names?"

"Interesting." Max nodded. "I'm sure they reviewed cameras, but probably to try to see if they could spot anyone suspicious that might explain the *explosion*, not as a victim identification tool. As you can imagine, a lot of the cars parked right in front of the hospital were destroyed; I heard with some of them you couldn't even tell what make and model they'd been. But maybe exterior cameras in both lots can help those working to identify victims."

He smiled at Rick.

"That's a brilliant angle, Rick. They may have already thought of it, but it never hurts to mention it. Give me one moment."

He stepped into the living room to make a call to Nathan, returning after a few minutes.

"They did check video, but as I suspected, not as a means to link victims with vehicles," he confirmed. "Good call, Rick. They're going to use it now to try to help speed up the ID process."

Max rejoined them at the kitchen table and opened his briefcase.

"If I could trouble you for more coffee and another lemon bar? And we can talk about the next puzzle I need you two to help solve."

Rick and Faith grinned in anticipation.

Alesha's boyfriend arrived home from his business trip three days after she was killed, found the body, and was inconsolable. He remained the primary suspect in her murder, until crime lab was able to identify two blood types on-scene – O positive, which was Alesha's, and AB negative, which they determined must have come from the killer.

Given that the boyfriend's blood type was B positive, this discovery moved him farther down the suspect list. Later developments would eliminate him as a suspect completely.

Following Max's suggestion, the FBI team assigned to the hospital scene began reviewing the parking lot videos again. Over the next few days, they managed to piece together enough data to pull medical records and compare against remains found to successfully identify four more people.

Mikel and Paula stayed on the list as unrecovered to date.

Refreshed, Mikel and Paula made slow circles in the mid-size mall's parking lot in Johnson City, Kansas. Eventually, they spotted what they sought.

Marsha was headed to meet a girlfriend for dinner and a movie. She never made it.

Two days later, on October twenty-first, her badly beaten body was found near the town landfill.

Chapter Nineteen

BELLA AND NATHAN'S wedding day had arrived.

"You know, it's weird. I don't know why I'm nervous about today. I mean," she looked around, then whispered, "we're already married, so, I don't get it."

"I do," Stacy told her. "It's because this is a more formal thing. All his family's here."

"I guess so," Bella said.

"Ouch," Stacy muttered, rubbing the right side of her belly. "Man, this kid is kickboxing today, I swear."

"How much longer, you think?"

"Doc says anytime now. We made it past thirty-seven weeks, so whenever he or she is ready we're all set to go."

"Still don't want to know ahead of time if it's a boy or girl?"

"Nope," Stacy grinned. "We want to be surprised. So long as he or she is healthy, that's all we care about."

She winced, sucking in her breath.

"I can tell you this, boy or girl, this kid's gonna need to play soccer or something. Powerful little legs already."

Faith, Rick, Jandy, and Tony came down to join them at the table.

"So, how are you doing, sis?" Faith asked. "Excited?"

"Sis," Bella repeated. "Man, I like how that sounds. I guess Brad and Nathan went to get his tux?"

"Yep," Stacy said. "And we're about to go get nails done. Want to join?"

Tony and Rick exchanged looks.

"I think we're going to help set up in the back yard, make sure chairs are lined up, that sort of thing," Rick offered.

"Rain check?" Tony said, and they all laughed.

The girls piled into Bella's truck and headed to the salon.

Mark Johnson, the detective working Marsha's case, was having a late lunch and reviewing the file so far. The evidence-collection team had been able to lift a partial palm print and two fingerprints at the scene that didn't match Marsha's, and they were running them through the Integrated Automated Fingerprint Identification System, or IAFIS, to see if they could find a match. Hairs and fibers not belonging to the victim had also been found and were being analyzed, but it would take some time.

He took another bite of his sandwich, closed his eyes, and thought as he chewed. Then inspiration struck. Why not check the NCIC (National Crime Information Center) for similar crimes just in case the killer wasn't already noted in IAFIS?

Setting his lunch down so he could type more quickly, he logged into the NCIC site and began to enter the particulars of Marsha's murder.

The ceremony began promptly at four p.m. on a perfect Virginia fall afternoon. After some discussion, it had been decided that the variety of color in the leaves left little else to be desired in the way of decorations. Nature's canopy had provided the perfect backdrop for the occasion.

Nathan looked striking in his tuxedo, waiting in the middle of their backyard for Bella to join him and the pastor. When she and Max came out of the house and down the steps toward him, she took his breath away. She'd opted for a white column dress overlaid with lace. The Bardot neckline and dramatic train were simplistic yet elegant. She'd left her hair loose to flow down her back, adorned only with a simple, delicate wreath with a fingertip veil trailing from it.

His smile grew as she got closer, until at last, Max took her hand from his arm, tenderly putting it into Nathan's hand. Then Max kissed Bella's cheek, tears shining, and took his seat.

Twenty minutes later, with many happy tears, the guests cheered and clapped as Bella and Nathan kissed, for what most in the crowd thought was the first time, as husband and wife.

Detective Johnson almost choked on his coffee when he returned from catching another call and looked at his search results in NCIC. Fourteen similar cases within the last four and a half months. All young, dark haired, blue-eyed females. He picked up the phone and called the FBI's Behavioral Analysis Unit in Washington DC.

The cake had been cut, pictures taken, and everyone was mingling and having a grand old time when Nathan's cell phone rang.

"Thomas," he said, and listened intently, then frowned and went into his home office to hear better.

Bella watched him go, eyebrows raised.

"What's that about?" Faith and Rick asked her.

"I think he might have caught a case," she said.

"*Oh...*" Stacy groaned loudly, and Bella could tell something wasn't right.

"Stacy. You all right?"

Brad had his arm around his wife.

Nathan stepped back into the room just then. Bella went to him when she saw the look on his face.

"Baby, I have to go in to the office. We've got a new case," he told her.

About that time, Stacy managed to say, "My water just broke," before starting to Lamaze breathe through the next contraction.

All conversation stopped.

Brad's eyes were huge. "*What?*"

"We need to go... to the hospital now..." Stacy forced out between breaths.

"Jandy, need help here, can you stay with her for a sec? I'm gonna get out of this dress. Breathe, Stace, give me two minutes, okay?" Bella yelled as she hauled it up the stairs, with Nathan following right behind her.

"Quick, help me get out of this damn thing," she chastised.

He hurriedly undid the back buttons so she could fling the dress to the floor. As she raced to the closet for jeans and a sweater, he got her some socks and brought them and her sneakers over to the bed since he knew she'd sit there to put them on. His timing was perfect; she was dressed and heading downstairs in the two minutes promised, with him on her heels.

"You go work your case, baby, I'll go with them, and I'll meet you back here at some point?" she asked, and quickly kissed him before helping Brad get Stacy out to the car.

As she ran around to get in, he grabbed her arm gently.

"Your veil," he laughed, and worked it out of her hair.

"Thanks, honey. I'll call you with updates."

"You bet."

They sped off. Nathan turned back to his sisters, brother-in-law, niece, nephew, and Max.

"I have to go, too," he said. "I caught a case. I'm so sorry, guys. I don't know when either one of us will be back."

"It's all right," Jandy reassured him. "You go. We're fine here. We'll straighten up everything. Tony and the kids and I don't fly back until tomorrow. We can entertain ourselves."

"Our flight back leaves tonight at eleven, so we weren't going to be able to stay much past eight anyway," Faith chimed in, with Rick nodding in affirmation.

"We get all this calmed down, Bel and I will come down for a visit," Nathan told them.

He hugged his family and headed to the car.

As he began to pull down the driveway, he rolled down his window and shouted to them "Save me some cake!" then headed toward the office to get up to speed on this new case he'd been assigned.

Two hours later, Nathan Thomas realized this was going to be a very, very long journey. Fifteen different women, in ages ranging from fifteen to twenty-five. Some bodies had already been found, but four of the women were still listed as missing. All the same hair and eye color. From all over the place. Some of the body-recovery scenes had turned up no physical evidence at all, while others had garnered blood, DNA, and fingerprints.

Sighing, he pulled up the next one on the NCIC list, and made another call officially requesting all data be forwarded to his attention at the BAU.

Twelve hours into labor, Stacy was exhausted. The nurse tending to her was overly chipper, and Bella could tell that it was really pissing her off.

"I bet *she's* never pooped a watermelon," she snarled to Lizzie the moment the nurse stepped out. "Or she wouldn't be so fucking bubbly about it all."

Bella knew Stacy's patience was depleted, so she started running interference before Stacy killed the poor lady. Brad was focusing on coaching his wife's breathing, rubbing her back, and supplying ice chips. Bella was proud of him; he was holding it together well. Stacy was, too, for the most part. Only the perky-as-hell nurse seemed to be getting on Stacy's nerves.

Finally, the moment came. At the doctor's urging, Stacy pushed with all her might, clutching Bella's hand on one side and Brad's on the other, crushing their fingers as she screamed with effort.

Crying filled the air.

"Congrats, Mom and Dad, you have a daughter," the doctor announced, handing the newborn to the nurse for weigh-in and cleanup.

"We have a daughter," Stacy gasped, crying and smiling.

"Five pounds, five ounces," the nurse said, smiling. She finished her measurements, gently cleaned the child, wrapped her in a pink blanket, and brought her to her mother.

"She's gorgeous," Bella whispered, tears streaming down her cheeks.

"She is, isn't she?" Stacy nodded.

Her daughter turned her head instantly when she heard Stacy's voice.

"Hi, baby," Stacy whispered, nuzzling her baby's cheek. "Hi, my love."

Then she looked up at her husband.

"Honey, hold your daughter."

With joyous, tear-filled eyes, Brad took his child into his arms for the first time, and he sobbed.

"You're so beautiful. You're just so beautiful," he told the baby over and over as he cradled her and cried.

"What's her name?" Bella asked.

"Emily Grace," Stacy and Brad replied in unison.

Two days later, Nathan had received twelve of the fifteen requested files. The remaining three would be delivered any time. He kissed Bella goodbye and drove to the office.

He waved at Charlie, the desk guard, and whistled to himself as he took the elevator up to his floor. Greeting other agents as he went, he continued down the hall to his office. Nathan had commandeered a large whiteboard on wheels he'd maneuvered into his space. It was vital. With fifteen cases' worth of data to look at, he needed all the area he could get to work with.

He knew the rough order in which the women had been reported missing and/or bodies recovered because of the basic data in NCIC. But Nathan found that sometimes he preferred to review out of order, because he often noticed little things that might be missed by proceeding down a timeline.

So, he picked the file atop the stack. Helena, Montana. Mary, twenty-four, single, body found September eleventh, coroner approximated TOD forty-eight hours previously. Cause of death was stab wound to the aorta.

He put her name, location, and date found on the board, added her picture beside it, then proceeded to the next file.

Ely, Nevada. Barbara, twenty-five, married mom of two. Reported missing by her husband when she didn't pick her kids up from daycare on July twelfth. Still missing.

He added Barbara's name, data, and picture to the board, too.

He continued in this manner, reading file details in each case, linking faces and names, getting familiar with the dead and the missing so he could better help them. He noticed that in the cases where a body had been found, cause of death was all over the place, which was unusual. Typically, serial killers had a favored method they tended to stick with. He also noticed that in each case, the woman was twenty-five or younger, white, with dark hair and blue eyes. At this point, the only commonality seemed to be the victim's appearance.

He leaned back, thinking it out. Jealous jilted lover done wrong by a woman with dark hair and blue eyes? He knew that often killers projected fantasy revenge scenarios onto their victims, and in those instances, usually there was a very sexual element to the crime. He quickly scanned the summaries of each case again. No sexual assault in any of them. In fact, no sexual overtones at all, not even torn clothing. Strange. He closed his eyes, mulling it over.

Nathan's desk phone rang.

"Thomas," he said.

It was the lab. Both the Johnson City, KS and Cedar City investigators had overnighted their blood, hair, fiber, and fingerprint evidence to the FBI's Washington office for faster analysis.

"Hey, Nathan, it's Betty," the tech said. "Got some interesting results for you. I'm still working up a full DNA profile, but I can already confirm your killer is female with blood type AB negative."

"Female? Really?" Nathan responded, surprised. "Female serial killers are quite unusual."

"Yep. But you've definitely got one, kid. That popped on my prelim tests right away. I'll be back in touch once it's all complete."

"Interesting. Keep me posted. Thanks, Betty, I appreciate you," he said.

"You got it," she replied, and hung up.

Betty had been helping catch bad guys through lab work since the late 1980s and called everyone in the Bureau 'kid' because most of them were young enough to be her children – or grandchildren. But she had a soft spot in her heart for Nathan; he bore a striking resemblance to her oldest grandson Jeremiah, who was serving with distinction in the US Army as a Blackhawk chopper pilot.

She turned back to her microscope, fine tuning it until she could clearly see the shaft of the hair sample sent.

"Now," she muttered under her breath, "Let's see what hair color you were born with, cause this black isn't natural, I can already tell."

The woman whose hair Betty was studying so intently had just completed another of Mikel's assignments for her in Pittsburg, Kansas, the previous afternoon. Now she sat slumped in the front passenger seat, head leaning on the side window, as Mikel turned the car north to start the eight-hundred-mile trek to Marinette, Wisconsin. He'd shut her off for a while.

She had mailed the souvenir photos on Tuesday morning, just as he'd instructed. By his calculations, it should arrive before the weekend did.

Time to step up his opponent's game.

Even with the whiteboard, the details of each case were beginning to get all jumbled together in Nathan's head. And another case file had arrived. The killer had struck again at the other end of Kansas from Johnson City. The count was now sixteen. He was going to have to plot them out, no way around it.

He walked down the hall to his unit secretary's desk.

"Hey, Charlotte, do we have a US map I can have?"

"How big do you need?"

"How big do you have?"

She smiled. "I know where I can get a five foot by ten foot, if you need."

"That would actually be perfect, I can stick it on the other wall in my office."

"Plotting out where they all are, huh? We've had to do that a time or two before. I'll bring it to you."

"Thanks, Charlotte. I need a break. I'm going for lunch. Be back in an hour."

When he returned, he found Steve looking over the whiteboard.

"Geez," Steve said.

"Yeah," Nathan ran his hand over his face. "Charlotte is bringing me a big map."

"I was gonna suggest that. You want help with this one?"

"As many as there are, yes. I need to not miss anything, so the more hands and eyes, the better."

"Well," Steve said, sitting in Nathan's visitor chair, "the rest of the team is working other things. But my desk is light right now. I can help."

"That would be great," Nathan replied, as Charlotte walked in with two long rolls. "Let's start with getting those tacked up and go from there."

Once the laminated map was firmly planted onto the wall, Nathan called out case data and Steve put a red pin in each city involved. They stepped back, looked.

"I don't see a pattern," Steve said. "It's completely random."

"There must be something," Nathan sighed. "We just have to keep looking."

He glanced at his watch. "It's almost seven."

"Go home," Steve said. "Let's resume tomorrow, ten a.m."

Nathan headed home to dinner and time with his wife.

Mikel headed toward victim number seventeen's hometown. He had no doubt they'd find another in Marinette who would do nicely. He checked the time. Ten p.m. They had traveled roughly halfway. Time to stop for the night.

By this time tomorrow, another trophy Polaroid would be in the glovebox, and he would be one step closer to what he really wanted most of all – Bella Amsel all to himself. The mere thought made Mikel Metzger as happy as could be.

He activated Paula so she could go rent the room in the cheap motel he'd found in Des Moines, Iowa.

Nine a.m. the next morning found Nathan once again making his way to his office.

"Morning. There was a package that came for you. It's on your desk," Charlotte remarked.

"Thanks."

He hung his jacket on the back of his chair, staring at the brown box in the middle of his blotter.

Hmmm.

This was not the case files he was still waiting on; those would have been stamped with the jurisdictional information at the very least and would probably have arrived via overnight courier.

He double checked with Charlie downstairs that the package had gone through standard security protocols to detect any explosives or other issues.

As he pulled on latex gloves, he reached over and pressed the intercom button.

"Hey, Steve," he said, when his boss answered. "Can we meet a few minutes early?"

Once the package was opened and the contents revealed, they looked at each other in disbelief.

"Jesus," Steve said as he carefully spread out the fifteen photos included with the note. He'd gloved up too as soon as he walked into Nathan's office and realized what was up.

"Yeah," Nathan breathed. "Question is, how did whoever sent this know I would catch these cases?"

"I don't think they could have," Steve replied earnestly. "Our rotation schedule for case assignment is not public knowledge. That means someone wanted you specifically to see this."

"The only person that this would make sense coming from is Mikel Metzger," Nathan paced back and forth. "He was very, very focused on Bella. Makes sense that he would send this to me; in his mind, he would believe she belonged to him and that I stole her away. But Steve, all the physical evidence in these cases is pointing to a female killer. Betty has already confirmed through prelim testing that the suspect is a woman."

He stopped, a glimmer of an idea forming.

"Steve. There's no way he could have escaped the hospital without help. It makes sense he's still on the missing list and nothing of him has been found at the scene. Because he wasn't there when it exploded. We need to find out for sure who on staff there had regular contact with him..."

"Because one of those people was his ticket out of there," Steve finished his thought.

They went down the hall where their coworker was still wading through the parking lot camera tapes.

"Brent, we've got something we want to try," Steve said. "You got that duty roster handy?"

"Yeah, it's right over there," he pointed to a table.

Nathan picked it up, flipped through pages.

"Here," he said, drawing his finger down the page then tapping the line that answered the question. "Two nurses on duty on the fourth floor that night. Abby, who was found alive and safe in the northeast elevator. The other one was named Paula."

He cross-checked the presumed dead list.

"Who is listed as missing, presumed. But what if she's not?" he asked out loud. "What if they haven't identified her remains because she wasn't there when it went up, either?"

The three looked at each other.

"Anything in the record about her car? What did she drive?"

Brent tapped a few keys. "Red Malibu, assigned spot D forty-seven."

"Roll tape on the lot from one hour prior to the explosion," Nathan suggested. "Something tells me we'll see our missing nurse in action."

He was right. Forty-one minutes before the hospital was destroyed, the camera clearly showed Paula – in street clothes, not scrubs – walk from around the building to her car, get in, pull out, and drive back the direction she'd walked in from.

"Since she wasn't wearing scrubs, she looked like just a visitor," Nathan mused. "And they didn't keep record of those, no sign-in required. We missed her before because she didn't look like someone on duty, and who really polices parking spots?"

"What's that way, the direction she drove? Any camera angles?" Steve asked.

"Not any good ones. And that direction," Brent checked his notes, "is the street-level ramp entry down to the basement where the morgue was."

Silence in the room as all three contemplated.

"Okay," Steve muttered. "Morgue. Wouldn't be unusual for a nurse to have to go down there, transporting a body from upstairs. No need to alter any security levels on her badge for that, and she wouldn't look out of place."

"We need her complete file," Nathan stated. "Anything we can find out about her. Friends, family, co-workers, all of it. If he managed to talk her into helping him escape custody, maybe he managed to talk her into much worse. Somebody needs to go to Arizona and dig."

He turned to Steve.

"I think we also ought to get with Phoenix PD. Give them her license plate, make, and model. See if we can't track where she went through traffic cameras."

"I agree," Steve said. "And by all rights I should be yanking your ass off every bit of this since it all seems to tie back to the man who stalked Bella. But," he held up his hand as Nathan started to protest, "I'm inclined to leave you on it. For now. I do need to read the AD in on what's happened, though."

Chapter Twenty

THEY SAT ONCE AGAIN in the AD's visitor chairs, with their boss seated behind his desk, fingers steepled as Steve and Nathan brought him up to date.

Steve finished the narrative, and the room fell silent. The AD gazed at Nathan. Nathan returned with a level visage of his own.

"So," the AD finally spoke. "When did you want to leave for Phoenix?"

"You're not pulling me off this?"

"Not at this time. Nathan, that package was sent to you directly. Whoever is behind all this *wants* you fully engaged in what's going on. As you have the best insight into Mikel Metzger, taking you off this right now would, I feel, hinder rather than help our investigation."

He stood, then came around the desk to perch on the corner nearest to Nathan.

"However, I reserve the right to reassign any or all of this at any time, if I feel you or the investigation has been compromised in any way. Clear?"

"Crystal," Nathan answered. "As to when I leave, the sooner I get out there, the better. If what I think is happening is correct, the more we know about this Paula woman the further ahead we will be. Also, sir, I think it would be a good idea if you sent someone to take another look around the Metzger Institute. If she did help him escape, that's the logical place they would have gone for him to stock up for what he was planning next."

"I can take that piece," Steve offered. "Let's make the trip out together. You follow up the Paula angle, I'll go reexamine the Institute."

"Off you go, gentlemen," the AD stated. "Full reports when you return."

"Yes, sir."

"I'll be gone a couple of days," Nathan told her as he packed his bag.

"You can't tell me much about what's going on, can you?"

He looked at her, saw the concern in those beautiful blue eyes.

What I am gonna say, Bel? That there's sixteen women dead who all looked like you, but hey, don't worry, I think it's just a coincidence? he muttered in his head.

"Babe, I can't."

"I know," she sighed. "It's okay. Just be careful, please."

"I know this must be a shock to you," Nathan told Abby and Miriam gently. "Take your time."

Paula's co-workers were with Nathan in Dr. Brindler's conference room on the top floor of the professional building. They'd been summoned by the Chief of Surgery personally and had been extremely confused as to why.

Then Nathan began to speak about the reason for the meeting, and confusion had turned to complete shock.

"Wow," Miriam said. "That just can't be right. I mean, Paula ran over a squirrel once as she was coming into work. She was devastated. That type of person couldn't possibly kill others. I don't see it," she finished, shaking her head.

Abby was extremely pale and quiet. She nervously fidgeted with the buttons on her jacket.

"Abby, what do you know that we don't?" Brindler asked her gently.

"I was going to bring it to someone's attention, I swear," she began with tears in her eyes. "About what I saw. I knew it was wrong."

"Abby, you're not in trouble," Brindler reassured her. "Just tell us."

She took a deep breath to steady herself.

"I saw it once on the monitor at the nurse's station. You know, the one that changes view from room to room? I had finished my rounds and gone back to the station and happened to glance at the monitor. Paula was in room four-two-five, and at first she just looked like she was doing her normal thing. Then she went back over to him and leaned over and kissed him."

Dr. Brindler's eyebrows went up.

"She did what?"

"She kissed him."

"When was this?"

Abby closed her eyes, frowning in concentration. "Umm... maybe June sometime? It was before he woke up, I know that."

She sipped the bottled water that had been offered.

"After he woke up, whenever she was on, she *insisted* on working that end of the floor. She'd get, like, snippy with you if you asked to trade. The night of the explosion, I asked her to trade wings with me – you know, break up the monotony."

Miriam nodded her head in understanding.

"And Paula was, like, really hateful about it. Completely out of character for her. I remember thinking, 'geez, don't have to get all huffy about it'," Abby finished.

Brindler and Nathan exchanged looks.

"Anything else you can tell us about her?"

Abby and Miriam thought, then shook their heads.

"Okay then." Nathan handed them each one of his cards.

"If you think of anything else, please let me know, no matter how minor it may seem. If she reaches out to either of you, let me know right away. And please, let's keep this conversation to ourselves. Okay?"

They both nodded their acknowledgement and left.

"Well," Brindler said, getting himself a bottled water. "It seems your instinct was accurate. What next?"

Out at the Institute, Steve and the Flagstaff agents had made it to Sub-Level Three.

"Would you look at that," he said, holding up a hospital gown with gloved fingers. "Nathan was right."

It was carefully placed into an evidence bag.

He also noticed and bagged an empty vial for testing, was just noting it in his log when his phone rang. It was the Phoenix police department.

He listened, then responded, "I'll be there shortly."

After hanging up with them, he called Nathan.

"Meet me down at the police station."

Within half an hour, they had convened at police headquarters and were able to review the traffic camera search results. Paula's car was on tape, passing through several lights, leaving town, headed in the direction of the Institute the night the hospital exploded. Then Steve shared what he'd found out there in Sub-Level Three.

"And the locks on the gate hadn't been disturbed at all," he finished. "So, there must have been another way into that building that we never found, and a hiding place where he stashed some stuff just in case, because we completely cleaned out Sub-Level Three last December."

"Twenty bucks says that vial contained his nanotechnology serum," Nathan stated with certainty. "If he injected Paula with it, he'd be able to get her to do whatever he wants, whenever and however he wants. Which would explain behavior so far outside her norm."

"So, you're saying she may be killing these women, but doing it on command?"

"That's exactly what I'm saying."

An officer came in and handed a note to Steve.

"Her car's been found," he announced. "Just the other side of Ely, Nevada."

"They need to impound it, collect any trace, dust it for prints," Nathan said. "My gut says we may get lucky and get Mikel's DNA or prints on or in it somewhere."

Steve nodded. "Already underway. They'll send what they find to DC for testing."

"Okay," Nathan said. "We need to get back to the office. I want to take those pins down and put them back up, in chronological case order. Mikel Metzger doesn't do things randomly. The case order means something, I can feel it."

Marinette, Wisconsin, had indeed produced another stellar addition to the lineup. Mikel had to glove up and jump in when Paula's grip fatigued, and seventeen-year-old Amanda had started to fight her way free. One quick swipe across the throat with the scalpel, and the fighting spirit left Amanda with her blood.

Paula made sure she captured Amanda's photo before rolling the body in plastic for disposal. Once she was loaded in the trunk, they waited until nightfall, then dumped the body next to railroad tracks as they headed out toward Jonesboro, Arkansas.

Back in Nathan's office, Steve took pins out while Nathan organized his cases in chronological order.

"Ready?"

"Ready," Steve replied. "Who's the first?"

"Barbara, from Ely, Nevada."

Steve placed a pin. "Next?"

"Bakersfield, CA. Megan."

Another pin.

It continued this way for Nancy in Sacramento, CA, Susan in Chico, California, Lily in Medford, Oregon, Tara in Salem, Oregon, Mandy in Boise, Idaho.

The next set pinned was Mary in Helena MT, followed by Patti in Miles City, Montana, Georgia in Idaho Falls, Idaho, Macy from Casper, Wyoming, Alesha the boxing champ in Cedar City, Utah, and Tiffany from Trinidad, Colorado.

Third group consisted of Rachel from Bismarck, North Dakota, followed by Kansas residents Marsha in Johnson City, and Tori, in Pittsburg.

They stood back and looked at the board.

"That's crazy," Steve remarked. "Why in the hell would someone drive from Trinidad to Bismarck for their next target? That's about nine-hundred miles."

"Oh, Christ," Nathan hissed as he saw it.

"What?"

"Connect the dots," Nathan said solemnly, and grabbed a dry erase marker.

Following the pin sequence, he began with Ely, Nevada, and drew lines to connect each pin, ending with Boise, Idaho.

"Do you see it?" he asked Steve.

"I think so. Draw a curved line from Boise back to Chico, and from Chico back to Ely?"

"Yep." Nathan did just that, then altered the top and bottom lines to curve also.

"Holy shit, Nathan," Steve exclaimed. "The first set forms a capital letter 'B'."

"Yeah." Nathan's features had turned to granite. "What do you bet the next set, from Helena, MT to Trinidad, CO, forms a rough 'E'?"

They drew lines, and sure enough, now they had a 'B' and an 'E' peeking at them from the map.

Repeating the exercise, they found the victims' locations from Bismarck, ND to Pittsburg, KS could be connected by lines to form the first 'L'.

"He's spelling her name, Nathan," Steve thought aloud in stunned disbelief. "He's spelling your wife's name with bodies of women who look like her."

Nathan's desk phone rang.

"Thomas," he almost whispered, eyes never leaving the board.

"It's Betty. The envelope you got in the mail. Female DNA only on the flap. Couple of prints off it, running those now."

"Let me guess," Nathan offered. "DNA matches the suspect's blood samples from the other scenes."

"Yep, same female, no question. And my other testing is far enough I can tell you, she's a white female."

"Thanks Betty, you're the best."

"You okay, kid? You don't sound too good."

"Yeah, Betty, it's just, the job. You know."

"I do know. Take care of yourself, Nathan." She hung up and went back to her analysis.

"So now we know for sure Paula sent you that package," Steve concluded.

"Yep. At Mikel's direction. Problem is, we won't be able to prove it or tie him to a single one of these cases. *Dammit.*" Nathan slapped his hands on his desk in frustration before running them through his hair.

"It's only her prints being left, only her DNA being found at the scenes. And I know that's on purpose. She's just a tool he's using that he will dispose of when he's finished with her. What I don't know is if he will go ahead and kill her or leave her alive to take the fall for all this."

He swept his arm out, gesturing to the wall map, then got up to pace.

"Sending me the photos. Why do that? That was a mistake, a big one, and he doesn't make many, Steve. It was very arrogant of him, not careful at all, sending *me* those pictures directly. I mean, think about it. What did that accomplish?'

"Well, it tells us everyone still listed as missing is already dead, and we just haven't found them yet," Steve chimed in. "And it hands us more physical evidence against Paula. I mean, any stronger, it should have had a big red bow around that box."

"Yes, and to anyone else, to any other investigator working on this, that might have been the end of it. But he had her send them to *me*. That's the arrogance and carelessness coming out. He wanted *me* to put it all together, Steve. And all that did was alert us to the fact that he is still very much alive, and that Paula's not doing this of her own accord. I need him to be cocky and make more mistakes like that one, before he can form any more letters. But Jesus, look at the map," Nathan gestured again. "Where would we even start?"

Steve said, "I can see it. He could start the next letter anywhere in half the US, from Minnesota down to Texas and all the way to the Eastern seaboard. How can we protect every white woman between fifteen and twenty-five years old with dark hair and blue eyes in *half the country?*"

"We can't," Nathan muttered despondently. "We can't. Which means more are going to die unless I can get ahead of him on this."

His desk phone rang again. Nathan answered it, closed his eyes, listened, and said "Okay, send it," and hung up.

Slowly, he shook his head, shoulders drooped, a long exhale before he turned and opened his eyes to look at his boss.

"Another body," he told Steve. "Marinette, Wisconsin."

Nathan went to the map and stuck a pin in that location.

"He's already started the next 'L'."

"We need to get Mitch in on this. Maybe he can extrapolate a target area based on the known locations," Steve suggested.

"I'll call him now," Nathan said, and dialed.

"Mitch, it's Nathan. Can you join us in my office? We need your brain."

Fifteen minutes later, Mitch was there, staring at the wall map.

"Mary Mother of God."

"Yeah," Steve and Nathan muttered at the same time.

Then Nathan said, "Any way to replicate this in the computer, maybe try to plot out anticipated locations so we can catch these two?"

"Two?"

Nathan and Steve filled him in.

"Jesus, Nathan, you just can't get away from this Mikel guy, can you?"

Nathan's mouth set in a tight line.

"It would seem not. He's determined to engage with me."

"Well then, we could certainly try," Mitch said. "Assuming certain factors like all the letters will be capitalized, roughly the same size, and so on, I should be able to provide some reasonable assumptions."

"I know this much," Nathan added. "Manassas, Virginia will be the last plot point. It may not be one of the outer points forming the letter 'A', but it will be the last one. He'll work the others out of logical order, outside his normal pattern, to make sure this all ends where Bella is."

"Nathan, you're going to have to send her somewhere safe until we catch them," Steve said. "How much are you going to have to tell her before she'll agree to that? I know she can be stubborn; she is Manfred's granddaughter, after all."

Nathan smirked in response to that, then sighed.

"You're telling me. Steve, I honestly don't know. She is very intelligent, makes me look like a complete dunce sometimes. And it's spooky how intuitive she can be. She'll know the minute she sees me tonight that something major is going on."

He turned to his boss. "What would you do?"

"If it was my wife, I'd do whatever was needed to keep her safe," Steve replied solemnly.

"Absolutely," Mitch answered also. "Not even a question."

"She'll be inclined to stay, to try to help and protect me, she'll be willing to fight it out if it comes to that," Nathan added heavily. "She's a warrior. She got that from Manfred, too. But I don't want her in this one. I don't want her anywhere near it, anywhere even close to here where Mikel can get to her," Nathan stated, walking back over to look at the map.

"Maybe between Max and I we can convince her to go to my sister's in Pantego, lay low for a while."

"Besides," he continued, looking at Mitch and Steve, "it's not just her I'm worried about. You guys know our first child is due in March. I'm not willing to risk either one of them."

"She might feel ambushed with you and Max both coming at her about it," Steve pointed out. "But that can't be helped. Her safety is your priority right now. I can see it. We both can," he indicated to Mitch.

Mitch nodded and told Nathan, "You won't be able to concentrate fully on catching this prick and his little robot until you're sure Bella is out of the line of fire."

"So, get with Max, and go get it done. Tonight," Steve told him, then glanced as his watch and winced.

Almost six p.m.

"I need to update the AD again anyway. Mitch, run the scenario we talked about. Let's reconvene at seven a.m. tomorrow. By then, the Marinette files should be here."

The three of them headed out toward the elevator. Nathan pressed the down button while Mitch and Steve waited to go up.

"I need to call Faith and Jandy and see if Bella can come stay with one of them until this is over. Let me get that part lined out first, and then I'll call Max and ask him to meet me at home. See you two in the morning."

Nathan stepped into his waiting elevator, cell phone already ringing through to Faith's number.

Steve and Mitch shared the next upward car that came. Steve went up two floors to try and catch the AD before he left for the day. Mitch returned to his lab to start the simulations and try to capture some possible target points.

"Of course, as long as you need," Jandy said. "Does Faith know about what's going on?"

Nathan had to leave Faith a brief message asking her to call him but hadn't gone into detail. Not that he was able to share much with Jandy either. Just that he was working a case that was particularly difficult, he felt the person he was chasing might decide to try involving Bella directly in retaliation, and that he'd feel better if she stayed in Texas for a while until this got wrapped up.

"I'll reach out to Faith, too," Jandy offered. "Between all of us, we'll make sure she's taken care of and protected."

"Thanks, sis. I owe you guys big."

"No, honey, you don't. This is what family does."

They hung up and he called Max.

"Hey, Max. What are your plans this evening?" he asked as he walked to his car.

"No plans," Max replied. "Why?"

Nathan read him in as he drove toward Manassas, using the brusque shorthand that investigators communicated in sometimes.

"I'll be there by eight-thirty," Max responded.

"See you then." Nathan ended the call and drove toward home, wondering how in the hell was the best way to break this all to his wife.

He sighed.

He wasn't going to be able to hold anything back this time.

His phone rang. "Thomas."

It was Steve. "Hey, I think we just caught a big break. Fleabag motel just outside Des Moines, Iowa. Owner got tired of being robbed, so he went all out and installed a mega security system, in the lobby and in the parking lot."

Nathan's antenna pinged. "Go on."

"On October twenty-sixth, he had a lady come in to rent a room. Said she looked stoned out of her mind, so he remembered her, and her car because it wasn't local. Beige sedan with Nevada license plates. She paid cash. But since she was acting squirrely, he watched her on camera. She wasn't alone. Some guy was waiting in the car. He got good, clear video of them, and the car, too."

"How did we even find out about this? Nothing's out in the media yet."

"He also happens to have a cousin who's on the police force in Marinette. Evidently, they talk on a regular basis. Cousin mentioned the Marinette case, and the motel owner said it struck him because his cousin could have been describing the woman that rented the room."

"Let me guess. White, mid-twenties, black hair, blue eyes."

"Yeah, except one blue eye, one green."

"Contacts. She dyed her hair, and went with blue contacts, and she's lost one somewhere."

"Yep. Best part? Pittsburg, Kansas PD listed one blue contact among trace evidence found at their victim's dump site."

"Video coming to us?"

"Marinette got it from him and they're sending it electronically to our lab."

"Excellent. That means we'll have pictures to distribute," Nathan said as he took the exit toward home. "I think our best bet to keep another murder from happening is to make this as public as possible. Names, previous photos, still shots from the video showing what they look like now, full car description, the works."

"Agreed," Steve said. "We'll have all that ready to go out by nine a.m. tomorrow. We might get lucky and get to them before there's a number eighteen. If it's Paula and Mikel on the video, that is."

"It's them," Nathan replied firmly. "I can feel it down to my core."

"Well, your gut hasn't been wrong yet. See you in the morning."

Nathan ended the call and pulled into his driveway. He took a moment to steel his nerves, then walked toward his front door.

Chapter Twenty-One

"You want me to what?" Bella asked incredulously. "I've got classes, Nathan, and they're all advanced. I can't do them by remote. I'm one more semester from being done. You want me to put my life on hold forever?"

"Not forever," Max said calmly. "Just for the next few weeks or so."

"*No*," she retorted, chin out, glaring defiantly at them both. "No. Not before Thanksgiving break. I *might* be talked into that, but I'm sure as hell gonna be back here when classes pick back up the first week of December."

Nathan and Max exchanged looks.

"Wait," she said. "What aren't you two telling me?"

Nathan had hoped to be able to just skim the surface like he had with Jandy. But that wasn't going to cut it. He would have to tell her all of it, so she'd understand why it was so important to send her away from him.

He'd already cleared doing so with his supervisor. He'd just hoped not to have to.

Now he came and sat beside her and held her hand.

"Okay. I'll tell you. All of it."

And he did.

Mikel and Paula's escape, what was found at the Institute, and their belief that Mikel had infected Paula with the serum. The killing spree. And what the kill locations were spelling out on the United States map once plotted.

Bella's face was ghostly white, and tears streamed unchecked down her face.

"Seventeen women are dead... because of me?" she managed. "Oh, my God."

Bella hung her head and sobbed.

He held her until her tears slowed and her breathing became less hitched.

She raised her head and looked at her husband, then at her godfather. "You have to draw him out before he kills another one," she said flatly.

"Yes."

"You're gonna go public, plaster his face everywhere, piss him off so he changes his plans and comes straight here next, aren't you?"

"That's the plan."

She sighed and wiped at her face.

"If I'm gone, what if he's casing this place? He'll figure out I'm not here, he's not stupid."

"We already have a female FBI agent lined up as a stand-in, for just that reason."

Her eyes widened in surprise.

"Nathan. I think I just felt the baby move."

"And that's the other reason I want you safe, away from here, until this is done."

He looked over at Max. "We both do."

"Okay," she said in a small, shaky voice as she placed her arms protectively over her child. "Okay. I'll go. It's the only way to draw him in close enough to stop him. Max, can you travel down with me?"

"Not only that, dear, I will stay down there with you, to watch over you. And we will come back, together, as soon as it's safe."

"Okay," she said again, a little stronger. "When are we leaving?"

"We can catch a flight tomorrow afternoon," Max said. "I don't believe we're of a need to leave right this minute."

He glanced at Nathan questioningly.

"That sounds right," Nathan confirmed. "We won't be spreading the news through media until tomorrow noon at the earliest. I figure he's somewhere south of Marinette, Wisconsin right now, probably heading due south to stay on his pattern. My gut says he's at least eight-hundred miles from here. Gives us time to get you down to Texas and safe."

"I'll reach out to my professors in the morning. I can just tell them I'm experiencing some small issues with the pregnancy and have been put on bedrest for a while. They'll be willing to work with that, including my emailing in assignments. Anything I can't handle remotely I'll deal with when I get back."

Max rose.

"Bella, I will arrange for us to fly out to Dallas-Fort Worth Airport around six p.m. Will that work? And I can pick you up here around three-thirty."

"That would be good. Thanks, Uncle Max. See you tomorrow."

She kissed his cheek before he left. Then she was silent, looking at Nathan for a long while.

"I understand now why you didn't want to tell me. Hearing it all... it's awful."

"I had hoped to spare you all that," he agreed. "It's completely horrible. But not a single bit of it is your fault, Bella."

"I should have been a better shot last year when I was face to face with him. If I had killed him outright, seventeen women would still be alive, and that poor nurse wouldn't be his personal robot."

"Baby, you can't take that on. None of it. *None of it*," he said, shaking her shoulders gently. "Not a goddamn bit of this is on you."

"I know that, up here," she said, tapping her temple. "It's here that it's sticking." She placed her hand on her heart, fresh tears coming to the surface.

"What's going to happen to her?" she asked.

"To the nurse? Paula?"

"Yeah."

"Well, she did help him escape, and it seems she did so freely. That was willful intent. As far as the murders go, if we can prove he infected her with the nanotech serum prior to the murders starting, that would establish she did them under duress, an altered state beyond her control. That might help her when it comes to the punishment phase."

"I sure hope they take that into account," she replied. "I mean, look at what that stuff made Tommy and Nate and Chris do."

"I remember." He held her close. "But right now, my priorities are keeping you safe and catching them, in that order."

Then she gasped. "The baby moved again. I can't wait until he or she gets further along so you can feel it, too."

"Me, too, Bella," he told her. "Me, too."

"Promise me, Nathan," Bella said, as they headed upstairs for a soak and sleep. "Promise me you'll be safe and that you'll stop them."

"I promise, love."

And I hope I can do that before anyone else dies, he thought to himself.

———

At seven the next morning, Steve, Mitch, Nathan, and the AD met up again, this time in the conference room. Nathan's office could only hold so many people comfortably.

Nathan had arrived at six-thirty and already had the US map with its revelations tacked up on the wall in the conference room, the whiteboard flanking it. When the others filed in shortly before seven, he was prepped and ready with his portion of things to talk about.

The meeting began with Nathan running down what they had to date. Then he turned it over to Steve.

"Just got this video in from our lab guys," he said as he brought it up onscreen.

Mitch got up and turned off the lights as Steve pressed play on his laptop.

"Pause," Nathan said on a close-up of Paula standing at the counter, and Steve complied.

"Can we print that?"

"Coming up," Steve replied.

Nathan pulled her photo out of her hospital employment file, walked over to the color printer, then turned the lights back on for a moment and held the two images up, side-by-side.

"That's her, all right," he confirmed, then passed the photos around.

All agreed. Paula was very much alive and well.

Nathan turned the lights back out.

"Continue, please. Boss." He grinned.

Steve grinned back and hit play again.

The video really was top notch. They got nice, clear stills of the car, including its license plates, and a crisp, clear front view and profile of Mikel. He had darkened his hair and put in brown contacts. But it was him.

"And that is *definitely* Mikel Metzger," Nathan stated, little flames of rage beginning in his gut. "So. Here's what I want to do. He won't head back west; he's tracking eastward. Mitch's simulations bear this out. I want every TV and radio station, north to south and from the east coast to Kansas, running their names, previous and current photos and descriptions, the car, and what they're wanted for every hour on the hour. Any electronic billboards along highways we can put this on, I want it there, too. I want to make their faces, their identities, so public they can't even turn around in their own *clothes* comfortably."

The AD smiled wolfishly. He liked the kid's spirit.

Nathan stood, pacing, and continued.

"I wanna piss him off to the point he abandons his original plan and comes straight here. Bella has agreed to leave the area to a safe location; she's flying out with Max this afternoon. Steve and I already found an FBI agent that closely resembles her in both appearance and build, and we'll plant her at my house as part of the bait."

"Jenny Taylor, I presume," Mitch said, and Nathan nodded.

"Great choice, she's got a good head on her shoulders and can handle herself just fine in a firefight if it comes to that," the AD noted.

"I agree, sir. If they get caught up by police between here and there, that's great," Nathan continued. "But my money is on him making it to Bella Amsel's address of record. The only part I can't tell is when. He may show up at my house this evening, or it may be a month. My gut says it will be sooner rather than later though."

"One caveat," the AD held up his hand. "We have four families out there whose loved ones are still listed as missing. We here already know they won't be coming home, because of the package of pictures you received. But their families don't know that yet. And I *don't* want our media release to be the way those families get that news."

"So," he continued, "before we run with this, we should reach out to the four jurisdictions where the missing women are from, bring those detectives up to date, let them tell the families as gently as they can but as quickly as possible. If we can take these two alive, maybe they'll tell us where to find those bodies."

"Absolutely agree," Nathan replied earnestly. "Those four are Barbara from Ely, Megan from Bakersfield, Tara from Salem, and Georgia from Idaho Falls. I can reach out to those police departments right after this meeting, tell them what we know and that we've compared the death photos we were sent with the photos provided by the families."

"Do that, ask them to make notifications as soon as possible, and tell them we're holding the media release until *after* all four families have been told. That should impart the urgency here. Once we hear back that part is complete, run with the press release, gentlemen. Now, Nathan," the AD intoned, "fill me in on the specific ideas regarding when Mikel Metzger shows up at your door."

By six-fifteen p.m. Bella and Max's plane had lifted off the runway, beginning its non-stop flight to Dallas. Faith and Rick would be picking them up from the airport and taking them to Jandy's house since she had more room.

Bella stared out the window, worrying about Nathan. She couldn't help it. She was terrified something would happen to him.

Max read her body language.

"Dear child," he comforted, taking her hand. "Your young man is a remarkable agent. Trust me, he won't take any unnecessary risks."

"I know, Uncle Max," Bella sighed. "But Mikel. He is completely unhinged. There's no telling what he will do, especially if he feels cornered."

"We just have to trust that it will all work out," he told her.

She squeezed his hand and tried to smile.

By seven p.m. eastern time, all four police departments had reported back that the families of the missing had been notified of the situation at hand. Nathan envied absolutely none of the people that had been selected to perform that task. The media release was sent out. Most news stations would begin broadcasting it at eight p.m. EST.

Now Nathan and Steve sat in the conference room bringing Jenny Taylor up to speed on the role she was to play in this charade.

She was twenty-eight, four years in with the Bureau, deadly accurate as a righty or a lefty with both firearms and bladed weapons, and could have been Bella's twin, right down to the hair length. As they read her in, her eyebrows raised a few times, but she remained quiet. Once they finished lining it all out, she asked two questions:

"When do we start?" and, "Are you prepared to use deadly force only if it becomes absolutely necessary?"

The answers she got were 'tonight' and 'absolutely'.

She grinned.

"That's all I need to know. Let me pack a bag and grab my tactical," she said, referring to her bulletproof vest and hand-to-hand combat knives. "I'll be ready in twenty, darling."

She smiled at Nathan, batted her eyelashes at him, then laughed out loud when he blushed.

"Sorry. Couldn't help myself. Should have seen your face though." She stood. "Meet you downstairs."

"I like her," Nathan said. "She seems solid, up for the task. And a sense of humor."

"She's really, really good," Steve told him. "She's already been on a few of these kinds of operations. Like the AD said, good head on her shoulders, quick thinker. She's tiny, and she looks harmless, which catches the bad guys completely unaware. She's also naturally ambidextrous, so she can fuck someone up left *or* right-handed."

Now Steve was the one grinning.

"She asked about deadly force because the very first op she was on, another agent hesitated, and it almost got them all killed."

"What happened?" Nathan asked.

"She *didn't* hesitate. Took out the main bad guy, and the other two surrendered without incident."

"Cool under pressure," Nathan mused. "That's good to know."

"Jenny is ice," Steve agreed. "Definitely someone I would trust to go through the door with, any day."

Max and Bella's flight had been uneventful, and they had arrived safely at Jandy's house. Bella texted Nathan to let him know. As soon as he saw her text, he called her.

"Hi, baby. Glad you made it down okay."

"Yeah, nothing out of the ordinary. I miss you already. Please promise me you're going to be careful. All of your team, but especially you."

"We will. Hopefully you and I won't have to be apart for very long, Bella."

"I hope that, too, Nathan. I love you."

"I love you, too."

"Well, listen, I'd better get settled in down here," she said, trying to end the conversation quickly because she knew she was about to cry and didn't want him to hear it and feel bad.

"Okay. I'll be in touch as much as I can, all right?"

"Okay. Bye."

"Bye."

She hung up the phone and, as anticipated, started to cry.

Jandy came and wrapped her up in a hug.

"Oh, honey," she soothed. "Please don't worry. Everything's going to be all right."

Faith joined, wrapping her arms around them both, with Rick and Tony following suit.

Max smiled at them all from the doorway.

"See there?" Tony quipped. "In this group you never, ever carry stuff by yourself – whether you like it, or not."

His remark had the intended effect of making Bella chuckle from the middle of the group.

"I love you guys," she said.

"We love you, too," they all said in unison.

"Now," Jandy offered as they broke apart, "who's hungry?"

Mikel and Paula stopped around three a.m. at a twenty-four-hour gas station just outside their destination of Jonesboro, Arkansas for fuel. They had lost a day in travel when a tire had gone flat and the spare, as it turned out, didn't have much more air in it than the completely flat one did. It was frustrating to say the least, but it had been dealt with once they'd found a tire repair shop in the middle of nowhere.

Ordinarily, Mikel wouldn't go into any businesses they stopped at; it wasn't wise to continually be caught on camera, but he had to this time. He'd had to power Paula down completely again. She was getting more and more twitchy, more resistant to commands, a little harder to control. He just knew it was because of the prolonged nanotech exposure. But although he really wanted to hole up, run some diagnostics on her to see exactly what was happening, the mission came first. End of story.

He walked into the store and noticed he was the sole customer and probably the first in a while tonight, since he had to wake up the attendant to prepay twenty dollars in gas. He went back outside but, before he made it to the pump, realized he needed to pee. He went back in to get the restroom key from the attendant. Afterwards, he stepped back inside the store to return the key.

But the attendant, whose nametag said 'Pete' and who didn't look old enough to vote much less drink, wasn't reaching out to take the key back. His already pale face had gone deathly white, his brown eyes bulging in horror as he kept glancing back and forth between the man standing at his counter and the TV monitor positioned at an angle above and to the left in the middle of the store.

Mikel turned his head to follow the guy's line of sight. He saw a split screen of his own face staring back at him; the original, and the way he looked right now. Then Paula's. Then the car and license plate number.

FUCK.

He made the decision in a split second. He noiselessly leaped the counter and sliced the attendant –from left to right across the throat with the scalpel he'd pulled from his pocket.

As Pete slumped to the floor, blood gushing, Mikel went through his pockets and found the dying man's car keys. He pivoted, then opened the cash register, grabbing all the twenties and larger bills. Then he went out and located his new ride.

A 2010 silver Mazda3. Nice.

He took off the pants and shirt that had good old Pete's blood on them, hurriedly put on clean clothes, and threw the bloody ones in the nearest trash can. Then, he moved their things over to the new car before he activated Paula long enough to get her transferred over to the passenger seat.

He checked the Mazda's gas level. Completely full.

Double bonus.

He didn't want to linger here much longer in case another traveler stopped. But he did take the time once he got in the Mazda to adjust the seat then quickly scan the car's other gauges. He was delighted to notice after-market GPS navigation. That was about to serve him very well because he was about to drastically alter his route.

Nathan Thomas needed to die as soon as possible, and he needed his property back as soon as possible. Enough fucking around.

Coldly furious, he programmed the GPS for the most direct route to the Amsel property in Manassas, Virginia. He smiled as the polite female told him it was precisely nine-hundred and twenty miles to his destination.

Around four-fifteen a.m., Trooper Wallis pulled into the gas station lot and immediately noticed the beige sedan with Nevada plates. He checked in with Dispatch and received the BOLO for that vehicle.

Calling for backup, he exited his squad car, drew his weapon, and visually verified the car was vacant. Then he cautiously approached the store. He could see no one at all inside. He crept back to the bathrooms, gently tugging each door to verify they were locked.

Then he made his way slowly to the store's front double doors. Nothing had moved or changed at all from his first look inside. He drew a deep breath, opened the door, and swept left, right, and back to left with his eyes and his weapon as he entered, using the mirrors placed strategically through the store to verify no other living soul was there but him.

Once he was satisfied that he wasn't about to be ambushed, he made his way to the counter. Peering over it, he locked eyes with Pete's vacant, staring ones. He clawed at the mike on his collar, requesting an ambulance, too. But he already knew it was just a formality.

Within an hour, the store's security video had been rewound and replayed, then copied for evidence to be uploaded and emailed straight to the BAU. Pete's death and the man that caused it were both graphically captured.

A very shaken store owner met the cops at her business, crying, offering to help any way she could. It was the first overnight shift she'd let Pete work since hiring on three months before, and she was riddled with guilt that she'd taken the night off and asked him to cover. She verified he had just turned nineteen in May, and that his missing car was a 2010 Mazda3 that he'd saved up for three years to make the down payment on.

Nathan was roused from sleep around six a.m. by his cell phone ringing. It was Steve, calling to tell him there'd been another development and he needed to come in early. He powered through his morning routine and was in his car within twenty minutes, heading to the office.

Steve met him in the lobby, and they rode together up to the BAU conference room.

As soon as they entered, Nathan noticed the AD and Mitch were already seated.

"Kill the lights," the AD instructed. Nathan complied, then took a seat.

"This happened around three a.m. CST in Jonesboro Arkansas," Steve led in, then pressed play, and they all turned to the big screen looming on the wall.

They watched the needlessly violent events unfold from multiple angles, including exterior view shots that clearly showed the victim's vehicle being stolen.

"Jesus," Nathan breathed, closing his eyes for a moment. "He was just a kid."

Chapter Twenty-Two

No one spoke for a moment.

Then, Mitch said, "Steve, I think I noticed something. Can you back up to the part where he goes back outside after the murder, and roll it from there?"

"Sure." Steve rolled it back to the spot Mitch had mentioned and played it again.

"Pause," Mitch said. "I don't know if you guys noticed, but she hasn't moved a muscle this whole time," he pointed at Paula's image on the screen. "Now, watch what happens. Play, please, Steve."

Steve continued to roll forward. They watched Mikel change clothes, grab some things from the tan car and bring them to the Mazda. Then he grabbed his laptop, opened it, typed something in, and she moved.

"Pause. Right there. Nathan, I think he's booting her up, for lack of a better word. I think *that's* your evidence she's been infected with nanotech. She looked dead, didn't move at all, until he used that laptop."

"I agree, Mitch, good catch."

They played the video to the end again.

Nathan cleared his throat.

"I think, based on what we saw, the kid behind the counter had a news channel playing on the TV in that store. Our news bulletin came on, he saw it, Mikel saw him see it, and that prompted this."

The AD, Steve, and Mitch all nodded in agreement.

"How far is it from that gas station to my house?" Nathan asked.

Steve typed in the addresses and hit enter. "Nine-hundred and twenty miles exactly; that is the most direct route."

"Roll back to when he finally sits in the car, and play, please," the AD said.

They watched.

"Pause. See it? He looks like he's programming the GPS," the AD pointed out.

"Yep, it sure does," Mitch confirmed.

"Does the kid's car have Lo-Jack or OnStar in it?" Nathan asked. "If it does, we can activate that, find them sooner."

"It does not," Steve replied. "I checked already. It's the base model. Kid must have added the GPS as after-market."

"Dammit. Okay, we stick with our original plan then. If he left there around three-fifteen a.m. and the highway speed limit is seventy, on average, how soon could he get here?" Nathan asked Steve.

"Little over thirteen hours, if he drove straight through," Steve said. "So, four o'clock this afternoon, or thereabouts. But he won't be able to drive straight through, Nathan. That little car gets thirty-three miles a gallon on the highway, but it only has a fourteen-gallon tank. That's around four-hundred and seventy-nine miles. He will have to stop at least once for more fuel somewhere around Kodak, Tennessee, give or take fifty miles."

"Okay, let's cushion that ETA a bit just in case," the AD directed. "From three o'clock onward, Nathan, you need to be at home, braced for an ambush. Jenny will be there with you, two additional agents as backup upstairs like we talked about, two more plainclothes outside the residence on either side, raking leaves and whatnot, and an unmarked car near the turnoff to your house that can signal you guys he's coming in."

The AD rose. "Be safe, and I expect a full briefing once they're caught."

Mikel's desire to power straight through was thwarted by fuel consumption. He had to stop about fifty miles past Kodak. This time he sent Paula in to pay with cash and, thankfully, no TV programs were playing to give them away this time.

Back in the car, he refreshed the GPS. About four-hundred and forty miles to go. He checked his watch. Should be there by five p.m. at the latest. It was all he could do not to floor it as he got back on the highway.

Roughly seventy miles inside the Virginia border, his laptop made a strange sound. He hadn't heard it make that noise in forever. Frowning, he pulled over into a mostly deserted rest stop, reached into the back seat, and brought his laptop forward. He opened it and was completely shocked at what he saw. The nanotech control panel was now registering *two* activations, not just Paula.

What the hell.

Then he remembered, and a slow smile crept over his face. The senior senator from Arizona had been infected with the serum by his father not too long before Mikel had personally sent Adolf to hell.

Which meant the senator was in range to have been activated, picking up the signals driving Paula's behavior. Mikel didn't have a precise way to gauge distance; all his toys had, until now, been in very close proximity, and he'd never gotten around to calibrating for longer range manipulation.

Interesting. Extremely interesting.

It also meant he had another pet he could put to good use.

He took a few moments to type in some commands specific to the new recipient. Then, he placed his laptop back where he got it and pulled back onto the road toward Manassas and his prize.

The senior senator was in session in Congress, hearing the latest debate on global warming. He'd had a slight headache all day and was reaching for the glass of water in front of him to take another aspirin.

At that moment, all conscious thought was lost. Mikel's instructions had taken over. He stood and, without a word, walked out to his car. He drove back to his overpriced condo overlooking the Potomac, packed up his handgun, checked the clock, and settled down to wait. His instructions were to head south out of town toward Virginia, and to time it so he met his commander onsite.

Bella and Stacy were on the computer, video chatting and catching up. Stacy and Emily had been released from the hospital two days after arrival, and the little family had flown straight home to get settled in. Now Emily was nestled in her mom's arms, sound asleep.

"Yeah, she's quiet right now. If you were here around, say, two-thirty a.m., it would be a totally different story. This little girl is *loud* when she's hungry. Or wet. Or mad." Stacy laughed softly. "But I wouldn't trade it for the world."

"I always knew you'd be a good mom, Stace," Bella told her best friend.

"Aww. Thanks, Bel. So, when are you two gonna have one of your own?"

The look on Bella's face had Stacy almost squealing in excitement.

"Easy..." Bella told her very softly, looking around to make sure she had this corner of Jandy's house to herself.

"No one knows yet, we were gonna make an announcement at the reception, and then, well..."

"All hell broke loose," Stacy finished for her.

Bella laughed. "Yeah, that pretty much sums it up."

"So... when?" Stacy asked, in code.

"Mid-March is the estimate," Bella replied with a twinkle.

"Girl! The *minute* this gets out you gotta call me, and let's talk about it in depth, 'kay?"

Emily started to stir and wail.

"Oops, someone's hungry. Gotta go Bel. Love you!" Stacy blew her a kiss and disconnected.

Bella sighed. She was so ready for that. Her and Nathan and their baby and just normal life. No evil lunatic stalking her or threatening him. Just her husband, their child, and day-to-day stuff. She was so afraid it was going to be taken away.

Maybe it was because she hadn't slept well since she left his side, but there was a deep undercurrent of foreboding she just couldn't shake. And she didn't know what to do about it, other than to go be with him.

But that wasn't an option, and she knew it. If she went back, Nathan would be distracted, and when it came to Mikel Metzger, distractions could get someone seriously hurt.

Or worse, her mind finished on its own.

Mikel glanced at the car's clock. Three p.m. Right around two hours to go. He pressed down on the accelerator.

Nathan's team had been briefed and were all in place. Weapons were checked and rechecked, as were communications.

Those inside the house settled in for the wait, while those outside the perimeter took their positions so they'd be able to move quickly when the lookout car gave the signal.

By a quarter to four, the senator was beyond ready. He took his bag to his car, placed it in the front passenger seat beside him, and began his drive southeast.

He was about seven miles into his journey on the freeway when a big rig started to merge without using a blinker. He cursed, swung left, and was almost even with the truck cab's back tires when the Peterbilt's driver-side front tire came apart.

The huge truck careened sharply to the left, then right as the driver fought to regain control, then left again. But the force of motion was too much. The truck jackknifed, folding itself around the car, and the momentum launched them both across the remaining lanes. They careened out of control for seventy-five feet, their progress halted only by a violent impact into the concrete and steel retaining wall. Metal and glass was flung into the air in every direction, raining down all over the roadway, and the screech of vehicles around them slamming on the brakes was an overpowering symphony of chaos. Then suddenly, a deafening silence descended.

Police working the fatal scene would later estimate their speed at point of impact at just over sixty miles per hour.

Fifty-one miles away from his destination, his laptop chirped again. Mikel pulled over to check it and noticed the Senator's signal had disappeared from his control panel.

Win some, lose some.

He shrugged and kept driving.

Nathan's team got the signal from the lookout car posted a half-mile away at five twenty-seven p.m. The plainclothes agent got a good look at both Paula and the license plate, so he was able to confirm it was on. But he warned them that Mikel wasn't with her.

"Guys, you know what to do," Nathan said quickly on his radio. "Alive, if possible."

Then he turned to Jenny and the two agents that were about to head back upstairs.

"Showtime."

"Yeah, but where's her puppet-master?"

Paula's handler had felt a strange vibe about five miles from their destination. Something didn't feel quite right. Change of plans. She'd go in alone, just in case.

He pulled over in a shopping center parking lot and looked at Paula.

"You ready?"

"Yes, baby," she said woodenly. "Kill him, capture her."

"Don't fuck this up," he growled at her.

Although he was not one-hundred-percent sure, Mikel had an inkling that something deep inside Paula had begun to actively fight the nanotech for control. He could see it in her eyes - the way she glanced over at him, then at the door handle, trembling, like she was about to leap out and run away.

He tapped some keys and watched with satisfaction as the hazy veil he'd kept her under clamped firmly back into place. Then he got out, grabbing his laptop and the backpack that held his money and a few clothes just in case the vibe he was feeling turned out to be accurate. She moved over across the console to the driver's seat.

"Go get it done and pick me back up here."

"Yes, baby."

He noticed the barber shop in the little strip mall wasn't busy at all. Time for a buzzcut to match the next identity he'd forged for himself.

Never could be too careful.

Nathan's outdoor group had informed him of the car slowing down about five driveways away.

"Here we go," he said into his communicator, as he flipped TV channels downstairs on the couch, Jenny seated right next to him like Bella would be.

"Subject car stopped two houses down, she's coming to your door on foot."

"Roger that. All outside units, maintain your cover, keep watch in case he shows up."

About forty-five seconds later, the doorbell rang. Then a "Hello?"

"Coming," Nathan said nonchalantly, like it couldn't be a life-and-death encounter. He exchanged nods with Jenny as he went to the front door. Opening the wooden one but not the glass exterior door, he said politely, "May I help you?"

"Hi," Paula said. "I'm new to the area, supposed to come see some friends, I'm completely lost, and my cell is dead. Can I use your phone?"

Wow, she's good. No alarm bells at all if I didn't know what I was looking at, he thought as he pretended to think about it.

Jenny chimed in, to make it believable that it was just another Friday. "Who is it, hon?" she called out.

"A lady, she needs to use the phone."

"Well, let her in, Nathan, I'm sure it's okay."

She winked at him since Paula couldn't see her, while giving him a smile that said *let that bitch in, and let's play.*

It was all he could do not to grin back.

"Sure, come on in, phone's in the kitchen. I'll show you."

He swung the glass door outward and stood to the right, holding it open. Jenny stood and angled herself behind the wooden door that had opened be able to monitor the situation as Paula passed him and walked inside.

Nathan pointed, saying, "Right through here," as he closed the glass door and reached behind him with his right hand to act like he was closing the front door.

Paula took about eight steps, then all hell broke loose.

Paula pivoted around left. Her right hand came up holding a 9mm pistol. She fired three rounds at him and caught him in the chest with each one. He crumpled to the floor.

Sensing movement to her left, Paula turned, slashing out with the knife she'd concealed in her left hand. She managed to slash a long streak up Jenny's right forearm from wrist to elbow before she was met with a roundhouse kick that sent the gun flying. Now Jenny pulled a knife of her own, brandishing it in her left hand.

Paula screamed and charged at her, lifting the knife over her head. She got in another kick, this time to her midsection, for her trouble. She stumbled back, and Jenny went on the offensive, stabbing, slashing, attacking from all angles.

When Paula dropped her guard, Jenny landed a brutal right cross that knocked her out cold. She went down harder than Nathan had, and her head hitting the hardwood floor echoed through the room.

The two upstairs agents rushed down and looked almost disappointed that it was over so quickly - until they saw Nathan had been shot from less than six feet away, and Jenny was dripping a fair amount of blood.

One of them went to Nathan, radioing for ambulances, and the other started to move toward Jenny to check her arm.

"Fucking... *hurts...*" Nathan managed through clenched teeth.

After a few minutes, Paula moaned, then started to get up. She stopped moving when the business end of Jenny's Glock was mere inches from her face.

"Try me, princess," Jenny muttered, holding her weapon just fine with her left hand while her right forearm streamed blood. "On your stomach. *Now.*"

Paula complied and was handcuffed and patted down. The search revealed two more knives.

Mikel had just paid for his quick haircut and walked outside when his laptop chirped. Opening it, he could see from her monitoring signal that Paula was unconscious, and therefore, most likely caught.

He was glad he had listened to his gut about letting her go in alone. He could hear multiple sirens in the distance. That confirmed he'd been smart to stay away.

"Time to go," he said. He was frustrated things hadn't gone the way he wanted, but he wasn't about to risk capture now. Plan B. Get out of the U.S., back home to Manaus where he couldn't be extradited, and regroup. He had more resources there anyway. The FBI had frozen all his assets here.

It was almost going to be better than the original plan, he realized. They'd grow complacent at some point, thinking he'd given up, and one day he would capitalize on that complacency in a big way.

But not today. And he could be very, very patient.

He walked nonchalantly through the lot until he spotted his next ride. He was in, had the ignition bypass made, and was heading south toward the Florida Keys in under two minutes.

"That's gonna leave a mark," the medic grinned at Nathan, pointing to where the bruises from the bulletproof vest pushing back against skin were already forming. "Bet you're glad you had that thing on."

"You know it," Nathan replied, wincing. "I think I cracked a couple of ribs, though. It hurts to take a deep breath. But better than the alternative."

Another medic was wrapping Jenny's arm. "This is just until we can get you to the hospital. She got you pretty good, this will probably need stitches."

"Goody," Jenny muttered.

Nathan looked at her. "You okay?"

"Yeah, not too bad," she said. "You?"

"Yeah. Hey, I want to say. Steve was right about you. You're ice. And I would go through the door with you, any day."

"Thanks, Nathan. You, too."

Paula had a concussion from her contact with the floor, three stab wounds, and multiple lacerations from attempting to take on Jenny. She'd been loaded into the ambulance and was already in route to the hospital – under police escort.

An APB was immediately issued for Mikel Metzger, his old and more recent pictures run time and time again on the air, to no avail. He had simply disappeared.

Paula's interrogation got underway as soon as she was released from the hospital and taken to the FBI's field office in Washington DC. Nathan and Steve sat across from her. She cast her eyes downward as she was informed of her rights. She nodded her understanding.

They also informed her that the session was being recorded; she shrugged her shoulders, then meekly said, "That's fine. And I don't want a lawyer. I'll tell you anything you want to know."

Then she lifted her head and gazed across the table at Nathan. "Are you okay?" she asked Nathan timidly.

"Yes," he replied, a little surprised by the question.

Now her eyes began to fill. "I'm so, so sorry. And I'm glad you were wearing a vest. Truly."

"Paula, what happened to you?" he asked her gently. "Can you walk us through it all?"

She sighed deeply. "Yes, I can."

She took several deep breaths, then began.

"It started when I fell in love," she said, eyes glistening.

She told them everything, from the very beginning. Seeing him and falling in love at first sight. The joy when he woke up. Him asking her to help him escape. The trip out to the Institute.

They interrupted her at that point to let her know that the man she loved had blown up the hospital to cover that escape, killing four-hundred and thirty-eight people in the process. She went stark white, her mouth hung open with shock and horror.

"I didn't know that happened. Any of it. I swear to you. I didn't know he had planned anything like that, or I would have stopped him. Oh, my God."

She started to sob violently.

They paused the interrogation and brought her some water. When she regained her composure, they continued.

She resumed her story. The Institute. Being passionately seduced. Then feeling a horrible stinging, burning at the back of her neck, and everything being foggy for a while. And having no free will, no control over her own actions.

"It was like being outside myself looking in, and I couldn't do anything about it," she said morosely, with haunted eyes.

Nathan and Steve looked at one another. She'd just described what it was like to be infected with Mikel's nanotechnology. Since they'd known to look for it, they'd had tests run while she was in the hospital to confirm that she did in fact carry nanotech in her system. The prevailing opinion from the medical staff that had treated her was that the concussion she'd experienced had somehow inactivated it.

When they got to the part of the story that happened in Ely, Nevada, Paula was able to give them specific details, up to and including where Barbara's body could be found. Nathan was shocked. He knew from the standoff at the Metzger Institute the previous winter that typically those inoculated with the nanotech tended to have no recollection of events that happened while it was activated.

But Paula had remembered everything since they left the Institute and headed west. The only logical conclusion to make was that prolonged exposure to the activated nanotech didn't have the same effects as short term exposure.

She was able to go into detail regarding each town pinned on the map on Nathan's wall. The other three women whose bodies had not yet been recovered would now also be given a proper burial.

Finally, they reached the point where she and Mikel had bypassed the rest of the first plan and headed straight to Bella's house.

"Why would he drive all that way and then not come to the house with you?" Steve asked her.

"He got a weird vibe, about five miles out, pulled into a strip mall parking lot, and got out and told me to go get it done, then come back and get him."

She looked at the agents.

"I guess he sacrificed me to save himself." She began to cry again, swiping at her face with her hands.

"And what was supposed to happen after you killed me and took Bella?" Nathan leaned his elbows on the table.

"He said we'd go home, because they don't extradite their citizens," Paula answered. "He said the name of the town he grew up in, but I don't remember it."

"Manaus?" Nathan offered.

She nodded. "Yes, that's it." Her head drooped now. "I'm really tired."

"I know. We're almost done, Paula. One more question," Nathan prodded gently. "Did he say how you would get home?"

"Tickle the Keys," Paula whispered. "I need to rest now. Can I rest now?"

"Yes," Nathan said, signaling for the man at the door to arrange her escort from the room.

"Thank you," she mumbled. "Agent Thomas, can you do me one favor? Can you please tell their families I am so, so sorry? If I had been stronger, I could have fought back more, maybe gotten my mind back, helped those women instead of hurting them."

"I will try to let them know," was the best he could do.

"Thank you."

She shuffled away toward a holding cell, agents on either side of her, bound in leg shackles and handcuffs as the man she loved had once been.

Nathan turned off the recorder, then sat with his head in his hands.

Steve blew out a long breath.

"Wow," he mused. "Kinda feel sorry for her."

"I do, too, Steve," Nathan replied ruefully. "I do, too."

"Do you think he's still going to try for Bella?"

"My gut says not immediately. It's too hot right now. I think he's headed home for a while until things die down, and he'll come at her and me again when we least expect it."

***

Bella raced to her cell phone. "Hello?"

"Hi, baby," Nathan said. "I really miss you."

"I miss you, too."

"Good, because I'm on the next flight down there to you."

"Is it over?"

"For the most part. I'll explain when I see you. I should be there in about five hours."

Max and Bella met him at the airport. He embraced and kissed his wife, hugged Max, and they drove back to Jandy's.

On the way there, his phone rang with an update on his case. Paula had hanged herself in her jail cell. A simple 'I'm sorry' was scribed on the wall with her blood. It served as her suicide note.

He closed his eyes and said a prayer for her.

Epilogue

LATER THAT DAY, Nathan filled Max in on it all. The CIA began some inquiries as to Mikel's whereabouts; among other things, they needed to know for sure that no one else had access to Mikel's remote-controlled nanotechnology.

One week and five-thousand dollars later, someone copped to having given a man who looked an awful lot like Mikel a private plane ride out past where the Florida Keys ended.

Meanwhile, Nathan Thomas was back with the woman he loved and surrounded by his family. As they sat down to dinner with Jandy, Tony, Max, Faith, and Rick, he and Bella held hands and finally got to make the pregnancy announcement to them all.

The room erupted with joy.

Mikel Metzger stood on the balcony of his father's complex in the Amazon jungle in Brazil. He lazily swirled a glass of brandy and admired the sunset over Lake Manacapuru, just as his father had done so many years ago. The first time Adolf and Mikel had met was that evening. Mikel enjoyed the irony of that recollection, knowing *he* was now the lord and master here.

It was good to be home. Here, he would be able to come and go as he pleased. His mind was already racing with ideas. How much more serum to make, how to best test the range of control. He wanted it all to be perfected so that when he did return north to claim Bella, nothing would be able to stop him.

The mere thought of her made him smile.

"To Bella, my Angel. I will return for you," he said aloud, lifting his snifter in toast.

As he raised the glass to his lips, savoring his future, he had no time at all to register surprise or pain as the sniper's bullet perforated the center of his forehead. It destroyed bone and brain matter before escaping through the back of his head and shattering the French door behind him.

Across the lake, the sniper's spotter keyed his mic.

"Thunder to Zeus."

"Go for Zeus."

"Target has been neutralized."

"Roger that, Thunder. Retrieve the package."

Zeus, also known as Max Jones, turned off his short-wave radio, smiled to himself, and returned to his book as he lounged on his hotel room balcony in Manaus.

Who *was* Adolf Metzger – and why did he hate Manfred Amsel so much?

Get 'Wall of Secrets', the Prequel to the Vital Secrets Series, and find out. It's exclusive to my subscribers, and it's *free* when you join my spam-free newsletter: Subscribe

Upon signup you'll also get a free bonus supplement to the series!

Sneak peek at <u>List of Secrets</u> is next!

<u>List Of Secrets:</u>

It could just be coincidence. It also could be revenge.

But hardened cop Frank Zimmerman doesn't believe in coincidences. Neither does FBI profiler Nathan Thomas.

A drowned lawyer, a fatal car accident, a heart attack and a socialite's lethal fall in front of a huge crowd all have their cop antennae pinging - hard.

They dig for evidence to support Frank's theory of a trail of bodies that lead into the past.

What's going on? And who will die next?

At her desk in Seattle's police headquarters, Detective Elizabeth Zimmerman finished typing out her case report on the one she'd finally been able to wrap today. A fatal carjacking two months earlier had given her quite the run. But she'd stayed focused, channeled the dogged determination she had inherited from her father, and the hours tenaciously racked up had finally paid off. She not only caught the man she'd been chasing, but she'd managed to hand Vice an extremely handy piece of intel; they had conducted a raid earlier in the evening that resulted in over three million in cocaine taken off the streets of Seattle.

She had just hit 'save' then 'print' when her cell phone rang. She glanced at the number.

"Hi, daddy," she said.

"Hey kiddo, what's up?"

"Just finishing up a report."

"You caught your carjacking suspect. I can tell by your voice. Good work, kiddo."

"Thanks Dad. What are you up to?"

"Not much, just got off. Gonna go hang with Joe, watch TV."

"Sounds fun."

"Yeah. Hey kid, I... I gotta go. Just wanted to check in on you."

"Thanks, Dad. I love you. Talk soon?"

"Talk soon," he confirmed, and hung up.

She smiled sadly.

He just wasn't the same as before. Before, Frank Zimmerman had been one of Fort Worth's best detectives, ever. It wasn't just her opinion as his daughter; he'd had several commendations over his twenty-five years doing detective work. One case, though, had broken him. One case from earlier in his career that haunted him enough to turn in his detective shield and go back to patrol work once new evidence came to light.

He just hadn't been the same since last fall, when the real killer in the 1985 case was finally identified through now more sophisticated DNA testing, and Frank realized that the man he'd helped put in prison back then - and who died while incarcerated - was innocent all along.

Now he walked a beat, and spent his off time with Joe Wallace, his former partner in the Detective unit. And, according to her last conversation with Joe a couple of months ago, Dad had become more and more dependent on whiskey to get through his days as a beat cop.

She sighed. She'd have to take some time, travel down to Fort Worth soon and check on him. Maybe over the holidays at some point. Although that was when the crazies seemed to peak around here.

She'd just have to play it by ear.

***

Buy List of Secrets

Or, save money and buy the collection!

Follow me on:
Bookbub
Goodreads

Also by D.F. Hart

Vital Secrets

Mystery, Suspense and Thriller written as D.F. Hart

Book of Secrets

List of Secrets

Web of Secrets

Path of Secrets

Carnival of Secrets

House of Secrets

End of Secrets

Vital Secrets, Volume 1-3

Vital Secrets, Volume 4-6

Raven's Path - Coming in 2023

Mystery, Suspense and Thriller written as D.F. Hart

Raven's Rise

Raven's Attack

One Last Gift – An Anthology by James N. Richardson (D.F. Hart, Editor & Publisher)

Love's Defender Series

Steamy romantic suspense

Saving Brielle

Minding Mari

Protecting Andria

Another Try Novellas

Contemporary romance

Never Say Sorry

Save Me a Dance

Falling into Place

Love Notes

Read My Lips

Out of the Blue

One Last Try

The Another Try Collection

About the Author

D.F. Hart resides in Texas. Her favorite authors include Frederick Forsyth, Ken Follet, and J.D. Robb. Other interests include hidden object and puzzle games -she loves a good mystery storyline!

Of writing, she says: "It's a lot of work, but also an escape. A lot of tears and sweat go into a story, building believable characters, shaping the plot so that the reader can't wait to turn the page. Sometimes I'll wake up at 3 a.m. with that perfect line that escaped me earlier in the day running through my head. But it's worth it. And the brilliant part is, you get to create a little universe of your own. Anything can happen; there are no limits."

She happily pens mysteries and thrillers under D.F. Hart, and contemporary and suspenseful romance as Faith Hart.

www.ingramcontent.com/pod-product-compliance
Lightning Source LLC
Chambersburg PA
CBHW031646100726

47898CB00006B/1993